ROGUE
ELEMENTS
THE GAMMA SEQUENCE, Book 2
a medical thriller

DAN ALATORRE

ROGUE ELEMENTS
THE GAMMA SEQUENCE, Book 2
a medical thriller

Edited by Jenifer Ruff

OTHER THRILLERS BY DAN ALATORRE

The Gamma Sequence
Terminal Sequence, The Gamma Sequence Book 3, *coming soon*
Double Blind, an intense murder mystery
An Angel On Her Shoulder, a paranormal thriller
The Navigators, a time travel thriller

CONTENTS

ACKNOWLEDGMENTS

A big thank you
to the editor of this work, my friend
Jenifer Ruff
whose patience has helped craft a series
readers all around the world
are currently enjoying.

Note to Readers

If you have the time, I would deeply appreciate a review on Amazon or Goodreads. I learn a great deal from them, and I'm always grateful for any encouragement. Reviews are a very big deal and help authors like me to sell a few more books. Every review matters, even if it's only a few words.

Thanks,
Dan Alatorre

CHAPTER 1

The assassin backed his stolen car into the parking space, exactly three rows from the target vehicle where the device would go. He tapped his fingers on the wheel. This was a good spot. Close enough to see his victim in the parking garage, but far away enough to not be noticed by her. He glanced at this watch for the third time in two minutes. Two twenty-seven A. M.

Taking a few deep breaths, he lowered all four windows of the sedan, letting the icy Minnesota winter rush in. The frigid air made his eyes water and dried the inside of his nose.

He ran his hands back and forth over his thighs, tapping his heels as he checked out the other cars. The nearest one had a light dusting of snow on it, compliments of the strong winds that blew nonstop through the airport garage's second floor.

Okay, I have something for that.

The assassin reached across the car and hauled a gray duffel bag from the floor and onto the passenger seat. White clouds formed with each rapid breath as he inspected the objects inside. His gaze darted past the magnetic metal box that would help kill his victim. Next to that, a homemade transmitter rested. Some clothes acted as cushions between the other objects, with a can of artificial spray snow and a can of spray-on window frost completing the inventory. They weren't technically necessary in the near-zero temperatures, but appearances mattered. He needed his stolen sedan to look as if it had been sitting in the parking garage for a while.

He swallowed hard and jumped out of the vehicle, shaking the can and spraying a fine layer of fake snow onto the car's hood and roof, then lightly coated the windshield with the fake frost. He glanced over his shoulder at the elevator.

Nothing yet.

With shaking hands, he leaned close to the glass, spit onto the driver's side, and cleared away a baseball-sized spot with the heel of his hand.

Midway up the glass. Just about perfect.

Another glance at the watch. Two-thirty. She'd be here soon.

His heart was racing. The chosen parking space was outside the field of view of the security cameras, but his victim's car was not. Grabbing the duffel bag off the passenger seat, the assassin dropped the cans inside and slipped the strap over his shoulder, walking towards the black Audi.

Walk normal. Walk normal.

As he passed the victim's car, he zipped up his jacket and pretended to drop the duffel bag. Bending to retrieve it, he snapped the magnetic box onto the underside of the car frame and shoved a remote stopper inside the exhaust pipe.

He stood up, bag in hand, and proceeded to the elevator. After pressing the button, the assassin waited, tapping his fingers on the side of his leg and holding his breath.

No cameras here.

An instrumental version of Jingle Bells played on the elevator speakers as he stepped inside. When the doors had closed behind him, the assassin pulled off his jacket and reversed it from gray to blue. His hands shook as he removed a knit cap from the duffel bag and placed it on his head, then reached into the bag for the glasses. The elevator doors re-opened on the second floor. He took a deep breath, stepped out, and took a different route back to the sedan. This time, he carried the gray bag low, at knee-level.

It was twenty long minutes before anyone came out of the elevator. At the sight of his victim, his adrenaline surged. He gripped the wheel and leaned forward, peering through the clean spot on his windshield as she headed toward her black Audi.

The woman tugged her coat around her as she walked, the wind blasting her black hair. Before she got to her car, she lifted the key fob, unlocking the doors and starting the engine. She opened the shiny black door and slipped inside.

His pulse pounding, the assassin lifted an electronic telescope from the gray bag, holding it to the cleared spot on the windshield. He swallowed hard as he reached out with his other hand and flipped the first switch on the transmitter.

Under the car, just behind the gas tank, the metal box's red light came on.

The assassin sat back, releasing a long, slow breath.

When the Audi's taillights came on, he started the sedan. When his victim pulled out of her parking spot, he drove out of his. A quick squirt from the windshield washers cleared most of the spray frost away, but left the window a little smeared. The second squirt finished the job.

He was right behind her, headed for the exit and the attendant. His heart raced.

Easy now. Take it easy.

The Audi slowed, and the driver shoved her parking card into the slot on the machine. When the screen displayed the amount due, she swiped a credit card across the protruding brackets. The striped arm of the automatic gate went up, and the Audi rolled out of the garage.

Pulling forward, the assassin paid as well—being careful not to lean too close and allow the security camera to catch his face.

The gate went up. He grabbed his phone, his fingers trembling. The screen was lit with a map of the city streets, a green dot blinking as his magnetic device relayed the Audi's location on 34th Avenue South. In a moment, it should turn onto highway 494 and drive toward Lynnhurst.

He drew a deep breath, a knot forming in his stomach. Slipping the phone into a cupholder on the console, the assassin drove the stolen car out of the garage.

The dot on the screen did as predicted, pulling onto highway 494 and heading west. He pressed the sedan's gas pedal a little harder, not wanting his prey to get too far away. Squeezing the steering wheel, he did his best to contain his nervous energy. He'd never killed anyone before.

Outside his window, snow-covered trees streaked by. Inside the car, the dot continued straight along 494. He drove past the on ramp to the highway and pulled behind the row of empty warehouses lining the street. Parking, he grabbed his duffel bag and slid the strap over his shoulder as he exited the car. He rubbed his hands as he headed to the big white tow truck that awaited him.

The cab of the truck was still warm, but the cardboard pine tree hanging from the rearview mirror wasn't effectively masking odors in the cab any longer. He started the truck and placed the bag on the passenger seat, withdrawing his transmitter and his cell phone.

His finger hovered over the transmitter's second switch. The device would work from this distance, he knew, but he preferred to be closer.

The dot on the screen moved steadily along 494.

Just a few more minutes and she would've been home.

Staring at the black night beyond the highway, he lowered his finger until it rested on the second switch. Around him, the world was silent. At this hour, in this part of the world, not much was happening. A blanket of white covered the trees and ground. Nothing moved.

The road was calm, wet from the melting snow and streaked white from the road salt. Highway 494—just a few feet away, really—was all but vacant.

All but for the one driver he was about to kill.

He swallowed hard and stared at the metal box in his hand. In a moment, it would all be over.

Gritting his teeth, he shoved the little switch forward.

His gaze darted to the highway, then to the phone. Silence. He held his breath. The green dot on the phone screen slowed and then stopped. The hush of the still night remained undisturbed.

Dropping the big truck into drive, he stomped the gas pedal and raced toward the highway on ramp.

The black Audi was on the side of the road. The hood was up, but only technically. She'd probably pulled the release from under the dashboard, but hadn't released the second latch under the hood. Maybe she didn't know where it was, or didn't want to search for it in the cold.

His heart thumping, the assassin flipped on the truck's yellow emergency lights and pulled to a stop behind her.

It was noticeably colder on the highway than it had been in the garage. The assassin shivered, the snow crunching under his feet as he crept toward the Audi. Flashlight in one hand and cell phone in the other, he shined the beam into the car. "Roadside assistance."

Can't have any surprises.

He kept walking, his pulse throbbing in his ears. The snow around the vehicle was undisturbed.

Good. She's still in the car.

When he reached the driver's door, the window powered down. "You certainly got here quickly," the woman said.

"Yes, ma'am. We, uh . . . we keep an eye on the roads around the airport."

He shined his flashlight into her eyes. She recoiled, squinting into the brightness. "Is that necessary?"

He raised the cell phone to the window, trying hard not to let it shake in his hand. The face on the screen matched the one behind the wheel. He lowered the beam of the flashlight, staring at the woman he was about to kill.

She huffed. "I'm sorry, but that's very rude."

The assassin slid the phone into his pocket and reached for the .45 holstered on his hip. "You're right, Lanaya. Or Dara Han—whatever name you're going by today."

Her mouth dropped open and her eyes went wide. He yanked the weapon free and raised it, pointing it at her chest. The woman pushed away from the open window, turning to run, to flee somehow, but her seatbelt held her—the shoulder strap moved freely, but the lap band kept her hips in place. Her hands flew to the clip, crushing the button as she strained to run away from the man outside her car.

He froze, staring at her, unable to pull the trigger. She screamed as she clawed at the seat belt.

"Stop," he said, stepping back. He dropped his flashlight and gripped the gun with both hands. "Stop trying to get away!"

The seat belt came free. The woman leaped to the passenger side of the car and grabbed the door latch.

"Stop it!" he shouted, his gun shaking. "Stop!"

The first gunshot boomed through the quiet night like a cannon. It ripped the shoulder of the woman's jacket, sending a tuft of white material upwards in a little cloud. The muzzle flash lit the Audi's interior. Blood splattered onto the shiny dashboard.

The gun bucked in the assassin's hand as he fired a second and third shot into his victim's back. She cried out as the rounds pounded her, ripping through her insides. She slumped across the console, gasping and groaning. The assassin stared at the dying figure, her back moving up and down as she fought to breathe.

He shook his head, reaching in and grabbing her jacket, yanking her upright. "Did you really think we wouldn't find you?" His voice quivered. "Did you?"

Blood dripped from the side of her mouth, her head sagging. Her eyes drifted in the direction of her killer, half open and unfocused.

He stepped back and forth on the snow, leveling the shaking gun at her chest. "This is a gift, to die so quickly. I'm giving you a gift! You—you should be thanking me."

He clenched his teeth and fired two more times, her body jerking with each impact. A trail of blood painted the back of her seat as she slid sideways, her eyes staring ahead at nothing, but he kept firing. He stepped forward, pulling the trigger over and over until the hammer clicked and the magazine was empty.

The Audi was now red inside, its owner dead and nearly unrecognizable from the amount of blood covering her face and body.

He stared, gasping, unable to move or to remember what he was supposed to do next. In the distance, over a long, grassy field, an airplane approached the runway. Its engines grew louder and louder, waking the assassin from his trance.

The card.

Tugging off a glove, the assassin shoved his hand into his pocket and withdrew an Angelus Genetics business card. He thrust himself into the Audi and jammed the card into the corpse's open mouth, then sprinted back to the tow truck. Jerking open the door, he flung the empty gun onto the blood-stained body of the first victim of the night—the tow truck driver, whose fat corpse now lay on the floor of the passenger seat. The *click, click, click* of the emergency lights were the only sound in the cab of the truck as they cast their yellow glow over his murder scene.

Cursing, the assassin slapped at the dashboard buttons until the flashing lights turned off. Then his knees buckled.

He put his hands on the seat of the truck and lowered his head, fighting back the urge to vomit. He closed his eyes, spitting to get the bile out of his mouth. A few deep breaths cleared his head. There were details to take care of.

He took off his jacket and heaved it onto the corpse, then stared at the dark, empty road.

What else?

After retrieving his flashlight and removing his equipment from under the dead woman's car, the assassin pulled a clean sweatshirt from the duffel bag. He gazed at the inside of the cab, remembering the plan, unable to let his eyes wander back to the black Audi.

Light filled the inside of the tow truck. The assassin gasped, whipping his head around. The headlights of an oncoming car lit the horizon. The killer crouched beside the open door of the truck, holding his breath.

There's nothing wrong. There's nothing wrong.

The car came closer. He forced himself upright and wiped his hands on his jeans.

Cross the road. Go to the car.

There's nothing's wrong.

He yanked the clean sweatshirt over his head and grabbed his duffel bag, running across the road and waving.

The car slowed to a stop and the driver's window went down. "Everything okay here?"

Reaching the far side of the car, the assassin opened the door. "Like clockwork." He thrust his bag over the headrest and plopped down in the passenger seat. "Let's go, Mika! And call Fuego. Tell him phase one is complete."

The driver nodded, made a wide, slow U-turn, and drove her car back the way it came.

CHAPTER 2

Hank DeShear stood on the sidewalk in front of St. Joseph's hospital, peering through the glass as he tried to get the knot in his stomach to subside. A large Christmas tree twinkled at the far corner of the nearly-empty lobby. DeShear shook his head, grimacing. The happiest day of the year for most people was about to be the worst for him.

Ho, ho, ho.

Taking a deep breath, the private detective stepped forward to the electronic doors. They parted, bathing him in warm air and holiday music.

As he approached the admitting desk, a slender woman in a white uniform walked toward him. "Mr. DeShear? I'm Candace Callander." She smiled, holding out her hand and gesturing toward the hallway. "This way, please."

"Oh. Okay." DeShear fell in line behind her as they walked past the admitting desk. "Don't I need to fill out some paperwork or anything?"

The nurse shook her head. "That's all been handled for you."

He nodded, massaging his abs. Spending Christmas in a hospital didn't appeal to him, and it wouldn't be a short stay, but the reason for his visit had caused the knot in his stomach.

"Merry Christmas, CC," the round lady at the admitting desk said.

"You, too, Abbie." She turned to DeShear. "You must be very important. It's not every day I get called into a meeting with the Chief of Medicine to be assigned to a patient."

"Uh, I'm sure there's been some mistake, then." DeShear increased his pace and stepped around to her side. "I'm definitely not important, nurse Callander. I'm just a guy who got some bad news recently."

"Please call me CC." She handed him her business card. "I understand we're going to be working together for quite a while."

He read the card and slipped it into his pocket. "Ten months of treatment, they told me." He rubbed his forehead. "That sounds like forever."

"Might as well be friends, then." She brushed a lock of auburn hair from her eyes. "And it's no mistake. Dr. Haverford even gave me your picture so I'd spot you in the lobby and you wouldn't have to wait."

"Well, thank you, then, CC." DeShear glanced at the clipboard, where an 8x10 head shot of him was clipped. The picture was at least five years old, from his private detective profile online with the Florida Department of Professional Regulation, but it still looked like him. "I appreciate the VIP treatment, too. I was never a fan of paperwork." He smiled weakly. "I guess they told you about my . . . *condition*, huh?"

"Yes, but there are some blanks I'd like you to fill in, if you don't mind." CC flashed a dazzling smile and increased her speed. She moved like she was in a rush, but she spoke in a calm, relaxing tone, like she was sipping lemonade on her grandmother's front porch. "I read your file. You're quite the hero."

DeShear shrugged. "I don't know about that." He looked into a few rooms as they passed. Each patient looked worse than the next. His heart sank.

"When you were a police officer, you ran into a library building that was on fire and rescued a bunch of people who were trapped inside. You also stopped a school shooting. The file goes on and on with things like that." Swiping her ID through a slot on the wall, she opened a door to an area marked Limited Access Only and continued down the hallway. A few doctors passed them, but no nurses. "In my experience, people like that are very rare. They're called heroes. Anyone in my business would be happy to save a hero's life, if given the chance."

"Ma'am, if you can do that . . ." He glanced at her. "It would be the best Christmas gift, ever. You'd be my hero."

"Then we'll be heroes together, because I have every intention of saving your life. And call me CC." She continued walking briskly down the endless hallway. "I won't get it done by Christmas, but I will get it done—with some help. I'm overseeing your entire treatment from start to finish, and a microbiologist from one of the hospital's benefactors is coming in. My understanding is you have a genetic condition that's causing issues with your internal organs. Is that right?"

He sighed. "That's one way to put it."

She opened a treatment room door, revealing a large examining table and a lot of medical equipment. "Have a seat." She stood by the round stool at the counter. "What else can you tell me about the condition, Mr. DeShear?"

"Hank." He smiled. "Since we're gonna be friends and all. How is it that you ended up working the Christmas Eve shift, CC? Seems like a nurse of your seniority and stature would have the holiday off."

She cocked her head. "Stature?"

"Your ID badge." He pointed to the credential clipped to the hem of her uniform top. "It's a different color than the admitting nurse and every nurse we passed in the hallways, but it's got the same color stripe across the top as the doctors in the Limited Access Area."

She looked down at her ID, her cheeks turning pink. "You're very observant."

"Comes with the territory for a detective, I guess. So what happened? You drew the short straw at the office party?"

"No." She took a short breath, clasping the clipboard and folding her hands in front of her. "I volunteered. They needed a senior person to work this case. I'm the best on the staff."

"Well, I'm glad I'm getting the best, but I hate to drag you out on Christmas Eve just to take my blood samples. They could have had somebody else do that."

"Yes, but I wanted to do it. It made sense to be involved from the get-go, so I'd be completely up to speed."

He nodded. "You're used to calling the shots, aren't you?"

"Usually. Around here, anyway." She narrowed her eyes. "Are you going to be this inquisitive the whole time we work together?"

"Sorry." DeShear held his hands up. "I'll behave. You're in charge." He leaned on the examining table, tapping his fingers on the side of the cushion. "You asked about my condition. There's not much to tell so far. I had some flu-like symptoms a few weeks back. Because of the specific genetic defect I carry, the doctors ran some tests and concluded my bout with the flu was actually the opening salvo of the gamma sequence, a little genetic time bomb. It activates in people my age who have the condition, causing their internal organs to shut down. It's like an instant, rampant cancer—and your microbiologist friend has supposedly developed some drugs that will help me survive it."

"I'm sorry. That's a lot to deal with." She lifted the clipboard and made a few notes, then took his temperature and blood pressure. "How are you feeling right now?"

"Right now? Fine." He shrugged. "That's the irony. I'm a little sleepy from an overseas flight yesterday, but otherwise I feel completely normal.

It's just—I . . ." His shoulders slumped as his words caught in his throat. "It's hard to wrap my head around it, but when I do—when I realize I could be dead in a few months . . ."

She set her pen down and turned to him, speaking softly. "You can rescue innocent people from a burning building, but you can't do anything about some rogue elements in your genetic makeup that may kill you. That's a very scary place to be."

He stared at the floor, nodding, as his hand went to rub his abs. "Yeah."

"The biologist we have coming is an expert in this condition. She and the people behind her have successfully steered a few others through the onset of the gamma sequence. My job is to gather every piece of information you can give us, so we can develop a treatment. It will be a long, hard road, but if we—if you—are brave enough to endure it, you'll save a lot of people."

His gaze went to the medical equipment—an EKG, an IV drip. The knot in his gut grew. "It's like you said, a strange place to be."

"I said it's a scary place to be, not a strange place. You can't even say the word, can you?"

DeShear sighed. "Does that make me weak?"

CC shook her head, her voice falling to a whisper. "It makes you human."

"I'm just . . . I'm not good at asking for help."

"If you were," she grinned, "you'd be the first man I ever met who was."

DeShear smiled at that.

CC sat on the stool and leaned back, crossing her legs and folding her hands over one knee. "You said you just got back from a flight. Where were you traveling?"

"Indonesia, but . . . I can't really get into that."

"It could be important. That's not a direct flight. Many foreign countries have diseases that we don't have, and their airports can be—"

"It was government business." He shrugged. "The folks in charge said we need to keep it quiet."

A hint of a smile tugged at the corners of her lips. "Ooh, you're an international man of mystery, are you?"

"I hope not." DeShear seated himself on the examining table. "The flight back really took it out of me. I'll stay in Florida, thanks." His phone rang in his pocket. He took it out and pressed the button on the side, sending the call to voicemail, then flipped the switch to vibrate. "Sorry about that."

CC stood, taking the clipboard from the counter and pulling an ophthalmoscope from the drawer. With a quiet click, a tiny beam of light came out of it. She went to DeShear and placed her hand on his forehead, guiding the light toward his eye. Her fingers were warm against his skin.

"Look straight ahead, please." Leaning close, she peered through the scope, then moved to his other eye. "Well, mystery man, the secrecy thing fits right in with this operation. I don't know much about the microbiologist they assigned to work with me, other than she's an expert on your condition and has major financial backing."

Her breath was soft on his face. Fresh, and gentle. She had good skin—smooth, with very few wrinkles—and she wore almost no makeup. Her high cheekbones framed her blue eyes nicely. DeShear assumed her to be in her mid-thirties, with the trim figure of a long-distance runner.

She clicked off the scope, placed it on the counter, and withdrew another instrument from the drawer. Moving to his side, CC guided an otoscope to his ear. "To be honest, I was a little down about working Christmas Eve, but now I'm kind of excited about it. Yours is an interesting case."

"Yeah?" DeShear asked. The ear inspection tickled, but only slightly. "Well, I appreciate your enthusiasm. They said it was imperative to start my treatment right away, but I still feel bad about making you come out on Christmas Eve. That's a time for family."

"Hmm." She checked one ear, then the other. "These days, my family consists mainly of my mom, my sister's family, and my cat Horatio. Mom and Horatio are both asleep by nine-thirty most nights." Returning to the clipboard, she scribbled a few lines.

DeShear sat forward, putting his elbows on his knees. "Why'd you name your cat Horatio?"

She smiled but didn't look up. "I didn't name him that. He was a rescue. I think he's named after the fictional sea captain hero, Horatio Hornblower."

"Well." DeShear leaned back. "I guess even a cat doesn't deserve to be alone on Christmas Eve."

"He's not alone. He's with my mother." She set the clipboard down and took a set of EKG sensors from another drawer. The wires and tabs dangled as she held them up. "Take off your shirt, please. We're going to check your heart."

DeShear reached for his buttons, suddenly aware that CC had gotten his nervousness to fade substantially.

"And no, there's no Mr. Callander, if you were wondering. So maybe I would agree to go have a friendly Christmas soda in the hospital cafeteria after your session ends—just to alleviate your guilt for making me work late on Christmas Eve, of course."

"Of course." DeShear gave her a crooked smile.

Placing the bundle of wires on the examining table, CC pulled the EKG cart closer. "Unless there's a Mrs. DeShear."

"Not anymore. We divorced about ten years ago." His phone buzzed in his pocket.

CC peeled a tab off one of the EKG contacts. "Someone's trying awful hard to get ahold of you, mystery man."

"Yeah, but since my new friend CC is about to commence a life-saving treatment for me, that gets top priority. I'll call them back."

The examining room door flew open. A slender, black-haired woman with an armful of file folders burst into the room. "Sorry I'm late." Setting the folders on the counter, the stranger pulled a phone from the back pocket of her skinny jeans and waved it. "I just got the text ten minutes ago."

CC turned to the woman. "And you are . . ."

"I'm Maya Rodriguez." She extended her hand to the nurse. "I'm your microbiologist." As the ladies shook hands, Maya turned to their patient. "You must be Hamilton DeShear. I've heard a lot about you. How was your flight back from Indonesia?"

"Uh . . ." He glanced at CC, but decided if the young microbiologist was discussing his trip out loud, then maybe his prior case didn't need to be so hush-hush after all. If they were going to work together for the next ten months, CC would probably learn all about it anyway. "It was a very long, very bumpy commercial flight." DeShear finished unbuttoning his shirt and took it off, draping it across the top of the examining table—and catching CC's eyes lingering on his muscular chest. He sat upright and looked at Maya. "Getting to Indonesia was much nicer. Private jet."

"I flew in private jets a lot with my former boss. It'll spoil you." Maya returned to the counter and leafed through her folders. "How was the hotel?

"It was great. Do I have you to thank for that?"

"It was arranged through Dr. Carerra at Angelus Genetics. She wanted us to commence the first treatment cycle immediately upon your arrival back to the States. Let me give you the low down." Maya spun around and leaned against the counter, holding a file folder to her chest. "You're going to be getting a lot of injections—steroids and HGH, among other things, so you can expect some mood swings and nausea. Initially, the sessions will last three or four hours, but expect them to get longer and more frequent with the onset of the disease. I'll dose you with specialized stimulants and antibiotics to ward off the onset of infection. Think of it like a bullet proof wall we're trying to erect between you and the disease attacking you, so it never gets a toehold, but where it does, we react with precision treatments in overwhelming force."

"If your treatment can keep me alive," DeShear said, "I can put up with all of that. Do I stay in the hospital the whole time?"

"I can do most of the treatments remotely, but it's better to do everything here. Nurse Callander needs to monitor your progress and reactions so she can properly interact with the medical experts we've retained from around the world."

His phone buzzed in his pocket. He took it out and glanced at the screen. Another call from the same number, a 612 area code. He pressed the side button and sent the caller to voicemail. "That's fine. It's not like I have a case to work on or an apartment to go home to."

"What happened to your apartment?" CC asked.

"It kinda got burned up before I went out of town. But the people Ms. Rodriguez works with— via your benefactors, I think—are helping to arrange for a nice big check to get me a new one."

"Lay back, please." CC prepared another EKG sensor and pressed it to his chest. "You look like you're in good shape."

"Thank you." DeShear watched her press the sensor onto his firm torso. "I run on the beach every—"

"No." CC shook her head. "I mean, you don't look like someone who's about to have multiple internal organ failures. They tend to look very jaundiced."

The last sensor went on the side of his rib cage. He tensed, trying not to react.

"And you definitely don't look your age," CC said. "At least, not what they wrote in the chart."

DeShear peered at the sensor stickers making a polka dot pattern on his chest. "I'd say it's good genes, but we all know that's not the case, since my genes are about to kill me."

"It is and it's not," Maya said. "You have good genetics, but you have some genetic defects, too. We all do."

"I'll trade you." His phone buzzed again.

CC stepped back. "Do you need to get that? We really need you still for this."

"Okay, I'll answer it." He pulled the phone from his pocket. It was the 612 caller again. DeShear mashed the button and held the phone to his ear. "DeShear Investigations."

"Hamilton? It's Raiden Han." The man's voice wavered. "I think you knew my wife. She went by the name Lanaya Kim."

DeShear bolted upright. "Yes, I know her. She's a client of mine." The knot returned to his gut. "Is something wrong?"

"There's been a terrible tragedy. My wife . . . she's been shot." He choked the words out as his voice broke. "She's dead."

A jolt of adrenaline went through DeShear. He jumped off the examining table, putting a hand to his forehead. "Where are you?"

"Hey!" CC said, putting her hands on his shoulders and stopping him. The EKG wires dangled loosely at his waist.

"The children and I are on our way to the safe house that my wife set up." He sniffled. "Mr. DeShear, before she went to Indonesia . . . she said if anything happened to her, I should call you."

DeShear squeezed his eyes shut, nodding. "You did the right thing, Raiden. Now, listen carefully. When we hang up, power your phone off and get a disposable one as soon as you can. Call me from that phone, and don't use this one again. I'm—" He glanced at the wires hanging from his chest and the medical machinery in the room. "I'm on my way."

He ended the call and grabbed his shirt.

"Hey! No, no, no." CC pulled the garment from his hands. "You aren't going anywhere. We need to start your treatments. Now. Tonight."

"The death of this lady means that something I thought we stopped in Indonesia *didn't* get stopped. Lives are on the line. I know how much I need this treatment, but I'm fine right now. Let me check into what's happened, and—"

"Look at me," CC said. "*Your* life is on the line. If Maya can't give you these medicines in the right doses, at the right times, you're not going to be around to help anybody. You said you were tired from your trip, but how do you know it's not the second tier of the gamma sequence starting? Maya said there'd be fatigue. We may need to start now if we're going to save you."

He turned away, rubbing the back of his neck.

"You don't have ten months, Hank. You may not have ten weeks—unless we start your treatment."

DeShear frowned, pacing across the room and holding his head in his hands. He wheeled around and looked at CC. "Is there a way to do both?" He faced Maya. "You said you could do mobile treatments. Come with me."

Maya's jaw dropped. "Well, yes . . ."

"What? No." CC stepped in front of him and blocked the door.

"CC, please," DeShear said. "The murder of Lanaya Kim could mean we didn't stop a cold-blooded killer called The Greyhound, or that a power-drunk sociopath named Dr. Hauser is still on the loose. He's responsible for the deaths of thousands. I have to check this out. Please."

"Hank—"

"We can't start the treatments. Not here." DeShear slipped his shirt on. "Whoever killed Lanaya Kim knows I was working with her. She flew back with me from Indonesia, and I told her she'd be safe. Now, less than forty-eight hours later, she's been murdered. Her killer might be looking for me— and a hospital isn't set up for that kind of attack. I can't be here when they arrive, and neither can either of you. Staying here with me puts you in harm's way."

CC looked down, shaking her head. "Yes, but . . ."

He lowered his voice and looked into her eyes. "You said your job was to help keep me alive. Staying here and starting the treatment could get us all shot to death. We'll come up with a plan B. That's what us hero types—you and me—that's what we do."

Sighing, she stepped aside. "Okay."

"Maya." DeShear glanced at the microbiologist. "You on board with that?"

"Yeah. I can make a remote treatment work."

"Good. Give me a number to call you at and head to the airport as soon as you can. Get out of this hospital. Now." He turned back to CC. "That goes for you, too."

Maya scribbled on a piece of paper. "I'll be at the airport in less than an hour. You can reach me at this number."

"You already have my card," CC said. "Call me so I can keep you alive."

"We'll get you any information you need, I promise." He smiled. "And I'll be back to have that drink, even if it's a soda in the cafeteria. Maybe for New Year's."

"Okay," CC said. "It's a date."

Maya handed DeShear her number. Shoving the piece of paper into his pocket, he turned and disappeared down the hallway.

CHAPTER 3

"Mind the gap."

The loudspeaker reiterated its message several times as the train pulled into Cambridge station. Jaden Trinn stood and joined a few other passengers as they exited the car, turning the head of more than one college boy as she did. Ten years older than most of them, she gently tugged the back of her short leather jacket. The coat barely covered the top of her slim hips, but it hid the blackjack tucked into her belt. Trinn rolled her shoulders as she walked across the small lobby, loosening up after the long ride. The station at Cambridge was smaller than she expected, and not nearly as tall as the one in London. The roof of Kings Cross must have been sixty feet up. The Cambridge station ceiling seemed barely fifteen.

The loudspeaker crackled again as the train doors shut.

"Mind the gap."

A quick swipe of her newly purchased "Oyster" card got her past the turnstile and into the chilly air waiting outside of the beige brick building. The station's grand arches and gingerbread roof line were a stark contrast to the dull, gray sky overhead. The wind cut straight through Trinn's skinny jeans and high heeled boots, whipping her brown hair over her shoulder. She winced, pulling the collar of her jacket close around her slender, athletic figure as she untucked the tails of the red scarf.

A smattering of other passengers trickled by, headed towards their destinations. Waddling past the blue safety barriers that lined the front of the building, a plump middle-aged man approached the big, arched doorway. He took a long drag on a hand-rolled cigarette and pointed to the red scarf. "Trinn?"

"Yeah." She looked the man up and down. Again, not what she expected. "You must be Hastings."

"Hollings, Miss." He narrowed his eyes. "You're American. They didn't tell me that. Or that you was a woman."

Trinn stood tall, bracing against the wind. "Does that make a difference?"

"Not to me it doesn't. I like Yanks. And pretty women." Hollings dropped the cigarette and crushed it under his foot. "Just didn't know, is all."

The Brit had a rough edge to his mannerisms. Trinn decided he probably wasn't as soft as he looked. "Most of my trip has been on a 'need to know' basis. Guess the people in charge figured you didn't need to know."

"Right." Hollings shoved his hands into his coat pockets. "Any baggage, then?"

Trinn shook her head. "Nope."

"Well, my car's just there." He pointed down Station Street, walking between the blue barriers. "Then it's three hours on the A-1 toward Leeds—or did you fancy a bite first?"

"I'm good." Trinn tugged her collar again. "Let's just get on the road."

Hollings' Ford Escape was easily five years old, but it was shiny and clean—and warm. Trinn settled into the seat on the left, debating whether to soften the old man up with some conversation. "I wasn't expecting it to be so cold in London."

"Christmastime. Can't be helped." Hollings pulled onto the nearly-empty street. "It's cold where you live, too, eh?"

"New York. Yeah, it's freezing there, but we've gotten a ton of snow this year. That helps, somehow." She turned to him. "What does 'Mind the gap' mean?"

"Oh, that's a warning to passengers to be careful when they step off the train. There's a space between the platform and the railway car as you exit."

"People ride these trains every day, but they need to be reminded not to fall into the hole?"

"I suppose so. Safety, you know." Hollings checked the rearview mirror. "Bit of a waste of time, us going all the way to Leeds, don't you think? Nobody's following us."

Trinn stared out the window as fields of short, green vegetation streamed past. "New boss, new rules, I guess."

Hollings glanced at his passenger. "If you don't mind me saying . . . this job doesn't make much sense. You, coming up from London to meet me in Cambridge, then us going all the way north to Leeds and back to Macclesfield again? Then out to Liverpool on the coast—to hijack one of our own trucks? I mean, the delivery driver works for us, don't he?"

Trinn nodded. "That's right."

"Then why, when our boys would be lifting his cargo between Macclesfield and Liverpool anyway, would we need to jump in ahead of them and snatch it first? Aren't we shooting ourselves in the foot?"

"Interesting way of putting it. But like I said—new boss, new rules, I guess." She glanced toward the rear hatch. "Now, let's see what Santa brought us for Christmas, shall we?"

Hollings smiled. "Ah, I was wondering when we'd get 'round to that. Here, it's in the boot."

He took the next exit and pulled onto a side road, driving until a muddy path cut between two falling stone walls. Shifting the car to park, Hollings opened his door and stepped to the rear of the car.

The icy wind blasted through the vehicle, erasing any hint of warmth. Trinn got out and cupped her hands to her mouth, blowing hot air through them as she walked to the rear of the Escape.

Glancing around, Hollings leaned forward and pressed the release. The shiny hatch raised itself with a long, slow wheeze, revealing a few cardboard boxes resting on a blanket. Shoving the boxes to the side, the old man grabbed the corner of the blanket and flipped it back.

He stepped back, smiling at his cargo.

Trinn stared at the weapons—a small pistol and a double-barreled shotgun. "That's it?"

"That's plenty for these parts, Miss. When we shove the business end of that blaster into our driver's face, he'll be too busy trying not to pee down his leg to wonder why we're robbing him."

"Does the driver know you?"

"Nah." Hollings dug a crumpled pack of cigarettes out of his pocket, shaking the pack to get one loose. He pulled it free with his lips and fished in his baggy pockets for a lighter. "Is he supposed to?"

"Can't have any loose ends." Trinn plucked the unlit cigarette from her new friend's mouth and tossed it into the brush. "Let's get back on the road. It'll be dark soon."

* * * * *

Trinn recognized the handgun. It held eight shots fully loaded, and the shotgun could hold two at a time, but that would have to do. She rubbed her hands together, staring out at the road. The sun had already set, and the scant traffic had dropped off to almost nothing.

Christmas.

"So there's a guy like you in Budapest and Athens . . . where else?"

"I don't know about Budapest," Trinn said. "We've started operations in Yemen, I know that. And Algeria."

"Can't say I care for either of those. Wouldn't mind a trip to Greece, though. Them other places are a bit manky, for my taste."

"I'll have to take your word for it." Her cell phone pinged with a text message. A moment later, Hollings' phone pinged, too. Trinn opened her phone's GPS app and studied the screen. "Pull over up here," she said, pointing. "At that deserted-looking hay barn."

Hollings glanced at her, slowing the vehicle. "Change of plans, hey?"

"Check your phone." Her GPS indicated that a crossroad was nearby. She leaned forward. About a hundred yards ahead, a dark road connected to the one they were on. "This is the place. That cutoff goes to Liverpool."

He stopped the car and dug a phone out of his pocket, reading the message. "This says there's a package waiting for you here." He stared into the fading light. "Never used this drop before."

"Let's go." Trinn opened her door. "Leave the car running so the heat stays on."

"Right." He put a hand on the door latch as she got out and walked in front of the car. The headlights illuminated Trinn and the rickety old wooden structure in the distance. Tall weeds covered the ground between them.

Hollings opened his door. "Probably in that old barn, eh? I'll just grab us a torch—ah, flashlight—Miss."

The wind blasted Trinn's face and ears as she shoved her hands into her pockets and stared at the barn.

Hollings waddled to the back of the car, the low engine noise of the exhaust pipe making the only sound in the quiet night. He opened the hatch and took a flashlight out of one of the cardboard boxes, tucking it under his arm. Flipping back the blanket, he grabbed the shotgun and raised it in the direction of the barn.

Trinn was no longer there. Hollings's jaw dropped as he gazed into the darkness.

"Looking for someone?" Trinn stepped from beside the car, her hand resting on the raised tailgate.

Hollings gasped, swinging the shotgun toward her. He thrust his finger onto the trigger. "Get on the ground, you!"

Trinn didn't move. "Why the double cross?"

"Get on the ground!" He leveled the gun at her, scowling. "I'll blast you to pieces, girl! I swear it!"

Trinn heaved the hatch down, crashing it into Hollings' hands and the barrel of the gun. The impact knocked the shotgun from his grasp as he pulled the trigger, firing the gun into the car's bumper. Trinn threw her shoulder into the tailgate, crushing Hollings against the car frame. He howled in pain.

Flinging the hatch open, she swung a long leg into his chest. Hollings arched backwards, arms out, as he crashed to the ground.

The old man lay in the weeds moaning, a trickle of blood running from his ear. Lifting the tailgate once more, Trinn pulled the pistol from under the blanket and held it up to the interior light to ensure it was loaded.

She walked to Hollings and put the sole of her boot on his neck, gritting her teeth as she lowered the gun to his head. "You know the driver of the truck, don't you?"

"I don't!" Hollings coughed, his trembling hands raised in surrender. "Honest."

Trinn cocked the gun and pressed it to his forehead, pressing harder with the heel of her boot. "This isn't a good time to test my patience. I'm freezing, and if my hand starts to shake, I might have an accident with this little pea shooter."

"Okay, I know him," Hollings whimpered. "Met a few times, is all."

"Well," Trinn narrowed her eyes. "If it makes you feel better, that won't factor into whether I kill him or not."

"He's a good fellow. Won't give us no guff."

"No, he won't." Trinn pulled the gun away and lifted her foot from Hollings' neck. His hands flew to his throat as he gasped and wheezed. She stepped back, shaking her head and glaring at the quivering old man, then raised the gun again and pointed it in his direction. "The truck driver won't give us any guff—and neither will you."

* * * * *

On the other side of the empty barn, a man sat in a car, waiting in the darkness. Three short bursts of light flashed across the trees, illuminating them like lightning from a faraway storm.

The man's phone hummed on the dashboard and the name *Trinn* appeared on the screen. He pressed the green button. "Hello?"

Trinn's voice was calm and even on the other end of the line. "Call Fuego. Phase two is complete. Now drive around the barn and come get me."

CHAPTER 4

DeShear glanced up from his phone and waved at Maya as she made her way across the Delta Airlines terminal. Overhead on the public address system, a female voice cut through the holiday music to announce a gate change for a delayed flight. Setting a large suitcase by DeShear's chair, Maya took the seat next to him. A large shopping bag rested at his feet, but no luggage.

"You went shopping?" Maya said.

"I got a few things. My apartment burned, remember?" DeShear finished typing and sent the phone to black screen. "I don't have a lot of clothes at the moment."

Crossing her legs, Maya tapped her hands on the armrests of her seat. "Hank, I understand the need to get out of the hospital—no sense in being a sitting duck—but why are you going to Minnesota?"

"Not just me—you're going, too, right?"

"Yeah, I didn't pack this steamer trunk because I thought I'd be sitting at home." She sighed, glancing at her big suitcase. "But I wish you'd reconsider. Your first few cycles of meds are in there. It's a lot of paperwork to get all this through security. But let's think about this. Can't we move to a different hospital and you not go flying off? Getting your treatment started is very important. If we wait, it could—"

"I don't think Minnesota can wait," DeShear said. "There are a lot of lives at stake. Besides, I feel fine. A little tired from my flight, but that's it."

"Is it, doctor? Do you have jet lag or are your kidneys shutting down and letting toxins seep into your bloodstream? Or maybe it's lack of red blood cell regeneration due to bone marrow failure. That's why we need medical assistance, like what we set up at St. Joe's. The symptoms don't necessarily happen in the same order each time, and they don't happen all at once in every patient. We need professionals to monitor you so we know what to treat based on what's attacking you." Maya leaned on the armrest between the seats. "Getting the treatment you need, it's not some kind of game. The cycles were very hard on my prior patient. He nearly died, more than once. Running all over the place . . ." She sighed. "We can do it, but it makes everything much harder."

DeShear pursed his lips and stared at the floor. "I need to see what happened. I owe her that. I was convinced she'd be safe. The local police won't know how her death might connect to . . . bigger things." He glanced at his cell phone. "Anyway, that's what I put in an email to Camilla Madison at the IRS. Cammy was in charge in Indonesia. She has the ear of some important people. She's also my ex-wife, so she knows me, and knows I wouldn't bother her with something that was probably a waste of time."

Maya shook her head. "Do you know what a failing liver feels like? Or a weakened pancreas? Maybe like jet lag. You have an insidious condition that will knock you to your knees without notice. It will kill you if you aren't—"

"Okay!" DeShear's voice cut through the airport lobby. Several tourists turned their heads and looked at him. He lowered his voice. "I'm going to Minnesota. I don't have a choice." He sighed. "But I'll do the treatments. I'll do my job and I'll make sure you can do yours. Okay?"

"Okay. It's not that easy, but it's a start."

A gate attendant in a Santa hat announced the arrival of a flight from The Bahamas. A small cluster of people in leather jackets and heavy sweaters got up, assembling themselves in a line near the counter as they awaited the subsequent boarding announcement. Outside the massive windows, a large passenger jet pulled up.

DeShear rubbed his chin. "Look, something is up with this murder, I know it. Maybe The Greyhound changed his mind and started his vendettas again, or maybe some deranged disciples of his are trying to carry on his original mission. But it might not even be his group. There could be people who were ousted from Angelus Genetics—angry factions, who are looking for revenge." He glanced at Maya. "I have to see if Lanaya's death was connected to any of them."

"Like who?" Maya asked. "I know about Dr. Hauser and how he was running a criminal enterprise at Angelus, but he's dead."

DeShear faced her. "Is he? We never saw a body. In Indonesia, the special assistant to the prime minister said Hauser died, and we all took her word for it. With Hauser's money and connections, he could have easily bought his way out of the country. But that's just one possibility. There are other places we'll need to consider."

She shook her head. "You keep saying 'we.' I'm not sure I can just pull up stakes and run around like that."

"Then we'll have to figure that part out as we go." He leaned forward, staring into her eyes. "Hauser's facility in Indonesia killed thousands of people. He could be anywhere on the planet by now, gearing up production in places we never even thought about."

"That . . . that's a pretty scary thought."

"Scary enough to get you on a plane to Minnesota and wherever else we might need to go?"

She got up from her seat. "I think I can sell that to my bosses. Where's the ticket counter?"

* * * * *

The flight attendant pushed the drink cart down the aisle, distributing soft drinks—and stronger drinks, for those so inclined. DeShear asked for a Mexican beer and Maya ordered a Sprite. When the attendant had placed the drinks on their tray tables and moved far enough away, DeShear leaned over to his companion. "How schooled did you get about all this? Hauser, Angelus Genetics, The Greyhound—how much do you know?"

It was a tricky question to ask, no matter what answer he got. Maya might know a lot; she might not. She seemed well financed, and acted like she was well connected, but that didn't mean the higher ups let her in on the big picture. She might bluff, too, when she answered . . . but with his life on the line, and Maya assigned to help him through, at some point DeShear would have to put his full trust in her. Now was as good a time as any.

Maya took a long sip of her soda and set it on the seatback table in front of her, rattling the ice cubes around in the plastic cup. "I worked with Dr. Carerra—you know her. She helped take down the corrupt regime at Angelus Genetics. Good enough?"

"It's a start. You act like you know more than you're letting on."

"How so?"

"Anyone who wasn't pretty well connected wouldn't have gotten on this plane with me. Not for the reasons I gave you. They'd have left the hospital, maybe, and gone home."

"I'm here to save your life."

"That's not all you're here to do," DeShear said. "I'm trusting you, Maya. You have to trust me, or when the bullets start flying . . ."

She winced.

"Yeah, this stuff is for real, too. A geneticist—a nice, hardworking scientist just like you, who wanted to help keep people all over the world from getting sick—she got brutally murdered.

Probably for no other reason than money." DeShear shook his head. "That's what we're dealing with."

"Maybe I should have stayed home."

"I'm glad you didn't. If what Carerra said about my condition is true, I'm in for a rough ride. She trusts you to get me through this thing, so do I. That means you can trust me, too."

"Hmm. That geneticist trusted you. Look what happened to her."

DeShear's phone pinged with a text message. He pulled it from his pocket and glanced at the screen. "Looks like the husband got to the safe house and picked up a new phone."

Maya slouched in her seat, staring at the ice in her plastic cup. "Will he know anything?"

"I doubt it." DeShear set the phone on the tray table. "I think Lanaya wanted him and the kids free and clear of this stuff, just in case. You can't tell people what you don't know. But somebody killed his wife. Her dying the second she set foot back in the U. S., that was no coincidence."

"If Hauser is alive, my money is on him."

"Not The Greyhound?"

Maya peered at DeShear out of the corner of her eye. "No."

"Why not?"

She gazed into her plastic cup, the ice cubes getting a little smaller each time she looked at them. "We're going to trust each other, right?" Maya sat up. "When the bullets start flying, you'll keep me safe?"

"You and Dominique Carerra are the best chances I have to stay alive, and she's not here. That pretty much makes you the whole world to me."

"Okay. Well . . ." Maya swallowed hard. "That former boss I mentioned? He was The Greyhound."

DeShear stopped breathing for a moment, letting the impact of those words settle on him. The Greyhound had been a cold-blooded killer, bent on revenge, who seemed to see the light—but did he? Lanaya might be dead for thinking so.

"Now you know," Maya said. "Dominique did what she thought was right at the time by helping him, and I helped her. But that's changed now. So I have some battle scars, too."

"Where's The Greyhound?"

"Underground. Nobody knows where, not even Dominique. But I don't think he killed your friend."

DeShear thought about it. If Maya was still working with The Greyhound, she could have killed DeShear at the hospital or staged a guy outside to whack him when he left. She'd almost certainly have known Lanaya was dead. Maya could poison him with the first round of drugs, but she wouldn't risk getting on a plane to Minnesota to do it. Not when there were easier ways to get rid of him. It didn't add up.

The tension drained out of his neck and shoulders. He could trust her.

"While I was getting to the airport," Maya said, "I checked the news. The police are saying your friend was shot multiple times at point blank range.

Killing someone like that . . ." She shook her head. "Why would one human being do that to another person?"

"The killer was sending a message. He wants people to *know* she's dead, and that she died violently. He wants people like her scared so they'll keep quiet about what they know."

Maya shuddered. "Pretty effective." She crunched through the remaining ice cubes in her plastic cup and grabbed DeShear's beer. "Better get us a few more of these."

* * * * *

Their faces said it all.

Raiden Han stood at the door with his grown children, his eyes red and swollen. It had been a sleepless night for all of them, and the day wouldn't be much better.

"Mr. DeShear." He swallowed hard, his voice quivering. "This is my daughter Sadka and my son Ronin."

DeShear shook the boy's hand and smiled at the girl. "I'm . . . very sorry to meet you under these circumstances."

"My son is a senior in high school and my daughter, my daughter is . . ."

The girl broke into tears. All of them had been crying, and at some point it would stop, but today wasn't that day.

"This is my associate, Maya," DeShear said. "We . . ." He stopped himself. He had no words.

The young man, trying hard not to cry, stood rigid and firm in the foyer of the safe house, hugging his younger sister and staring at the floor. Their father wrapped his arms around the two of them.

DeShear looked into Sadka's eyes, his voice falling to a whisper. "I knew your mother. She was my friend." He blinked hard, forcing a smile. "You look like her."

Sadka peeked out at DeShear from her father's arms.

"Your mom was smart and strong," DeShear said. "And very brave. I didn't know her long, but . . ." He swallowed, a knot forming in his throat. "She saved my life by telling me about a condition I have, and by connecting me with people who could help. She wanted to help others like me. That's who she was. That goodness, that strength, is part of you, too." DeShear's gaze went to Ronin, then the father, then back to the Sadka. "I can't offer you much, but I promise you this. Whoever killed your mom, I'm going to find them."

CHAPTER 5

A large wreath adorned the wall of the police station. In front of it, the desk sergeant checked DeShear's credentials. "Okay." He handed Deshear's ID back to him and gestured to a row of wooden chairs and benches lining the wall of the empty lobby. "Have a seat. The investigating officer is Jack Coleman. He'll be right down."

Maya sat on a bench; DeShear paced back and forth across the lobby until a tall, dark-haired officer appeared. "Are you folks inquiring about the double homicide?"

"Yes, sir." DeShear stood and shook hands with Officer Coleman. "I've been asked by the victim's family to look into it. She was Dara Han. Can we talk for a moment? I think I might be able to help your investigation."

"Sure." Coleman nodded to the door. "I was just headed out for a smoke. Been working nonstop on this case."

"You deserve a break, then." DeShear waved toward the exit. "Lead on."

"Outside?" Maya said. "I'll wait here. I'm not a fan of cold weather if I can avoid it."

"There's hot coffee and tea in the hallway, ma'am," Coleman said. "Help yourself."

"Thanks." Maya wrapped her arms around herself. "I may try to bathe in it."

An icy wind blew nonstop across the station's front steps from the municipal parking lot next door. Several officers and a few staffers had gathered on a corner to smoke.

When the first breath of cold, dry air reached DeShear's lungs, it burned. He coughed reactively, swallowing a few times until the feeling subsided. "From what I saw in the news, the shooting was out by the airport. Dara Han was alone in the car and was shot several times."

"She was shot *eight* times," Coleman said. "That's what we call overkill—the mark of a killer whose emotions got carried away. Usually, that's because it's personal, somehow. There was a tow truck driver killed, too. Same gun, but only two shots—one to the head, one to the chest—so the killer had calmed down by then." He shook a cigarette out of the pack and lit it. The wind whisked each ribbon of smoke from his lips and streamed it over his shoulder. "But the double homicide kicks it out of my pay grade. I'll be turning the case over to our investigative unit this afternoon. Detective Nillson will be handling it from there. I asked her to join us."

"Thanks." DeShear hunched his shoulders against the wind. "You were the first one on the scene, right?"

"To the female victim? Yes, sir," Coleman said. "So, what can you share that might help us?"

DeShear sighed. "Well, your female victim had several aliases. Lanaya Kim, was one. Akina Cho was another. She used them for travel and hotel reservations. Maybe for other things. She had money—cash—stashed in airports. Atlanta, for sure, and Tampa."

The officer took a drag on his cigarette. "Was she involved in some sort of illegal activity? Drugs, or identity theft? Was she a . . . was she turning tricks?"

The burn in DeShear's lungs loomed again, sending him into a second fit of coughing. He put a fist over his mouth and turned away. The knot in his stomach had returned.

Is this it? Is this how it starts?

Coleman leaned forward. "Can I get you some water?"

DeShear shook his head, clearing his throat a few times. "It's just a tickle," he wheezed, blinking a tear out of his eye. He righted himself. "The cold air here is really making my throat go crazy." Taking a deep breath, DeShear tried to clear his airway again, but the icy chill hit his lungs and launched him into another coughing spell.

He recovered, cleared his throat a few more times, and patted his chest. "Geez."

The officer smiled. "Minnesota winters aren't for everybody."

"Wow." Deshear sniffled. "I'm sorry about that. It's like when I had the flu a few weeks ago. I did nothing but sleep and cough for a week." He cleared his throat again. "Anyway, to answer your question, no. Lanaya Kim was clean as a whistle. She was a respected scientist, but she feared somebody was after her."

"Guess she feared right." Coleman took another puff of his cigarette, turning to exhale away from DeShear and cupping his cigarette low by his thigh. "The shooter killed her at close range and didn't leave a fingerprint anywhere. Not finding prints isn't unusual this time of year, it being so cold and all. Everybody's wearing gloves. But so many shots at such close range—that's what detective Nillson calls interesting."

"What about the ballistics?"

"Standard .45." Coleman shrugged. "Nothing special."

"Ten shots between two victims . . . that requires reloading. Any fingerprints on the shell casings?"

The officer glared at DeShear. "We know how to do our job, sir."

"I know you do. I'm sorry." DeShear lowered his head and stared at the gray horizon. "It was a long flight and guess I'm still a little tired from it."

A leggy blonde approached the men, dressed in a slender wool overcoat. Tufts of short-cropped hair stuck out from under a North Face beanie. "Mind if I join you, gentlemen?"

Coleman glanced over his shoulder, smiling. "Please do." He nodded to DeShear. "Detective

Erika Nillson, this is Hamilton Deshear, a private investigator out of Tampa."

She shook DeShear's hand. "You're far from home, Hamilton."

"And hating it." Coleman chuckled. "Our frosty atmosphere has been giving him fits."

DeShear cleared his throat, shaking his head. "It's a combination of things. Mostly I'm drying out from the lack of humidity. It's tickling my throat and making my face feel like it's cracking."

She studied his cheeks and jaw. "You have to moisturize up here. I'd be a prune if I didn't."

"Can you do me a favor?" DeShear said. "I read in the news that you're understaffed at the moment, but would you ask the coroner to run an advanced toxicology screen on your two victims? We're looking for the drug Propofol, and maybe traces of chloroform. It's a long shot, but Propofol won't show up on a regular toxicology test."

"That's interesting. Sure, I'll request it." Nillson narrowed her eyes. "What's your angle on this? How do our shootings relate to anything in Florida?"

"I'm playing some hunches right now. The victim was a friend of mine, and in Tampa we had a killing that was linked to some others—the one I was looking into was a headmaster at a private school. How'd your killer get the tow truck?"

Coleman stuck his cigarette between his lips and pulled a notepad from his pocket. "The driver got called to a T3—a car with a dead battery. Pretty standard in this weather. The road service dispatcher says she sent him out to the warehouse district near the airport around ten o'clock, but they never heard back from him after that. She figured he called it a night and went home without calling in. He'd done it before."

DeShear nodded. "Any tire tracks in the snow or signs of other vehicles at the address?"

"We're not sure he got to the location." Coleman flipped his notebook closed. "According to the tow company, when a driver arrives on scene, they're supposed to radio in with an arrival code, and when he gets the account information of the car he's servicing, he's supposed to call that in, too. The dispatcher never got any of that from him."

"So . . ." DeShear rubbed his chin. "He got dispatched and never got to where he was going?"

"Or the stranded motorist wasn't there anymore," Coleman said. "Or they didn't have their membership card on them, or he got lazy and didn't call it in."

DeShear shook his head and folded his arms. "On the night you get shot in the head with a .45, it's not a coincidence you forgot to do things. More likely you didn't get a chance to do them. Same as the female victim. She never saw it coming. Eight bullets at close range is an ambush."

"So," Coleman said. "Our killer knows what he's doing."

"Killers, plural." Detective Nillson looked down, rocking back and forth on her feet. "One person didn't do all this. First, the murders were done in different styles. Eight shots all over the place on the woman versus two precision shots for the truck driver. That tends to indicate different shooters.

Second, to appear and disappear—that requires coordination and planning. The gunman couldn't have known where the victim's car was going to stop—not exactly—so he couldn't have had a vehicle stashed there. Somebody might have seen it. My guess is, they had to get the tow truck first, in order to stop the Audi driver. So, two precision shots for the truck driver—just enough to get the job done—followed by eight scattered shots for her . . . that kind of overkill indicates someone else did the second murder. A novice, probably. New to murder." She glanced at DeShear. "My guess is, the woman's killer got picked up when the job was done. That means we have two people involved in the killings."

"At least." DeShear nodded. "And for a set of killers to go take out a tow truck driver and then a geneticist who have nothing in common, that means it's part of something bigger."

The officers glanced at each other.

"Anyway, it ties to my dead guy in Tampa."

"Like how?" Nillson asked.

"Like the murder in Tampa was staged to look like an accident."

She shook her head. "This was no accident."

"No," DeShear said. "But the geneticist was the one who told me the dead headmaster in Tampa wasn't, either."

* * * * *

DeShear found Maya at the coffee machine. "Ready to go?"

"Maybe we should stay here." She gripped her coffee cup with both hands and held it to her chest. "It's warm and there's coffee. But . . ." she glanced at the wall clock. "We have to start your first round of meds. And you look like you need them. Your face is gray. How are you feeling?"

He reached for the coffee pot, trying to ignore the knot growing in his stomach.

No need to overreact. Maya's tests will tell us if anything's happening. Until then, it's just a cough.

"It's cold out there," he said. "You'd be gray, too, if you'd have tagged along."

"Uh-uh." She shook her head. "I'm no detective."

In his pocket, DeShear's phone rang. He pulled it out and glanced at the screen.

Camilla.

Pressing the green button, DeShear put the phone to his ear. "Hey, Cammy, thanks for getting back to me. Did you get my email?"

"I did. Dash, this is not an IRS matter. We don't do murder investigations."

"I know." He poured some coffee into a paper cup. "But if it links up to your Indonesian situation, then you're right back in the middle again."

"If that's what pans out, then yes. Until then, it's a police matter and I can't help you."

He winced.

"I'm sorry," Camilla said. "I know that's not what you want to hear."

Detective Nillson rounded the corner. Raising a finger, she mouthed, "Got a minute?"

DeShear nodded. "Cammy, can you hold on a sec?"

"No. I'm pretty busy here, Dash. I'm mopping up an international crisis for the Vice President, remember?"

He lowered the phone. "What's up?"

"We held some information back from the public," Detective Nillson said. "But based on what you've been looking at, I thought you should know." She took a deep breath. "We found a business card in the female victim's mouth. It was from Angelus Genetics."

DeShear's jaw dropped. "Angelus . . ."

"Officer Coleman wasn't sure if he was allowed to release that to you. That's why he didn't. And I wanted to check you out first before I said anything." Nillson folded her arms and leaned on the wall. "But obviously, it changes things."

"It sure does. Thank you." He put the phone back to his ear as the detective left. "Cammy, the victim here had an Angelus Genetics business card stuffed in her mouth—just like The Greyhound did to his victim in Canada."

"Oh, no you don't." Camilla huffed. "Don't ask me what I think you're about to ask me."

DeShear smiled. "Not a lot of people knew about that."

"Dash . . ."

"Just mention it to the Vice President." He shrugged. "If the answer is to ignore it, I'll ignore it. If not—"

"If not, I'll be responsible for unleashing you on Washington, D. C. I hate to think about what could happen then."

He pressed the phone close to his ear. "So you'll make the call?"

"Promise me I won't look like an idiot if I do."

"Right now, you are riding high. You took down Angelus Genetics in Indonesia, exposed their human trafficking ring and their illegal organ harvesting program—you're practically a national hero."

"Except this latest information makes it look like I didn't do anything except stop one leg of it."

He nodded. "All the more reason to call the Vice President."

"Crap."

A wide grin stretched across DeShear's face. "Have I told you how smart you sound over the phone?"

"I'm hanging up now."

"But you'll tell the Vice President?"

"I'll call. Now go."

DeShear took a deep breath and let it out slowly. "Thank you."

She groaned. "Thank me when it's over and I still have a job."

CHAPTER 6

In her hotel room, Maya's phone alarm clanged. She reached past a crumpled Chick Fil A bag and tapped the screen to stop the noise, then leaned over to peer into the adjoining room. "Time for your meds, Hank."

"Okay." Deshear sat on the edge of the bed, phone in hand. "I just have to make one more call."

"No." She entered his room. A large array of bottles had been arranged on the desk, and a portable IV drip rack stood near the bed. "We had a deal. You said you'd drop everything when I needed to give you the treatment, so let's get started. You belong to me for the next three to four hours."

He dropped his hands to his lap, staring at the assembly of vials. "Okay. Can I make calls while you do . . . whatever it is you're about to do?"

"You can try." She pulled an IV rack toward him. "Good luck staying awake. I'll need your shirt off, too, so I can monitor your heart."

DeShear leaned back on his elbows, tossing his phone to the mattress as he reached for his buttons. "So how bad does all this get?"

"Bad." She lifted a bottle and inspected its contents. "But not right away. You aren't fooling anyone, by the way. I saw you coughing when you were talking to those cops. Your face is ashen. You've mentioned fatigue several times." Setting the bottle down, she pursed her lips. "If I had to guess, I'd say those are all signs of the sequence beginning, but I won't know for sure until I run some tests."

DeShear nodded, lowering his head.

Maya went to him and placed her hand on his shoulder. "Hey."

He peered up at her.

"My job is to get you through this," she said. "And I will. But it's not just me. There are experts waiting to look at everything I do."

"I know." He pulled his shirt off. "CC in Tampa, Dr. Carerra . . ."

"Among others." Maya picked up a pen and made some notes on a chart. "We have top people, from all around the world, and our sole interest is to keep you—and people like you—alive. And we will."

DeShear sighed. "Okay."

"You know . . ." Maya set down the chart and faced him. "Dr. Carerra didn't ask you to come in to St. Joe's on Christmas Eve for nothing. We wanted to start countermeasures. The thinking is, get the patient as strong as possible before the gamma sequence takes them down. Early indications show it may increase success rates by as much as thirty percent."

"Yeah?" DeShear nodded. "That does make me feel a little better."

"Good." She dabbed his arm with an alcohol swab. "Now, let's start the IV drip that's going to make you want to puke."

He narrowed his eyes at her.

"Just kidding," she said. "That part's not until later."

On the mattress, his phone rang. He glanced at it, then to Maya.

She rolled her eyes. "Go ahead."

Pressing the button, he answered the call. "DeShear Investigations."

"Good afternoon, Mr. DeShear," a calm, male voice replied. "Please hold for the Vice President."

A chill went through him as the line went quiet. He sat up, clearing his throat. Maya glared at him.

He pointed to the phone, whispering. "It's the Vice President of the United States."

"Uh-huh." Maya put her hand on her hip. "Thought you were going to be good."

DeShear lowered the phone. "I'm serious!"

"So am I. Your treatment is starting." She held up a needle for the IV drip and plunged it into his arm. "Talk fast, because these drugs are going to knock you for a loop."

He glared at the IV and raised his phone back to his ear.

"Dash, are you there? It's Camilla. They conferenced me in."

"Oh, hi, Cammy. Thanks for doing this." He lowered his voice. "Hey, got any tips for this kind of call?"

"Be brief and don't speculate too much. If the Vice President asks what you think, shoot straight."

The knot in his stomach grew.

A short burst of static rolled through the line, followed by the unmistakable voice of Vice President Hunter Caprey. "Hello, everyone," she said. "Thanks for letting me intrude on your holiday."

"Merry Christmas, Madam Vice President," Camilla said.

"Thank you, Bureau Chief Madison, and again, congratulations on uprooting that mess in Indonesia. How's the operation there going?"

"Very good. Still lots to dig through."

"I bet. Now, Mr. DeShear, Camilla informs me that you think the Angelus Genetics operation in Indonesian might have grown some legs and spread to another location, is that right?

"I think that's a real possibility at this point, ma'am." DeShear swallowed hard and wiped the palm of his hand on his pants. "In Indonesia, Angelus ran an international human trafficking ring, illegal organ harvesting, performed mass euthanasia to hide failures in their genetic experimentation . . . We shut that down. But Hauser's a business guy. It makes sense that he'd create other locations as a backup. He even indicated as much when we were recording him. Angelus could have hidden labs across the globe."

"Always have a backup plan," the Vice President said. "We used to say that when I was a Naval aviator."

"Yes ma'am."

"Okay, people. How do we find out for sure if it's spread?"

Camilla went first. "I was thinking, ma'am. We could start with our allies and Interpol. A medical facility of any size can't operate in the dark. It has to acquire supplies. In Indonesia, they masked the illegal organ harvesting program by making its purchases look like they were for a school and orphanage. Our allies could look internally and report back about entities making large pharmaceutical purchases, couldn't they?"

"Good," Caprey said. "I'll have Perlicia Jackson at CDC make a call. What else do we know?"

The line was silent.

"Dash?" Camilla said. "Any thoughts?"

"We need . . ." DeShear cleared his throat. "Hauser's operations need drugs to operate, but there are other things. Milk, for example. Angelus was buying it by the truckload for the orphanage and school. And there would be big tanks of medical gasses on site for surgeries. Purchases like that would be done through large hospitals or government agencies, maybe even directly through the pharmaceutical manufacturers themselves. Most of those are in western Europe, but Hauser would have a system in place to hide it. What we really need is someone on the ground who knows what to look for."

"Okay, then," Caprey said. "Let's get you on a plane, Hank."

"Me?" DeShear recoiled. "No, no, no. We need someone who can move around unfettered over there, in different countries. Someone with government contacts that would be willing to help us. And we have to assume Angelus has some leverage to use against anyone who'd talk. That's what they showed us in Minneapolis."

"Let me worry about that," Caprey said. "There's a routine diplomatic goodwill mission headed overseas. The first stop is Paris. Our ambassador to the UN was supposed to head it up, but now I think I will. We can launch our operation from France and add stops in Tel Aviv and Ukraine, changing the schedule as needed."

"Tel Aviv?" DeShear asked.

"Israeli intelligence. Mossad is the best in the world. As for Ukraine, well . . . in Russia, everything is for sale—especially information. When you're talking to Kiev, you're talking to the Kremlin. DeShear, we'll attach you to the goodwill tour as a special liaison. My office will get you the access you'll need when we get over there. And don't worry about people talking. One thing about government— there's always an unhappy element willing to divulge what they know to move up in the ranks."

Frowning, DeShear peered at the IV attached to his arm.

"We can talk more about everything else when I see you in the morning, detective."

"Excuse me?" He sat upright.

"The goodwill mission leaves tomorrow," the Vice President said. "Wheels up at 10 A. M. Get to D. C."

* * * * *

The Vice President's Chief of Staff closed the door behind him as he exited Caprey's office. Pulling his phone from his pocket, he dialed a number and put the phone to his ear.

"Jameel Pranav calling for the Director of National Intelligence, please."

A moment later, the call went through.

"Jameel?" Bob Richards' voice was rough. "What's the situation?"

"This is a request to authorize a Tampa private investigator to conduct an off books operation for Vice President Caprey."

"Son of a gun." Richards chuckled. "She went for it? You are a miracle worker, boy."

Pranav smiled as he walked into his office. "She resisted initially, but DeShear does have specialized knowledge gained from Indonesia about Dr. Hauser and The Greyhound. And while some of our people do, too, I explained to the Vice President it would be difficult to get career government types to risk their jobs to embark on what could end up being an embarrassing wild goose chase. Enabling DeShear to run around, on the other hand . . ." Pranav shrugged. "If he ends up being successful, we step up and take credit. If he messes up, we dump him—and we all maintain culpable deniability."

"Caprey's a former Navy officer. Hard to believe she went along with that last part."

"The Vice President doesn't know anything about that," Pranav said. "She's far too honorable to screw over a colleague and leave him on the battlefield. That part was all me, Mr. Director."

"Creative as ever, Jameel. So how stable is this PI?"

"He's perfect. He's the kind of guy who runs into burning buildings to save women and children."

"Hmm. That could be useful when the time comes. What about Hauser's drones? They almost ready?"

"More than that." Jameel smiled. "They're active. The latest series is so advanced, they're indistinguishable from what you'd see in a park or on the street—anywhere at all. He plans to release them any time now."

"Heaven help his enemies after that," Richards said.

"So." Jameel went to the window and stared out over the south lawn of the White House. "All the information from DeShear will come through Caprey—which means it will come through me. I just need you to make sure your many field assets will be on board."

"As I understand it," Richards said, "this is a personal request from my good friend Hunter Caprey—so don't worry, my people will do what they're told. British Intelligence, Mossad, you name it—we all do special off book favors for each other from time to time. Any doors your boy needs opened, they'll open."

"Thank you, Mr. Director." Jameel lowered the phone and ended the call.

CHAPTER 7

Maya was able to administer the first part of DeShear's treatment before leaving to catch the red eye from Minneapolis to Washington D. C., finishing the session on board the plane. When they finally touched down around 6:00 A. M., a staffer for Vice President Caprey waited at the gate. "Mr. DeShear, this way, please." The young man pointed to two Marines holding metal-detector wands. "And if you and the lady will give me any baggage claim check tickets, I'll have your luggage brought to you."

DeShear held his hand out to Maya. "This is Ms. Rodriguez, my healthcare professional. She needs to come with me if I'm to make this trip, and she needs access to the medical supplies in her bags."

"Yes, sir. I'll update the Vice President." The man turned and walked ahead of them.

"That was easy," Maya said.

"I guess they're used to people who bring a group with them." DeShear handed his shopping bag to one of the Marines. "Good thing. I'm not sure what I'd have done if they said no."

"I do." She straightened her jacket. "You'd have gone without me. And you'd have died."

As the young man led them down another hallway, DeShear lowered his voice and leaned near Maya. "About that coughing you saw yesterday. The cold air irritated my lungs, but when I went to cough—each time I tried to inhale between coughs . . . I couldn't get a deep breath. It was like someone was sitting on my chest."

She nodded. "You may have fluids building up. Probably not in your lungs, but in your abdomen, or chest cavity, from a secondary infection. We'll need to get some x-rays. How do you feel otherwise?"

"Pretty good, actually." He passed an oversized Christmas tree and a cartoon sign welcoming travelers to Virginia. "A little pressure in my chest, but otherwise I feel . . . strong. Refreshed. Your stuff works. Just don't ask me to take a deep breath."

"We'll take it step by step," Maya said. "But no more holding out. I'll run my tests and treat you accordingly, but information like that is important. We're a team now. If you tell me your symptoms, I can give you something to counteract them and keep you on your feet."

"Got it. Keep building that bullet proof wall."

A blast of cold air refocused DeShear on the other task at hand. The Marine escorts opened a security door, revealing a small motorcade pulling up outside. Police motorcycles and several black SUVs formed a parade line centered by a black limousine bearing the seal of the Vice President of the United States.

The staffer opened the door, and DeShear peered inside.

"Change of plans." The Vice President smiled from the back seat. "We're headed to London. Get in."

* * * * *

Vice President Caprey studied a folder as her limo sped down the highway. "CDC started making calls for us last night." She crossed her legs and faced Maya and DeShear. "Turns out, our friends in the U.K. had a big truckload of pharmaceuticals get hijacked two days ago on its way from Macclesfield to Liverpool." Removing a glove, the Vice President massaged her left knee. "The main cargo was cylinders of surgical gasses. Sounds like your guys."

DeShear put a hand to his beard stubble. "Following the truck would tell us a lot. Maybe Hauser is alive and stealing supplies while he relocates to a friendlier country."

The Vice President shook her head. "We'd have to find it first. It disappeared."

"A lot of commercial carriers have location devices on board," Maya said.

"The driver sure won't be telling us much." Caprey handed her folder to DeShear. "They found him unconscious in a ditch. All he remembers is the gun they pointed at him. Local police are searching for the truck now."

"Can we ask them to not move on it when they locate it?" DeShear turned to her Chief of Staff.

"Let's get a call to the trucking company and see if they have a tracker on the truck. And call whoever's order got stolen, too. They're gonna need another delivery. We definitely want a tracker on that."

As Jameel scribbled some notes, the Vice President's vehicle pulled to a stop next to a large jet with its engines running. It was decked out in blue on blue.

"That's my ride." Caprey's door opened and another frosty blast of air filled the car. A young marine stood at attention outside. "I have to get briefed on a few matters of state," she said. "But there are phones in the rear of the plane. I'll see that you're hooked up with a secure computer. Let's get airborne and we'll talk again in a few hours.

* * * * *

DeShear set his coffee on a small table, taking a seat in a leather chair. Maya sat across from him, typing on a computer marked Office Of The Vice President.

The rear of the plane was designated for news reporters, but a small area had been sectioned off for DeShear and his "medical professional." Maya took a bite of her Danish pastry and stared out the window of the plane. The skies were pale blue as far as the horizon, where they connected with the deep blue of the Atlantic Ocean.

She turned the computer so Deshear could read the screen. "Check this out. There are only two manufacturers in the U.K. that make the medical gasses that were stolen. One is in London, and the news says they're in the third week of a labor strike.

The other is in Macclesfield, in the north part of the country. That's where the truck disappeared from."

"Bingo." DeShear shove the last bit of bagel into his mouth and clapped a few crumbs from his hands.

Maya smiled. "Their biggest customers are Royal London Hospital, and Freeman Hospital in Newcastle. They both buy and sell volumes of gasses used in surgeries."

"Well." DeShear rubbed his chin. "Whoever the bad guys are buying from, they actually have to account for stuff. That means accounting clerks at the hospitals will be involved in hiding phony paperwork."

"So . . ." Maya stared at the computer screen. "How do we get a bunch of accounting clerks in British hospitals to talk about what they know—if they know anything?"

"I don't know yet, but the longer we wait, the worse it gets. In Indonesia, I saw the mass graves. Kids, thrown into holes like discarded trash. Acres and acres of it."

Maya put her hand to her mouth.

"I'm not letting that happen again." DeShear gritted his teeth and stared out the window. "Whoever's running supplies out of London, they'll be doing it in other parts of Europe soon. We need to find them. Fast."

CHAPTER 8

"Sir, the Vice President will see you now," the young staffer said. He turned and headed toward the front of the plane. DeShear and Maya followed.

Several sections of the plane were walled off for employees of the Vice President's office; others were for dignitaries and official entourages. The plane's conference room consisted of eight leather seats surrounding a wood-colored table, and another half dozen seats lining the walls on each side. A TV monitor in the far corner broadcast a live feed from one of the national news networks. Vice President Caprey sat at the head of the table, with Chief of Staff Pranav on the left.

"It's one of those days. Lots going on." Caprey waved to the chairs to her right. "Have a seat." Maya and DeShear sat as the Vice President rubbed her eyes. "Any progress to report?"

DeShear cleared his throat. "We think we have an idea on how to find the supply links. But it involves a lot of stops at big hospitals, which doesn't seem practical. Was there any word on our truck?"

The Vice President turned to her Chief of Staff. Jameel opened a folder. "So far, not much. The transport company's insurer required trackers on the vehicles, but the device on the truck in question failed a few days before the hijacking."

"That's a heck of a coincidence." The Vice President frowned, drumming her fingers on the table. "That driver knows more than he's letting on. We need to talk to him again—with one of *our* people asking the questions. Jameel, get Nick Barrings on the line." She gave Maya and DeShear a half smile. "Let's see who the CIA has available in the U.K."

The Chief of Staff went to a chair on the perimeter and picked up a phone.

"You know . . ." Maya stared at the conference table and cleared her throat. "It's a pharmaceutical truck. The hijackers or the driver may have disabled the tracker, but pharmaceutical transportation is highly regulated. No thief would have the time to re-license and re-register the vehicle, they'd probably just alter the manifest." Her gaze moved to Caprey. "Ma'am, if the truck moves through anything like a weigh station or customs house, that would create tax paperwork we could follow."

"To Dr. Hauser or whoever's doing the buying." The Vice President nodded. "I like it."

Jameel tapped the buttons on the phone. "On it."

"Okay, that's one." Caprey stretched out, putting her arms behind her head. She looked DeShear up and down. "What was your other idea?"

He licked his lips, suddenly very thirsty. "To interview the accounting clerks in the major hospitals. There will be recordkeeping discrepancies in the books—if the clerks will talk to us."

The Vice President smiled. "Yeah, I can see why you kept that one in your pocket. Well, what's the biggest issue with that, from your viewpoint?"

"There would be multiple hospitals in each country to visit." He shrugged. "We could be doing interviews until next Christmas and still not learn anything, provided we could get access in the first place."

Caprey rocked forward in her chair, drumming her fingers on the table again. "I know people, detective. It's my job. Most folks want to do the right thing. We just have to give them the chance."

"Yes, ma'am," DeShear said. "How?"

Her fingers stopped and she looked at him. "We use our goodwill mission to inspect hospitals, and we ask. Bigwigs love showing off their technology—but they rarely understand it. Their people do, though, and if one of our people was to ask about the recordkeeping systems, I'm sure they'd show us. That will put us next to the accounting clerks you want to talk to."

"Based on the what we've seen Dr. Hauser do to people in the past, they might be too afraid to talk to us."

Caprey jabbed the table with her index finger. "We say we're issuing a notice to the general public that the cylinders are being recalled. Then we let it leak to the accountants that the recall is actually a cover story and the cylinders are dangerous somehow. Something that stays with it all the way through the supply chain to hospitals."

"Tainted gas, maybe," DeShear said. "But it'd be impractical to say all the different gasses were affected."

"The cylinders!" Maya bolted upright. "We can say there was a toxin introduced into the cylinders that hold the gas. Something very dangerous, like it causes cancer."

The VP smiled, pointing at Maya. "There we go. A cleaner used on the cylinders in the manufacturing process causes cancer, and when it reacts with the gasses, they become lethal to patients. Anyone even touching the cylinders needs to be screened immediately. We set up a confidential hot line—for phones, internet, social media, the works. Between our physical presence and the hot line, any accounting clerk with direct knowledge about the stolen cylinders would come forward—or contact the thieves directly. I'll see about getting some sort of audit team together, to hit every major hospital in Europe. Meanwhile, we keep looking for the missing truck."

"Well, ma'am," DeShear said. "How confidential is a confidential hotline?"

Caprey's smile grew wider. "The system will grab all their information the instant anybody makes contact. Anyway, even if they call from a pay phone in a pub, all we want to know is where they work."

DeShear nodded.

"Okay, that's it." Caprey clapped her hands, turning to her Chief of Staff. "Jameel, this is top priority. Anyone we can spare, put on it."

"Yes, ma'am."

"Detective." The Vice President stood, facing DeShear. "Can I speak with you for a moment?"

"Uh, I may need to call you back." Jameel leaned into the phone as he got to his feet. "I may be going into a meeting."

Caprey held up a finger. "I'd like to talk to the detective alone, Jameel." She turned and exited the conference room.

DeShear followed her past a section of empty seats and a long row of operation rooms. Uniformed military personnel worked radar and viewed monitors as they conversed with other government officials. At the end of the hallway, Caprey opened a door and went inside. DeShear stopped to read the placard.

Vice Presidential Suite.

The room was compact, like one on a cruise ship. It had what looked like a twin sized bed, a small table with two chairs, and a door that opened into a tiny bathroom. Caprey slid out of her suitcoat and dropped it in the bed while walking to the sink. DeShear let his eyes drift over her crisp white blouse and past her trim hips, pausing to admire her well-toned legs.

After digging through a small leather bag, Caprey produced a toothbrush. "Make yourself comfortable." She squeezed a dot of toothpaste onto the brush and put it in her mouth. "What do you think of my plane?"

He smiled at her folksy informality, taking a seat in one of the pub-style chairs at the foot of the little bed. "It's nice. To be honest, I thought Air Force Two would be . . ."

"Smaller?" She leaned over the sink and rinsed a foamy ring from her lips. "It usually is. When President Brantley flies in this bird, they call it Air Force One. He pretty much gives me free reign to use it these days. A year after winning re-election, he concluded that having me succeed him in the White House would be the crowning achievement of his presidency. This time next year, I'll be doing nothing but eating corn dogs in Iowa and kissing babies in Montana." She splashed some water on her face and patted it dry, draping the towel around her neck. "But that's not why I asked you here." Leaning on the bathroom door frame, she held the ends of the towel with both hands and looked at DeShear. "Something's on your mind. What?"

Her tone was casual, but firm. She wanted a straight answer.

"I'm happy to be playing such a key role in this investigation, ma'am, but . . . why me? Wouldn't an operation of this magnitude be better handled by the CIA or something?"

The Vice President clicked the bathroom light off and seated herself on the edge of the bed, lowering her voice. "We need to keep a low profile on this deal. I can't give my enemies across the aisle anything embarrassing that could impact my future candidacy. It wouldn't be unheard of for some of our intelligence people to scuttle a mission brought forth by an unpopular Vice President."

"I, uh . . . didn't know you were unpopular," DeShear said.

"All Vice Presidents are." She shrugged. "I told a reporter I wanted to end our latest war in the Middle East, so now my critics think I'm soft. They seem to forget I used to fly combat missions."

DeShear leaned forward, resting his elbows on his knees. "I read that you got shot down. That can't be fun and games."

"Literally shot down in flames, but they say any landing you can walk away from is a good landing. That's how I got my little souvenir." Caprey patted her knee. "Funny, my back healed up okay, but the knee still bothers me. I'm almost to where I can predict the weather, like my grandma." She leaned back onto the headboard and folded her hands in her lap, her eyes half closed. "Politics should be more like combat, instead of people smiling to your face while they try to stab you in the back." She glanced at DeShear. "Know who said that? An upstart Senator named Jim Brantley. He visited me at my hospital bed in Bethesda after the crash. Talked me into retiring from the Navy and running for congress. Four years later, Jim helped me take the Indiana Governor's mansion." A smile crossed her lips. "He's always trusted me, for some reason."

DeShear smiled back. "Because you're smart. Anyone can see that."

"Eh." She waved a hand. "Brantley knew my wings were going to get clipped after that crash.

What about you? My people tell me you were a cop for a long time and had a pretty solid reputation. Why'd you leave?"

"I broke the jaw of a drug dealer," DeShear said. "His dad turned out to be a big attorney in Tampa, so . . ."

"Leave it to a lawyer to ruin a hero." She shook her head, gazing at him. "Washington's full of lawyers. That's why the place smells so bad."

"I thought your husband was a lawyer."

"He was." She nodded. "We met when I started doing postgraduate work—on the way to doing this. Cancer took him thirteen years ago."

"I know. I'm sorry."

"I understand that's kind of like what's going on with you. If you ever need anybody to talk to about it, I'm available. I know from experience, people forget how to make normal conversation when they think you're dying." She folded her arms and eyed him up and down. "But if I'm going to be honest, you really don't look like you're sick at all."

"I can see what makes you such a good politician. The country is lucky to have you."

Caprey stood, rubbing her back and moving to the door. "I've got some meetings scheduled, so this suite is going to go to waste. Feel free to grab a shower or a nap if you want. It's five more hours to London. This cot they call a bed may not look like much, but it is very comfortable."

DeShear stood. "Oh, I . . ."

"Detective." She folded her arms and lowering her voice. "There's an old saying in the Navy—if somebody offers you a bed, take it. You

75

look washed out. You could probably use some rest, and even on Air Force One, airplane seats suck for sleeping."

There was a knock on the door.

"Ma'am?" the Chief of Staff said from the hallway. "I'm sorry to bother you, but MI-6 found our missing truck."

Caprey sighed. "Good news with bad timing." She reached for the doorknob. "Back to work, detective."

CHAPTER 9

"Here's what we know, ma'am." Jameel Pranav stood at the conference table, reading from a legal pad as the Vice President sat down. "Mr. DeShear's hunch paid off. British Intelligence was able to locate the truck from some cargo tolls and a shipping registry."

DeShear looked over the Vice President's shoulder as a staffer ushered Maya into the room.

"So where's the truck?" Caprey asked.

"Port of London, ma'am." His finger slid down the paper. "According to MI-6, it came in yesterday. Security cameras show it's just sitting there among a bunch of crates and cargo containers."

DeShear leaned forward. "Do we know if the original cargo is still on board?"

"No, sir. Local authorities were instructed to keep watching remotely until they hear from us."

Caprey faced DeShear. "What are you thinking?"

"Well . . ." DeShear rubbed his chin, pacing back and forth in the little room. "There's not much point in shipping an empty truck. That's an expensive decoy. So the cylinders are probably still on it." He turned to the Vice President. "We land in a few hours, right? Let it sit for now, but keep eyes on it. Nobody here knows me, so as soon as we land, I'll get down to the port and put a tracker on the truck. When it ships, we can follow it right to Hauser."

"What if they offload the cylinders?" Maya asked.

"They probably will." DeShear nodded. "So we'll have to be ready for that—after it gets out of the country."

The Vice President looked at Maya. "What are your thoughts?"

Maya cleared her throat. "I know from experience, medical supplies are hard to move, especially from country to country. I bet they've left everything on one vehicle for a reason—paperwork. Unloading it before it leaves the U.K. means additional vehicles and a bigger paper trail at the port. That's more ways to get discovered. Freighters leaving Liverpool go to places like the U. S. and Canada, but barges use the port of London to head to other parts of Europe."

"So . . ." the Vice President leaned back, drumming her fingers. "If we can follow this truck, when they finally unload it, they might lead us to every hidden operation that Angelus has in western Europe."

He nodded. "Yes, ma'am."

"Okay, then." Caprey stood, eyeing DeShear. "Get yourself to the port of London and get a tracker on that truck."

* * * * *

The cat peeked out from under the bush, the streetlight at the corner illuminating the raindrops that battered the shrub's wet leaves.

"Come on, silly." Trinn held a piece of cracker in her hand. She sighed, shifting her weight on her feet. "If you don't come out, you don't get your treat."

The cat eyed her, but didn't move.

Trinn's phone rang in her pocket. She stepped inside the back door of the dingy flat, shaking water from her jacket as she pulled her phone out. Glancing at the screen, she lifted the phone to her ear. "Yeah?"

"It seems we have a bit of a problem." Road noise accompanied the British man's voice.

"France is always a problem. It's full of French people." Trinn squatted and held the cracker out to the cat again. It turned and looked down the alley, as if she wasn't there.

"Different problem. Someone has asked MI-6 to go talk to our truck driver again, but this time with a CIA agent along to ask the questions."

"Hmm." Trinn stood up, tossing the cracker to the cat. It jumped out of the bush and grabbed the treat, disappearing down the wet alleyway. "Where's the driver now?"

The man chuckled. "The dolt complained your pistol gave him a fright, so they said he might have PTSD and they transferred him to the Royal

London Hospital for observation. He's in the south wing, eighth floor."

"Guess I'm on my way to London." She held the phone in place with her shoulder, opening a cabinet door in the tiny kitchen. She grabbed a taser and shoved it into a leather handbag, along with a pair of round-lens glasses. Then she picked up her pistol.

"Handle it quickly, eh Miss?"

Pulling the gun's release, she flipped open the barrel to ensure it was fully loaded, then snapped it shut. "Don't I always?"

* * * * *

As the little car rolled to a stop, the driver held a small package out the window. Trinn walked up and grabbed it, leaning over. "Got a room number yet?"

"Eight twenty-two," the man said. "Call me when it's done."

She nodded, and the car drove off. Tucking the little package into her handbag, she walked into the lobby of the Royal London Hospital.

The main admitting area was relatively quiet, but more than a few people waited in the lobby to be seen. A red-haired woman and her family crowded around the admitting desk, barraging a nurse with questions as she held paperwork out to them. Trinn found the ladies room and entered it.

Placing her handbag on the side of the sink, she pulled out the package and ripped open the paper. The white nurse's uniform and platinum blonde wig glowed bright under the fluorescent lights of the bathroom. She stepped into a stall and changed clothes.

With her gun tucked into the back of her pants and the taser in her pocket, the uniform still fit well enough. She opened the stall door and checked her look in the mirror, putting on her glasses. The long, shaggy bangs of the wig helped hide her forehead, brushing against the rims of the glasses. Her gaze went to her feet. She had no idea what type of footwear nurses wore at Royal London, but her running shoes would do for now. Jamming her leather jacket into her handbag, she pushed open the restroom door and walked across the big lobby.

Trinn glanced at the hospital layout on her phone. The elevators were straight ahead, just past the admitting desk. She held her purse low on her hip, walking quickly. People in hospital uniforms went in and out of rooms on the other side of the admitting desk.

The admitting nurse held up a hand. "Excuse me."

Trinn kept walking. The lady raised her voice. "Excuse me!"

As Trinn went past her, the admitting nurse stood. "Security!"

The red-haired lady threw the paperwork onto the nurse's desk, shouting. "Pay attention! I said I don't have my identification with me. Does that mean my son can't get admitted?"

The admitting nurse turned to the woman. "Just a moment." She turned back to yell at Trinn again, but a large security officer had already jumped up from his chair.

"Her!" the nurse said, pointing in Trinn's direction. "She didn't check in."

Trinn slipped into the group of uniformed employees. The big guard stopped, looking around. "Which one?"

The red-haired lady slammed her hand on the desk. "Will you listen to me! My son could be dying!"

"That one!" The nurse pointed. "Platinum hair."

Trinn kept walking down the hallway, her heart pounding. At the first empty room, she ducked inside and pressed herself to the wall. Panting, she glanced around, sliding her hand behind her back. Her fingertips found the butt of the gun. She swallowed hard. No need for that yet. Not unless things get out of control.

Footsteps raced down the hallway.

Her hand went into her pocket, grasping the taser.

The security officer burst into the room. Trinn leaped forward, jamming the taser into his ribs and pressing the trigger.

The guard's head whipped back, his eyes wide. Groaning, he twisted around and broke contact. He backed away, rubbing his side, then lunged for her weapon. Trinn ducked, knocking his hands upwards while plunging the taser into his gut. She pulled the trigger again. Convulsing, the huge man's eyes rolled back in his head. He grabbed his side with one hand and strained to reach her with the other. Trinn stood, gritting her teeth and slamming the taser into his neck. She leaned into him, forcing the device to deliver its load deep into the guard's flesh. He dropped to his knees, gasping, his hand slowly swinging in her direction.

The taser clicked in her hand. No charge released.

The guard put a hand on the floor and propped himself up, gasping as he reached for his radio. Stepping to his side, Trinn grabbed the radio and jerked it from his belt.

Breathing hard, he lifted his head to stare at her, his mouth hanging open and drool dripping from his chin.

The LED on her taser flashed red. Still no charge.

The guard lunged again, reaching for her throat. Trinn jumped back, grabbing his hand and trying to force it away, but the thick fingers still found their mark. The pressure in her throat shut off her airway. The guard thrust forward, slamming her sideways into the wall, and sliding his forearm across her windpipe, grabbing his wrist with his other hand and forcing her into a choke hold.

Fear rippled through Trinn's insides. She felt like her eyes would pop.

Scowling with fear and rage, the guard breathed hard on the side of her face.

Trinn twisted her head away as he pressed his weight into her, crushing her against the wall. Her glasses clattered to the ground. He grunted as his forearm pressed harder into her throat.

She could not inhale. In a moment, she would pass out. She clawed at his arm as she lifted the taser one last time. The LED flickered green.

Trinn jammed the tip into his arm and shut her eyes, mashing the button. The taser buzzed and his hand opened, the electricity passing through him. Gasping, Trinn leaned against the wall and pushed him away.

He staggered back, holding his hand as he glared at her. Sweat rolled down his neck and stained his collar. He slowly reached out again.

With both hands pressed to the wall, she gritted her teeth and swung her foot to the side of his head, connecting with a hard jolt. He dropped to the floor.

Trinn leaned back, rubbing her throat and gulping the air.

Too close. Too sloppy.

She bent over and grabbed the guard's ankles, dragging him behind the bed, then turned off his radio and laid it on his chest. Wiping the sweat from her throbbing brow, she retrieved her glasses and went to the door. She held her breath, listening.

No sounds indicated anything severe was happening on the other side of the door. She pulled off the wig, shoving it under the mattress of the bed.

Straightening her glasses, she went to the door again, took a deep breath, and stepped into the hallway.

The elevators were straight ahead. A clamor of voices came from the lobby behind her. She reached the elevators and pressed the call button, waiting. Her pulse pounding, she kept her eyes on the elevator doors as several people in white uniforms raced past her toward the admitting desk.

When the doors opened, she stepped inside and pressed number eight, tapping the "door close" button. Beads of sweat gathered on her brow.

"Hey!" Another security guard ran toward her. "Hold on."

Trinn's heart thumped. She pressed the "close door" button again, holding her finger on it and reaching for her taser.

The guard got closer. "Stop!"

Her pulse pounding in her ears, Trinn stepped back from the console and pulled the taser from her pocket. The LED still flashed red. She slammed her hand into the "door close" button.

"Stop!"

She kept her eyes on the elevator control panel, reaching behind her back as the guard raced closer. She put her hand on her gun. The doors inched forward.

"Stop!" The guard loomed in the hallway.

As he reached the elevator, the doors slid shut.

Trinn held her breath, staring at the doors. The elevator didn't move. The guard pounded on the other side. She stared at the seam of the doors, her fingers wrapping around the butt of the gun.

"Open the lift!" The guard banged on the elevator door. "Open up!"

Swallowing hard, Trinn lifted the gun from her belt.

The elevator jolted. Trinn yanked the gun out and held it by her hip. A gap appeared between the metal doors. Shouting came from the lobby. The guard's face appeared in the gap, then the doors slammed shut again. He swore, banging on the elevator, the sound of metal on metal filling the air. The doors shuddered as they parted a few inches, a security baton prying them open. Fingers reached inside, groping for her. Trinn gasped, throwing herself backwards into the rear wall of the tiny compartment.

An electronic motor whirred, and the elevator jerked upward.

The doors slammed shut.

Trinn froze, staring at the indicator lights. The lobby button remained lit. After an eternity, the next higher button lit up. Then the next . . .

Sagging against the wall, Trinn shut her eyes and took a deep breath, shoving the gun back into her belt.

She pressed the buttons for floors six and ten, in case anyone was watching to see where the elevator stopped, then she dropped the taser back into her pocket.

On the sixth floor, the doors opened again. Trinn stepped out and looked for the stairs. There wouldn't be much time now. The guards would be scouring the hospital. The last one saw her face.

She cursed herself for being so sloppy.

Finding the stairs, she sprinted up the two floors to level eight and cracked open the door. The hallway was quiet. No one seemed to be in much of a fuss. The hospital wasn't on lockdown yet—but it would be soon.

She stepped out, reading the room numbers as she hurried down the hallway.

Eight ten.

Eight twelve.

A waiting area with restrooms crossed her path after number eight eighteen. On the other side, the numbers resumed.

Eight twenty . . .

She glanced up and down the hallway, then entered room eight twenty-two, recognizing the man whose truck she had hijacked a few days before. He laid on top of the bed, eyes focused on a TV mounted high on the wall. The other bed was empty, a wooden chair resting in the corner by the window.

Trinn turned her back to the patient and eased the door shut until it clicked, sliding her glasses into a pocket.

"It's about time," the truck driver said. "I've been pressing the call button for nearly ten minutes. I think the kitchen's forgotten my supper."

"Very sorry." Trinn mustered her best British accent, choosing to say as few words as possible. She turned quickly and walked to the window, keeping her back to the truck driver.

Drops of rain dotted the glass. Two blocks away, the streets were aglow with the bright lights and neon signs of nighttime London. Below her, the large campus of the hospital stretched out, its shiny blue and white façades climbing high above the long rows of dark brick buildings that were its start.

In the reflection of the glass, the truck driver pushed himself up in bed. "Any idea when I can get out of here, Miss?"

"Soon." She slipped the taser from her pocket and held it in front of her. The LED glowed green.

Turning to the truck driver, she held the taser up. "Remember me?"

His eyes widened.

Leaping toward him, Trinn shoved her hand over his mouth. He fought to scream.

"No, no, no," she whispered, lifting the taser to his face. Holding it an inch away from his nose, she moved closer and pressed the button, sending a blue-white flash between the taser's metal tips.

The man's chest heaved up and down as he stared at the device.

Trinn leaned into him, squeezing his mouth to keep him from crying out. "Look in my eyes. Memorize this face. In a few minutes, some people are coming to talk to you. I'll be with them. If you answer anything they ask, if you say anything at all—" she sparked the taser again "—I'm gonna shove this thing down your throat and hold the trigger until your brains come boiling out your ears. Do you understand?"

Whimpering, the man nodded.

"You will say nothing, or you die. Look in my eyes. Do you think I'm lying to you?"

"Mm-mm." He shook his head.

"Quiet, now." She stood up, slid the taser into her pocket, and went to the door. Cracking it open, she peeked outside. The hallway was quiet.

Trinn put on her glasses and slipped into the hall, moving quickly to the restrooms at the waiting area. Once inside, she yanked off the white uniform and dialed her phone. "Are they here yet?"

"They're walking in the front door right now. Young blond guy with a dark blue sweater and an old fat guy in a tan trench coat."

"Got it." She stuffed the uniform into the trash can. "I'll watch for them to come down the hallway and join them right before they get to his room.

CHAPTER 10

The driver pulled the car to the curb as a light rain drizzled down from the night skies of London. Putting his arm over the back of the seat, he opened a metal clipboard and turned to Maya and DeShear. "This is the rally point." He pointed to the corner pub. The lights were off, and it was dark inside. Striped awnings dripped rain onto the wide sidewalk out front. "Ma'am, there's an alley behind the bar. Go up the stairs to the black door. They're expecting you." He handed her an envelope from the clipboard. "Good luck, Doctor."

Maya took the envelope. "I'm not a doctor."

"You are now, ma'am." He handed a second envelope to DeShear. "Sir, there's a train station down the street. You can grab a cab to the port from there." The young man handed them each a slip of paper with a phone number on it, and held up a butane lighter. "This is your contact in the Vice President's office. Memorize that now, please."

DeShear studied the number on his paper, then handed it back to the driver. The young man flicked the lighter and held the flame to the edge of the paper, dropping it onto the metal clipboard, where it curled up and turned to ashes. Maya passed hers to the driver, watching as it went up in flames as well.

"You have new passports," the young man said. "And some cash inside the envelopes. Good luck."

DeShear winced as he got out of the car, the wet cold air irritating his lungs. He dashed to an awning at the front of the dark pub. Maya pulled the collar of her jacket over her head and stepped to the curb, clutching the laptop from the plane. Her breath created little white clouds that sailed over her shoulder as she joined him.

"Check in so you don't get weak." She shook the water from her jacket and pushed a wet strand of hair from her forehead. "I'll need to draw blood and dose you on a regular basis now that we've started." As the car pulled away, she peeked around the corner toward the back alley, then faced DeShear. "You have about twelve hours, but don't push it."

"Twelve hours." DeShear glanced at his phone to note the time. "Got it."

She headed toward the alley, dodging puddles.

"Maya." DeShear stepped from the awning, raindrops soaking into his hair and rolling down the side of his face. "Thank you. For everything. I know all this hasn't been easy on you."

"It won't be easy on you if I don't see you in twelve hours." She jumped across a tiny river spilling out of a drainpipe. "Go."

DeShear waited in the shadows until the black door at the top of the stairs opened for her, and then he hurried toward the train station.

* * * * *

A short, gray-haired man in a thick wool sweater greeted Maya as she came through the door. "Welcome, Doctor Hughes." He gestured to the living room of an apartment filled with hospital machines and surveillance gear. "We were able to get the equipment you asked for, and a bed."

"Thank you. I could sure do with a shower, too." She walked into the large, open space and looked around. "Where's the hematology analyzer? I have a blood sample we need to run as soon as my suitcases get here."

"That's on the way, ma'am." He hooked his thumb toward the former kitchen. "We'll hook it up right in there. And your bedroom's down the hall, first door on the right."

"Okay." She put her hand out to the old man. "What do I call you?"

"This week I'm Carl Bennis with the CDC, Doctor." He shook her hand.

"Nice to meet you, Carl," she said. "I'm Maya. This week I'm a doctor."

* * * * *

Trinn paced back and forth in the restroom, waiting for the elevator bell to ding. Every time it did, she cracked open the door and peered out, worrying about whether she'd need to jump into a stall if someone entered the bathroom—or run for the stairs if security arrived.

The bell sounded again, and the elevator doors opened. Two men approached. One was thirty-ish and blond, in a blue sweater and with the fresh, almost wide-eyed look of a recruit. He had to be some sort of new plainclothes officer looking for a promotion. The other man was older, heavier, and wore a tan raincoat.

She adjusted her glasses and pulled an identification badge from her pocket, clipping it the lapel of her shirt as the men passed.

Slipping from the bathroom, she rushed up behind them and clapped them on the shoulder. "Hi, boys. Sorry I'm late. Cassie Pomeroy, CIA." She glanced at the security camera in the middle of the hallway, her heart pounding.

The older man stopped, glancing at her ID. "I'm Officer Davis and this is Officer Grant. We're supposed to help you extract information from this truck driver. How do you want to play it?"

"Bringing in CIA to question a hijacked driver seems like overkill," Trinn said. "Who's got their undies in a bunch over this guy?"

"This straight from the office of Vice President Caprey. She thinks he may be linked to international human trafficking ring. He didn't say much during our first round of questioning, so they want to see what you can get out of him."

Trinn shook her head, sighing. "I doubt a truck driver knows much, but it's worth a shot. Let's go. You take the lead. I'll jump in when I think the time is right."

The two men nodded and walked into the truck driver's room, approaching the bed. The driver glared at them. "You two again? Where's my supper? I—"

Trinn stepped into the room, her eyes locking on the driver. His jaw dropped open.

"This is Agent Pomeroy from the CIA." Davis scratched the back of his gray head. "She's going to observe our session." He pulled a notepad from his coat pocket. "Now, when did you first see the hijackers? Did you recognize any of them?"

He looked at Trinn, trembling.

"Don't look at me," she said, folding her arms. "The officer is asking you a question."

The older man stepped closer to the bed. "How many hijackers were there? What could you see?"

Trinn put her hands on her hips, glaring at the driver. He quivered, keeping his mouth shut, and turned his head to the window.

Davis stood up. "Is it your intention to not answer any of our questions today?"

His chest heaving, the driver kept his eyes on the far wall.

Davis glanced at Trinn.

She nodded, stepping to the bed. "You're in a lot of trouble, pal. We think the people who stole your cargo intend to do some bad things with it. Illegal organ harvesting on little kids—then they dispose of the bodies in mass graves. I hate to think of what kind of demented people are involved. If someone can maim and kill innocent children, they're capable of just about anything."

The driver gripped the sides of the bed, breathing hard but not looking at her.

Trinn leaned closer. "If you help these men—if you answer their questions, then the people involved can be apprehended. If you talk, that's what will happen. And the right people will know it was you who gave up the critical information."

Davis nodded. "Judges tend to look kindly on that sort of thing, son."

"All you have to do is talk," Trinn said. "People—very powerful people—are interested in what you might say. So . . . is there anything you want to say to me, or to these officers?"

He shook his head, a bead of sweat running down the side of his forehead.

"Well, just remember, I'm a phone call away here. If you change your mind and decide to talk, these boys will let me know."

The driver quivered, not taking his eyes off her. A whimper escaped his lips, and he was silent.

She got up from the bed and went to the far corner, gesturing for Davis and Grant to join her.

"That was about the nicest interrogation I ever saw." Davis put his hands on his hips and shook his head. "CIA has changed."

Trinn shrugged. "Good cop, bad cop. I think this guy's a bust, but if either of you wanna rough him up, I can shut the door and keep people away. A few bruises and he might crack open."

Davis winced. "We . . . were told to assist you."

"Well, he's scared to death of something, so he won't say anything here." Trinn glanced at the truck driver, his chest rising and falling as he watched them. She faced Davis. "We should cut him loose and see where he goes. Can you arrange a tail?"

"I'll handle it." The older man nodded. "We've been stuck watching him while he sits here and does nothing."

"Okay," Trinn said. "Have them process him out, then stick to him. If the hijackers or someone from their organization are going to make contact with him again, they won't wait long. Let's go."

Trinn stayed with Davis and Grant as they went to a hospital administrator's office. Security watched the lobby and conducted a floor-by-floor search for the rogue nurse while she sat with her hands in her lap not twenty feet away. After a few minutes, she and the two officers were outside.

"Can we drop you somewhere, Agent Pomeroy?" Davis asked, pointing to a small sedan at the curb. "We have a car."

"Thanks, but I have business across town." She wrapped her arms around herself and hunched her shoulders, a stream of white trailing from her lips in the chilly night air.

"You sure?"

"I'll grab one of these cabs. It'll be plenty warm in there, don't worry."

He shugged, opening the car door. "Okay. Goodnight."

"Yeah. Cheers." Trinn walked to the corner and waved at a taxi as the officers got into their vehicle. The cab pulled over to the curb, and Trinn climbed into the back.

"Where to, Miss?" The taxi driver tapped his fingers against the wheel, glancing at his passenger in the rearview mirror.

She giggled, swaying a bit and slurring her words. "Oh, just a moment. I have the address here somewhere." Falling backward into the seat, she pulled her phone from her pocket and scrolled through it. "The text is right here . . . somewhere . . ."

The driver sighed.

"No, it's in my email. That's right. One sec . . ." She let the phone fall from her fingers onto the floor. "Oopsie!" Sloshing forward, she bent down to retrieve it. "Ooh. I don't feel good."

"Easy there, Miss." The driver peered over the seat. "I don't want any messes in my car, do I?"

She sat up, winking and brandishing the phone. The cab's wipers cleared tiny raindrops off the windshield. A block away, Davis and Grant's car finally pulled away from the curb and drove off.

Trinn coughed, putting her hand to her mouth. "Oh, I think I had too many shots of Schnapp's."

"No, please. Not in my car. My shift just started!" The cab driver stretched across the seat and grabbed the latch, pushing the door open.

Trinn staggered to the side of the building, leaning over and letting her hair fall over her face. The cab pulled away, its door slamming shut from momentum as plumes of foggy exhaust drifted over the cold, wet street.

Standing, Trinn pushed her hair from her eyes and took off her glasses, tucking them into a pocket. As she walked away from the corner, she pressed a button on her cell phone and held it to her ear. "Tell Fuego not to worry, the truck driver got the message."

"Good," the man said.

"I'm on Cavell Street, headed north. Come pick me up—and bring me a jacket. It's freezing out here."

CHAPTER 11

DeShear's taxi rolled up to the main gate of the port of London, a light rain dotting its windshield. He jumped out and ran to the security hut as the cab pulled away.

A guard with a big, bushy mustache glanced at his credentials. "Right." The guard put on a blue and yellow rain slicker and stepped outside. "Been advised to give you access, *suh*." He pointed to a door at the far end of the dockmaster's building. "Our boys will meet you inside, *suh*."

A truck pulled up, blocking DeShear's way. Another guard checked it and raised the gate, allowing it to pass.

"Busy night." DeShear hunched his shoulders against the rain.

"Always busy here, *suh*." He handed DeShear's ID back to him. "Never quiet at the port."

DeShear nodded, trotting through the rain to the dockmaster's building. Beyond it, cranes loaded boxes of cargo onto waiting barges and freighters.

The little bit of jogging didn't bother him like he thought it might. He enjoyed running, getting in his miles each morning at dawn along Tampa Bay, but when his coughing fit started in Minneapolis, he thought he'd be sidelined for a while. Maya's drugs were doing a good job.

A man in a long raincoat stood outside of the dockmaster's building, smoking. He nodded at DeShear and let him enter the room. Warm air flowed over him as he stepped inside. A dozen uniformed officers sat at a long counter, staring at computer monitors.

"You must be the American." A man in a shirt and tie stood up. Two epaulettes decorated each of his shoulders. "I'm your liaison officer." He walked over and shook DeShear's hand. "Nigel Pratt, MI-6."

DeShear noted the officer's stripes. "Nice to meet you, Lieutenant. I'm Hank DeShear."

Pratt nodded. "Your truck's been quiet, mate. But I suspect that's about to change now that you've arrived. Look here." He went to a desk and unlocked a drawer, removing a small cardboard box and handing it to DeShear. "Clips right onto the underside, this device does. Press it onto anything metal and we'll follow that lorry wherever it goes, eh?"

DeShear opened the box and took out the tracker, a black metal box about the size of a pack of cigarettes. He slipped it into his pocket. "Where's the truck right now?"

"Section thirty-two, near the rail line." Pratt waved at a series of monitors at a desk where a young uniformed officer sat.

She pointed to each screen as she spoke. "We've got a high range camera mounted on a building behind it, staring right up the boot. Another one on building C can view most of the bonnet. Then we re-directed two rooftop cameras to get it from each side." She spun her chair to face DeShear. The name Kensington was stitched over her uniform pocket. "With all that, we've seen every inch that *can* be seen, since we were alerted. It's surrounded by cargo on three sides, the platform drops straight off to the river on its left. Nobody's bothered it."

DeShear studied the screens.

"And you'll need this, sir." Officer Kensington hoisted an eighteen-inch bolt cutter from a drawer and laid it on her desk with a clunk. Clicking the mouse, she zoomed the rear camera in on the truck's cargo doors. The infrared lens showed two padlocks. The officer handed DeShear the cutters. "This'll get you past those, sir."

Pratt handed him two padlocks. "These aren't identical, but they're close to what's on there—best we could do on short notice."

DeShear slipped them into his pocket. "Nice work, everyone." He took the bolt cutter and glanced at Pratt. "Now, Lieutenant, if you'll point me toward section thirty-two."

"You'll catch your death going out like that." Pratt looked over DeShear's attire. "Even a thief would wear a slicker on a night like this, sir." The Lieutenant went to a closet and pulled out an old, long raincoat like the one on the man smoking outside. "You can get right close to your lorry by keeping near to the warehouse. This'll keep you dry for the rest of it."

* * * * *

DeShear crept along the brick edge of the warehouse with his bolt cutters, his long raincoat flapping with each icy gust from the river. His lungs burned in the cold air, but he refused to give in and cough, aware that it might set off another choking fit. He pulled his phone from his pocket and glanced at the screen. More than ten hours to go until he needed to report back to Maya. Plenty of time.

He craned his neck and peered through the rain to a long row of wooden crates. The truck was just ahead, maybe another hundred feet, parked in front of a red truck and near the wall, just as the Lieutenant had indicated. DeShear crouched low, scurrying through the puddles between the crates, and looked up again. The truck was now about thirty feet in front of him, and maybe fifty feet to the left. Cargo containers stood to the right, and the river churned past on the left.

He scanned the dock. No one appeared to be anywhere around. Crouching low again, he weaved his way between the cargo bins until he was beside the red car at the rear of the truck.

The river's icy breeze blasted his face, carrying his foggy breath over his shoulder. He put a fist to his mouth and blew hot air onto his fingers, then slipped around to the front of the red truck.

Raising the heavy bolt cutters, he guided the tip over the long shaft of the first lock. With a hard squeeze, the lock broke. He knocked it from the door. The second lock offered more resistance, but fell away equally fast. Grabbing the door latch, DeShear flipped back the securing lever and swung the door open. He climbed onto the rear bumper, laying down the bolt cutters and pulling his phone from his pocket.

The light shined into the truck's cargo bay, illuminating racks of hundreds and hundreds of gas cylinders. A narrow walkway ran between them, going the length of the truck. He read the labels. Nitrous oxide. Entonox. Heliox.

His heart jumped. This was the cargo that would be delivered to Dr. Hauser—and deliver Dr. Hauser to him.

Sliding his hand into his pocket, he withdrew the tracker. Raindrops fell onto its sleek black face.

DeShear slipped the new padlocks through the cargo doors, locking them shut so whoever ended up driving the truck wouldn't notice the truck had been entered.

He dropped from the truck's cargo hold and dropped to one knee. He shined his light across the thick metal underside of the big truck. Flipping the tracker over in his hand, he located the activation button and pressed it, inching forward under the bumper.

Need to place this far away from any prying eyes.

He eased forward, holding his breath, looking for a dirt-free spot, so the magnets would hold it in place all the way to Africa and back, if necessary. He put his hand down and lowered his head to crawl further under the big truck.

A piercing pain shot through his palm. DeShear yanked his hand off the ground, wincing as he brought his light up. Blood dripped from a short, deep cut in his palm. He cursed, shining the light over the pavement. Several pieces of metal rebar jutted out from the edge of the dock like giant, bent nails.

DeShear wiped the blood on his raincoat and moved forward. A few feet ahead, he spied a large flat space near the axle, and scooted to it. As he lifted the tracker to the frame, the device shot from his hand and snapped itself onto the truck frame. He tugged it a few times, but it didn't move.

That sucker isn't going anywhere.

He glanced at his bloody palm again, balling his hand into a fist a few times to get the sharp stinging to subside. Turning off his phone's light, he typed a text message and sent it to the Lieutenant. "Bird is in nest."

His phone vibrated a moment later when the reply came back. "Signal being received. You are clear to exit."

He lowered the phone and turned to go, the wind blasting another cold gust into his wet face. In the corner of his eyes, a tiny red light flickered.

DeShear looked, but saw nothing. The phone light and the texting screen had dulled his night vision. He glanced around under the truck, trying to spot the little red light again.

It flashed, not six feet away from him. An LED—but it disappeared again.

He leaned closer. The wind from the river blew strong under the truck, grabbing his coat tails and shaking the wires along the chassis. Then he saw it, a piece of cargo strapping caught underneath the truck, swaying back and forth as the winds blew. It obscured the red light, making it appear to flash. Shifting to his left, he caught full sight of the light.

A red LED screen displayed a count down.

Thirty-three.

Thirty-two.

His stomach jolted. Heart pounding, he flung himself backwards, crashing onto his butt and elbows. He scurried away from the red light, gasping. The bumper was about ten feet away. Rolling over, he crawled on his belly toward the back of the truck.

He jerked to a stop, his raincoat pulling tight across his shoulders. He thrust himself from side to side, unable to move forward. Gritting his teeth, he glanced back. The old coat had snagged on the rebar. DeShear flipped onto his back and grabbed the edge of the slicker, yanking hard to free it. It ripped a little, but didn't come loose. His gaze went to the LED.

Twenty-two.

Twenty-one.

Slipping his right shoulder out of the jacket, he rolled over again to free his left arm and crawl out from under the truck. Whatever was going to happen when the LED hit zero, he didn't want to be around to find out.

He scrambled forward on his belly, his heart in his throat. The truck's rear bumper got closer and closer.

Get out, get to the side of that red truck, and get to the cargo bins as fast as you can—without being seen.

In his head, he marked the countdown.

Ten.

Nine.

The bumper was above him. He swung a hand up and grabbed it, hauling himself from under the chassis and launching himself to the side of the red truck.

A woman raced toward DeShear at full speed. She lowered her shoulder and crashed into his chest, knocking him backwards. Her arms wrapped around him and her legs thrust outward against the dock. DeShear grabbed at her with one hand, thrusting his other hands out to break his fall—but met nothing. Cold air rushed over him as the edge of the dock went by, the woman's head buried in his ribs, until the hard, wet crash of the river knocked them apart.

The water slammed over him, icy daggers jolting through his system and knocking the breath out of him. He plunged under the dark waves, the crush of water roaring in his ears. The woman shoved him downward, kicking her way to the surface. Wavering lights from the dock gave glimpses of her slim silhouette as she swam away from him.

He held his breath, groaning and pushing his hands through the icy water toward the surface. His clothing clung to him, dragging him downward and fighting his every move.

A massive boom filled the air. The surface turned orange as a giant fireball rippled across the water's surface, lighting all objects around and below.

Lungs burning, DeShear fought his way to the surface in time to see huge flames curling upward from the truck. Shredded cargo soared through the sky as he gulped breath after breath of the ice cold air, coughing and choking as it assaulted his lungs. The night was bright with fire, glowing orange and white and hot.

He gasped for breath, swallowing hard to fight back the coughing fit that wanted to overtake him. The river slowly dragged him seaward. DeShear churned across the current and caught the last pilon at the end of the pier, reaching for a scurryway ladder and pulling himself from the water.

He struggled up the metal planks, wheezing and dripping, exhausted from his swim and sore from the hit the woman laid on his rib cage. At the top of the ladder, he flopped over onto the edge of the dock, looking back toward the burning truck. Car alarms blared from a car-carrier truck and its long trailer filled with vehicles. The roaring fire lit everything around it like a bright summer day.

DeShear's lungs burst forth in pain. He gagged, putting his head down and coughing hard. Each breath was a fight, his insides on fire and his eyes watering.

Beyond the burning wreckage, a motorcycle roared into view. Its driver was tall and athletic-framed, his helmet whipping back and forth as he raced down the pier, scanning the debris. He stood, raising himself on the foot rests as the bike rolled forward, releasing the handle bars. Swinging his leg over the frame, he let the bike fall onto its side. It slid to a stop on the wet pavement. Standing near the flames, he held his hands up, shielding his eyes from the heat. He cupped his hands to his face, limping forward and shouting into the fire.

DeShear gasped and wheezed, pushing himself upright onto his knees. A black shadow cut in front of the flames. The woman from the truck raised her fist, filling DeShear's view. He swung his hand up, but the punch connected, blasting pain through his temple. His head whipped back as white streaks dashed across his field of view. He slumped forward, putting his bloody hand out to keep him from crashing face-first into the dock.

She stood over him, gasping, as water dripped from her drenched clothing. "Stay out of my scene, man!"

Lifting her foot, she put it to his shoulder, shoving him sideways onto the deck. Then she turned and ran away.

DeShear coughed, gathering information as best he could. His eyes blurred and faded.

Female. Average height. Slim. Dark hair.

He coughed again and forced his eyes open.

Black jacket. Running shoes. Maybe blue jeans. Strong. Athletic.

Her words echoed in his head.

"Stay out of my scene, man!"

The accent—or lack of it—said she was an American.

The truck exploded again, sending a fireball into the air and blinding him. When he looked up, the woman was sprinting toward the motorcycle, her dark hair whipping in wet strands in the icy winds of the Thames.

DeShear leaned on one hand, putting the other to the side of his throbbing head. When he took his hand away, it was streaked with blood.

He narrowed his eyes, fighting to see. The tall man turned in the woman's direction and waved. He lifted the motorcycle, threw his leg over the seat, and revved the throttle. The rear tire smoked and the bike spun around. As the woman got to him, she leaped onto the back of the seat, throwing her arms around the man's waist.

The motorcycle engine whined as the man leaned forward, launching them past the flames and away into the darkness.

CHAPTER 12

Maya walked through the alley, hopping around puddles as sunlight peeked between the old buildings. The rear of the ancient pub reeked of stale beer and grease.

Eyeing the buzz-cut neck of the young Marine in front of her, she clutched her computer bag to her side. "I am not ready for this."

"You'll be fine, ma'am." He reached for the door of the limousine. The tailpipe of every vehicle in the block-long motorcade sent its own thick, white exhaust cloud into the chilly air.

She stopped and rubbed the goosebumps from her arm. "Do you really think so?"

As he stood at attention, a smile tugged at the corners of the man's lips. "Yes, Doctor. Everything's been arranged."

Taking a deep breath, Maya leaned over to climb into the limo. The Vice President looked up at her from the back seat. "Ready to go put on a show?"

Wearing the businesslike dress that had arrived an hour ago, Maya squeezed into the back of the crowded limo. The tall, square-shouldered man to the left of the Vice President spoke in a strained whisper. "They had an incident last night, Madam Vice President. We're working on it, but it's still unresolved."

"Oh, nonsense," Caprey said. "I can't let a runaway nurse keep me from my schedule. If word got out that I could be disrupted so easily, my career would be over."

"But ma'am, proper security dictates—"

"We're going. That's the end of it." She faced Maya. "Now, about your speech. The Brits are nothing if not proud of the NHS. I mean, they put it in the Olympics, didn't they? And if the vendors who supply it to them think they have a shot at a customer as big as the Uncle Sam, they'll gladly show us anything we want to see."

Maya nodded. "Yes, ma'am. But what if one of the real doctors asks me some . . . technical things?"

The tall man tucked papers into a briefcase. "We'll handle all that, Dr. Hughes."

Maya shuddered. *Doctor Hughes*. It would take a while to get used to that. She checked her phone to see the time. There were still a few hours before DeShear needed a treatment—if he showed up for it.

Again, thoughts of disaster plagued her. "What if—"

"Don't worry." Caprey waved her hand. "First, the British are very cautious about offending anyone, so the folks you'll be presenting to probably won't ask you anything except what you like in your tea. Second, all sorts of folks work for our government agencies, just like theirs. Not all of them are talkative."

The man snapped his briefcase shut. "On a short notice play like this one, we need to keep the circle tight and move as quickly as possible. You know what we're looking for, and you may know some of the players when we get higher up." He handed her a computer tablet. "This contains a list of cogent questions you can ask about invoicing procedures. Reference them by pretending to make notes. The screen is micro-louvered, like a venetian blind, so people standing near you won't be able to peek over your shoulder and see what you're doing."

"A hospital will have lots of cameras," Maya said. "What if they zoom in on me and see the tablet?"

"No one will see anything, Doctor. The screen is optically fractured. They use that technology to defeat high optic lenses and facial recognition. Abe Lincoln could wear a pair of glasses made with that stuff and walk right past the best facial recognition system in the world. Remember, this is all about putting a bug in the ear of anyone with direct knowledge of the cylinder thefts or how the hospital is hiding the phony invoices. If we all do our jobs convincingly, someone may come forward."

"That would be a happy stroke of luck." Caprey scanned a folder, massaging her left knee. "Mostly, you're part of the dog and pony show—a kind of important-looking distraction, to make everything look official."

* * * * *

Lieutenant Pratt pointed to a port security computer monitor as DeShear sat on a cot close by, a blanket wrapped around him as he coughed uncontrollably. DeShear stared at his bandaged hand while Officer Kensington squatted in front of him, dabbing a cloth to the side of his face.

Pratt shook his head, turning from the screen. "Sorry, mate. No plates on that motorbike. Can't figure how they got it past our security gates, neither."

DeShear cleared his throat a few times. "The motorcycle . . ." He winced as he inhaled, his lungs burning and his insides aching. "Must've already been inside. One of the cargo bins, most likely. They just opened the container like I did with the truck, and drove it out."

Another coughing spasm seized him, sending daggers into his lungs, but the breath wouldn't come. He sucked in hard, working to get air. Exhaling produced a long wheeze deep inside his chest.

Kensington walked away, returning with an ice pack. She pressed it to DeShear's forehead and handed him a tissue. DeShear cleared his throat a few times and wiped his mouth. When he pulled the tissue away, there was blood on it.

She gave him another tissue. "Time to get you to hospital, eh?"

Barely able to speak, DeShear shook his head. He managed to squeeze a word out between the gasps. "Can't."

"No time to be a hero," Kensington said. "You've had a shock to the system from the cold water, and you're coughing up blood. Maybe got yourself some broken ribs."

DeShear forced himself to laugh in spite of the pain. "I'd know if I had broken ribs. I'll be okay." He stood up and stretched to show her, repressing the grimace threatening to give away his agony.

Sighing, Kensington stepped away. She signaled to the Lieutenant and walked to the rear of the room.

Pratt's radio crackled on his hip. He nodded at Kensington and held up a finger, lifting the radio to his face. "Lieutenant Pratt here."

The man on the other end was half-shouting, with rumblings in the background as he spoke. "Sir, the boys need another hour or two on the fire, then they say the inspectors can start going through it. Where do we want to move the undamaged freight?"

"Hold the line, Colin." He faced DeShear. "Have you seen what you need to from the videos, then?"

DeShear nodded, holding his side and coughing. "Can you download it so I can have it analyzed? Someone might know her, or the man on the motorcycle."

"Done. They were too far away from our cameras to identify their faces properly here, but we'll send it to the lab and see what they can do with it." He pressed the button on the radio. "Colin, I'll have some forklifts brought 'round. Move everything to dock ten."

"Aye, sir."

Pratt stepped to Kensington at the far side of the room. She lowered her voice. "Bit of a situation here with Mr. DeShear, sir. He's becoming a liability to the mission."

"Aye." Pratt nodded. "But he's got clearance from all the way up. Somebody big wants him in the front seat, so we're to help as best we can. Still . . ." He frowned, looking at DeShear. "I'll have a word with him."

"Sir, if it's that way, I do know a doctor in London. If it's the hospital that's got him bolloxed, I can ask my friend to come down. Bit unusual, but under the circumstances . . ."

"Right," the Lieutenant said. "Ring up your friend, then."

"No." DeShear grimaced, leaning forward on the cot. "There's no time. And a doctor can't help me, anyway. Neither can a hospital." He put his hand on the edge of the mattress frame. "I brought a medical attendant with me. I just need to get to Maya Rodriguez."

DeShear rocked on the cot, attempting to stand. A uniformed officer rushed over to keep him from collapsing to the floor.

Pratt frowned. "You'll botch the whole thing, the condition you're in."

"You have your orders." DeShear got to his feet and stared the Lieutenant in the eye. "Please."

The lieutenant stared at him. A fog horn on a distant ship echoed through the night.

"The coughing will pass, Lieutenant. It did before, and Maya has the drugs to keep it at bay.

Other than that, I'm a little banged up, but I'll manage."

"Okay. It's your arse." Pratt said. "Where do we find this Maya Rodriguez?"

"Thank you." DeShear gasped. "I'd call her myself, but I think I lost my phone in the river." He propped himself up on one shoulder to get a full breath. "Maya is traveling with the Vice President."

Pratt took out his phone. "MI-6 ought to be able to locate her for us, then. Kensington, organize a car. Get the Yank to Ms. Rodriguez straight away."

A port security officer handed a thumb drive to DeShear. "Here's the download, sir. Noisy sod, revving the motorbike like that. He wasn't worried about getting away unnoticed."

"He might have gotten excited," DeShear said. "If he's a pro, he won't let that happen again. Question is, what excited him? The bomb he planted, the woman he almost got killed, or me?"

* * * * *

Detective Nillson stomped the snow from her boots and walked through the entry to the police station. A warm gust of air blasted past her, repelling the Minnesota winds outside. Before she was able to settle behind her desk with a first cup of coffee, Jack Coleman was knocking on her office door.

"The tow truck and the black Audi are both processed, ma'am" Coleman handed her a file. "The woman's car didn't give us anything, but the other vehicle had a few items for us. The serial number of the attacker's gun shows it was reported stolen a few days ago in a residential robbery. I'm interviewing the homeowner later today." As Nillson sipped her coffee and flipped through the file, Coleman continued. "We got DNA samples from sweat that was on clothing found in the cab of the truck, and from traces of saliva that were taken from the bottom edge of the door panel. There was also blood splatter and gunshot residue on the sleeve of the jacket."

She sifted through the papers. "Any of the clothes belong to the driver of the tow truck?"

"The driver was about a size forty-eight in the chest and waist," Coleman said. "The jacket is an extra large, but it's a designer brand and the label says it's an athletic fit. I measured the waist. It's about thirty-two inches."

"So." Nillson set the file on the desk. "Unless our tow truck driver was planning on a crash diet, the jacket's not his."

"No, but the perp's a pretty big guy. I'd make him for a bodybuilder or athlete."

"Interesting." She leaned back in her chair. "How soon will we know about the DNA?"

"I asked them to rush it," Coleman said. "They think we'll get it back in about four hours."

"That's good work, Jack. Thanks." She took another sip of her coffee, reaching for one of the reports filling her in box. "Stay on top of it."

"Detective, what about that PI from Florida?" Coleman asked. "He helped hide the family. Think he knows anything else?"

"Maybe." She opened the report and glanced at the cover page. "I know you're anxious for something to happen, and—"

"Oh." He stood up straight, his cheeks turning red. "I just thought—"

"It's okay. I like ambition." Nillson turned a page on the report, not looking up. "Right now, we need to be patient and work the evidence. Cases get botched and bad guys go free when we focus on the wrong things." She lifted the next page, peeking under it. "You say we'll have the DNA results in about four hours, right? Maybe we'll get lucky and our killer will be in the system." She smiled at Coleman. "Then you and I will pull out all the stops and hunt this murderer down."

* * * * *

The ride from Maya's new dwelling to the Royal London Hospital was a short one, made shorter by the police escort. They sailed through traffic lights—as she avoided glares from London drivers who'd be late for work.

The entrance into the building was equally swift. Rope lines cordoned off sightseers and well-wishers who came out for a glimpse of the woman who might be the next President of the United States. Flashbulbs popped as Caprey waved to the small crowd, walking briskly with her secret service escorts through the large main doors of the old building.

Royal London Hospital was a study in contrasts. Some parts were hundreds of years old, made of brown bricks that rose like sentinels to a mere four stories high, but filled with some of the most modern technology in Europe. Other parts were shiny skyscrapers, blue and white glass structures standing nearly three hundred feet above their short brown cousins.

It was a massive and busy campus, all held quiet for the presentation that Vice President Caprey and Dr. Hughes of the CDC were about to give.

Maya followed the parade of people across polished floors and down a corridor, to an amphitheater. Overhead, the PA broadcast an elegant-sounding woman announcing—in the most polite of tones—for employees to please keep their identification badges on at all times and sit in their designated sections.

As she stepped backstage, Maya peeked through the curtain. Hundreds of people in hospital scrubs filed down the aisles. A shudder went through her. Any of them—a doctor, a nurse, an orderly—could spot her as a fraud at any time.

"Nervous?" The unmistakable voice of Vice President Hunter Caprey came over her shoulder.

Maya swallowed, turning to look at the Vice President.

"Don't be." Caprey put her hand on Maya's arm. "I'll introduce you here, on the big stage. Then we'll announce a meeting with a smaller group. That's where we'll make our little situation known."

The Vice President's Chief of Staff came up to them, his finger pressed to his ear. "Ma'am? They're telling me five minutes."

"Thank you, Jameel." Caprey took a deep breath, raising her eyebrows. "Guess I'd better have a look at whatever they wrote for me. See you onstage."

As the Vice President walked away, Maya let the curtain slip back, shutting out the large crowd, but their voices came through the cloth, and the polite lady on the PA reiterated her recorded announcement. "Employees are reminded to please keep their identification badges on at all times and sit in their designated sections."

Maya paced back and forth near the edge of the stage.

"Dr. Hughes?" an American man said. His words nearly went past Maya before she realized he was talking to her.

She turned around. "Yes?"

"This way, Doctor." A man in a suit led her toward the center of the stage, where a podium stood with a table on either side. A long row of microphones lined each table. "Here we are." The man pointed to a seam in a second curtain, behind the podium. "If you'll stand back here and wait for the Vice President to announce you."

She moved to stand with the others, wondering who they all were. Offstage to the right, the man from the Vice President's limo waved at her. She walked to him as a thunderous applause filled the auditorium.

"Welcome." A British man's voice boomed over the theater. "Thank you all for assembling on such short notice. We have a very special guest with us today . . ."

The show had begun.

"Doctor Hughes," the man said. "When the main presentation is over, come off stage this way. I will take you to the classroom where you'll be doing your presentation."

He pointed down a hallway to a door, and as he gestured, his suit coat buckled, revealing a shoulder holster and the butt of a gun.

Maya nodded. Secret Service. Of course.

"Just look for you, then?" she said.

"That's right. I'll be right here."

The words "Doctor Hughes of the CDC" came from the stage.

Maya froze, staring at him. The crowd in the auditorium gave a smattering of applause as the words echoed in Maya's ears. The Vice President's words. Maya's introduction.

She stood rigid in front of the Secret Service agent. He glanced toward the main stage. "I believe that's your cue, ma'am."

Butterflies erupted in her stomach. She turned and walked as casually as she could muster, her mind racing as she stepped past the slit in the curtain and out into the blindingly bright auditorium lights.

CHAPTER 13

Caprey spoke boldly, telling her British audience about her admiration for their country and how she hoped to learn about better ways to help deliver health care to millions of Americans. Her British counterparts thanked her for the visit and lauded praise on the American group that accompanied her, offering open and forthright answers to any and all questions they might have.

It was almost a blur. Maya stared at the microphone in front of her, forcing her eyes not to wander onto the big crowd assembled in the seats. After a few hour-long minutes, it was over. The crowd applauded politely and the others at the table stood up and made their way backstage.

The Secret Service agent stood on the right side, waiting for Maya. "This way, Doctor Hughes."

Overhead, the polite British woman announced, "If all members of the Accounting Department will please form a queue at room seventeen, section B. Your administrative session with Dr. Hughes of the CDC is about to begin."

"Just wait here, Doctor." The Secret Service agent stepped around a mobile metal frame, not unlike a doorway, with wires running off it and disappearing down the hallway. Hospital employees passed through the frame before entering the classroom.

Further down the hallway, two men in dark suits waved metal detector wands over the people in the line, asking them to raise their arms or take off their shoes, just like at the airport.

At the furthest point, a woman stood by a basket on a table, collecting phones. "Please turn your personal phone to vibrate and place it in the basket. You'll get it back after the presentation. We can have no pictures or recording devices present during the meeting."

That seemed to strike several people as odd, but no one was audibly annoyed about it.

The woman held up a list. "Miss Anders?" She glanced up and down the line. "Lily Anders? Your phone, please."

A petite blonde woman stepped forward. "I've forgotten mine at my desk. Should I go and fetch it?"

"Hurry, please. The presentation is about to start." The security woman raised her voice, addressing the people in the line. "May I have your attention, please. We have been provided a list of accounting department employees attending today's meeting. If you brought a cell phone to work today, it was logged when you entered the building. You must bring it and turn it in to us during the presentation to ensure no cell phones are unaccounted for."

"Ready?" The secret service agent had reappeared. Maya nodded and followed him into the classroom.

* * * * *

When the doors had closed, the Secret Service agent nodded to Maya. She turned to face the thirty or so employees in the classroom, reading to them from her tablet.

"As Vice President Caprey mentioned, I am from the Center For Disease Control. I have two points to deliver to you today. The first, is to thank you for your hospitality and to ask your patience as I ask questions about your healthcare delivery system. The second is a bit more delicate."

Maya cleared her throat. "It seems that an American manufacturer used a cleaning solvent on the insides of gas cylinders used in major medical surgeries. The residue of this cleaner has been shown to react with the gasses inside, creating a life-threatening cancerous situation to anyone who would inhale the gas. Naturally, we wish to keep this information as quiet as possible, and for now the risk appears limited to cylinders filled and distributed in the last thirty days. I have those batch numbers, and as a precaution we want anyone who has come into contact with the cylinders to be checked immediately. The cleaning residue was also found on the outsides of the cylinders, potentially causing dangerous levels of exposure to anyone handling the cylinders at any point. For this reason, we have already taken all of the hospital's loading dock workers in to be examined."

A man in a white jacket raised his hand. "I'm sorry, Doctor Hughes. No one in the accounting department would handle cylinders."

"No," Maya said. "But you'd record the cylinders entering the hospital and exiting to various stations on surgical floors, as well as any that were later shipped offsite or loaned to other hospitals. Bulk purchasing may get a discount from a supplier, but it can also allow a tainted object to pass through many hands. We're hoping that these batch numbers can be run through your system and pulled quickly."

"All that required a visit from the CDC?" the man asked. "Over a few dirty tanks of nitric oxide?"

"No." Maya shifted on her feet. "Some of the gases on the list . . ." She swallowed hard. Stick to the script or drive the point home? What would get these people's attention?

What would make them come forward?

She took a deep breath. "Some of the gasses are used exclusively in adolescent surgeries, and operations to correct heart malformations in newborn babies. Your hospital buys the cylinders, but may resell them to other hospitals around the country or even into parts of Europe, where over forty thousand surgeries will be performed on children this year. Some of the cylinders will be mislabeled or recorded incorrectly, and not found out until an annual audit is done. We don't have that kind of time. The effectiveness of the people in this room in locating these cylinders could save thousands of innocent children from contracting cancer in the next thirty days, possibly next week—maybe even later today. But we don't want to cause a panic. We just need all of you to help us track down these batches as fast as we can."

Maya stared at the faces of the people in the room. No one seemed irritated anymore, and several were tearing up. "I . . . I've said too much." She stepped backwards, toward the door. "Please keep the real story to yourselves. I'll be meeting with you as we—"

The Secret Service agent held up his hand, walking toward Maya. "We need—I mean, we have—a few more minutes. Are there any questions?"

A man in the back raised his hand. "How long do we expect contamination to take?"

Maya blinked for a moment, then glanced at her tablet.

The question and the answer were both there.

Q: How long do we expect contamination to take?

A: Contamination is expected to be contained within one standard deviation of the exposed population, with approximately ten percent displaying initial symptoms within thirty days. These symptoms include, but are not limited to . . .

She read the answer aloud, trying to focus on what she was reading and not how the exact question and answer got onto her tablet.

The next question was from a woman. Her question and its answer were also on the tablet.

In all, ten questions were asked, by ten different people, in the same order they appeared on her tablet—while the tension level of the audience visibly grew. Folded arms. Frowns. Shifting on seats. Tapping toes.

They want to save the babies, Maya thought. Why is the Secret Service delaying?

When she concluded, the accounting employees moved quickly out the door, taking their phones as their names were called out by the security guards.

"Dr. Hughes," the Secret Service agent said. "Would you come with me, please?"

She followed him into the classroom next door, where a panel of monitors showed various scenes around the hospital. The Vice President was on several, videoed from different angles, as she gave a talk to the hospital's chief administrators. Another camera showed the accounting employees filing back into their cubicles.

One displayed the people exiting the classroom Maya had just left.

"How'd you get that one?" Maya pointed to the screen. "I didn't see a camera in there."

"We had three in there, ma'am." A technician pointed to the wall of screens in front of him. "A Pinhole camera in the ceiling tile, and a camera in a fake smoke detector by the door."

"What about the third?" Maya asked. Her head and back appeared onscreen. She turned around to face the Secret Service agent.

He pointed to his lapel. A pin in the shape of the United States' flag had a shiny, round bead in the center. "Smile for the camera."

She shook her head, whistling. "You guys are impressive."

"Here's the really impressive part," the agent said. "Listen. When they turned in their phones before your presentation, we opened them and put a broadcast chip inside."

Two men sat at a second table, wearing headphones and staring at monitors.

"We have an engagement," one said. "I'll patch it through for you."

The Secret Service agent leaned forward. "Bingo."

A British woman's voice came over the computer's speakers. Her voice trembled, and she spoke in hushed tones. "It's me. The American CDC was just here. The shipment you stole is contaminated and anyone handling it might get cancer."

"It's crap, the lot of it," a British man replied. "Don't get mental."

"The phone's a burner," the technician said. "But the location is in Surrey. West end. Might be that truck driver they had upstairs. He got released yesterday."

"But they were just here. Why would they say that if it wasn't so?" The woman's voice fell to a whisper, the strain in her voice growing. "A doctor all the way from the CDC, and the Vice—"

"No, it's crap," the man said. "And it's not your concern, is it? You done your part with the paperwork, so don't get all up and buggered 'bout the rest."

The call ended. The Secret Service agent clapped his hands together. "Okay. What did we get?"

"Hold on," the technician said. "She's making another call. Stand by." He punched a button on his computer and static came over the speakers.

A phone rang, then the call connected. A pre-programmed, generic response asked the caller to leave a message.

The British accountant ended the call without leaving a message.

Cursing, the agent leaned forward and pounded the desk.

"Hold on. Tracking," the technician said. "Also a burner. Still tracking . . ."

The agent held his breath.

"Got it." He typed on the screen, reading as he scrolled through the information. "The call went to a phone at an address in Northeast London, near Victoria Park . . . owned by Marvis Faris. A rental unit. Cross checking . . ." He typed again, web pages flying on and off his screen. "And the renter is . . . Amelia Dansing."

"Check to see if they filed a copy of her driver's license when they recorded the lease."

The technician nodded. "They did. Here she is."

He leaned back and clicked the mouse, sending an image of an attractive brown-haired woman onto the big monitor. A dot flashed in the corner of the screen. "Hold on, she's got an alias." Leaning forward, he clicked the dot, opening a smaller page inside the bigger one. "This lady is an

American. A teacher at a mixed martial arts school in upstate New York—if that's real."

The agent frowned. "I don't want her resume, Kirby. The accountant just connected her to the hijackers and probably Hauser. That makes her a key player. So, what's her name?"

"Sorry, boss. Our renter goes by the name of Jaden Trinn."

CHAPTER 14

Jack Coleman held a coffee pot in his hand, staring out the window of the police station. Gusts of wind pushed thin waves of snowflakes back and forth over the street. The bright sun bouncing off the white scenery made it almost too bright to look at.

He glanced at his watch again. After pouring himself a cup of coffee, Coleman headed back to his work space. His desk phone rang, so he increased his pace, being careful not to spill his drink, and managed to grab the receiver by the third ring.

Ten minutes later, he was in Nillson's office.

"The lab called, detective," Coleman said. "All the DNA collected from the tow truck belonged to the driver and one other person—a Caucasian male, the guy who wore the sweatshirt covered in gunshot residue and blood splatter. Looks like we have our killer's DNA."

"Nice." Nillson smiled. "He in the system?"

"Yeah—the lab tech says the computer dumped a whole truckload of data on his desk. I've been sorting through it with Sergeant Mallory on my share screen, but some of it's not adding up."

Nillson typed on her keyboard, bringing up a list of documents under Coleman's name. He walked around the desk and pointed to the monitor. "This file. The suspect's name is Lorenzo Tarrante."

Clicking the file, Nillson scrolled through the links. "When you link up local, state and federal databases, there are always communication issues. We don't all use the same operating system." Her gaze darted over the screen. She put her finger to a blue mark on a criminal records file. "This indicator means his passport is flagged in the FBI database. Not sure by who, because the user has a redacted login." She leaned back in her chair. "What about basic background? Did you do an internet search on this guy?"

"Yes, ma'am," Coleman said, counting them off on his fingers. "Newspaper articles show Tarrante was a high school football star in Memphis and was a starting running back for the University of Tennessee on a scholarship. Next thing you know, he quits the team in his second year and moves to Spain to study in Madrid. That's as far as I got. I thought I should bring it to you. Murder is a federal rap, but I don't have authorization to access those databases."

"Did he get injured?" Nillson entered an access code and opened the federal links. IRS, DEA and FBI tabs turned from gray to green on the screen. A second tier of tabs did, too, for agencies accessed less often by law enforcement. "That can be why a kid quits college sports and takes up real study—like sports medicine. It's a way to stay involved with their passion." Nillson ran her finger across the top of the screen. "These tabs can tell us if he's paying his taxes on time, or if he has any arrests. Let's see what our federal friends have on Mr. Tarrante." She opened several links on her screen.

"No tax returns?" She glanced at Coleman. "Using the newspaper articles as a reference, if he was eighteen in high school, he's about mid-twenties now. Normally, a guy is paying taxes by then." She clicked another IRS tab. "Let's see if mama still claims him as a dependent . . ." Nillson stopped typing. "That's odd."

"What?"

"No mama. IRS records show the parents are deceased." She clicked through to state records. "No inheritance. Looks like our boy has been generating his income through off-record sources. And here's another FBI flag. This one cross references to the State Department. What gives?"

Coleman leaned over her shoulder, reading the files as she opened them.

"Well, I'll be." Nillson shook her head. "According to passport records, he's been living in Madrid. That explains the lack of IRS info, but we can't see his income there. Not at my level. But . . . he travels regularly from Spain to Paris, for weeks at a time. That can't be cheap."

"Must be a salesperson," Coleman said. "Or involved in some sort of international business."

"Could be. There's more here." She rubbed her chin. "You were working this with Sergeant Mallory?"

"Yes, ma'am."

Nillson punched a button on her phone. "Mike, it's Erika. Can you come to my office for a minute?"

"On my way."

She turned to Coleman. "All that international travel probably put him on the FBI's watch list. But he's been doing that for a while now, so I'm wondering—what triggers it all? Normal kid, athlete, gets injured and starts a new career—fine. Why fly all the way to Minneapolis to shoot a stranger the minute she gets off a flight from Indonesia?"

"Time to call that PI from Tampa?" Coleman asked.

She took a sip of her coffee. "Not yet."

An African American officer walked into Nillson's office. "What's up?"

"Mike, how was this guy Tarrante in the DNA registry?"

"Oh, he did one of those ancestry DNA tests in college." Mallory shrugged. "They offer them free on campus as a data collection thing."

"Interesting," Nillson said. "When did he do that?"

"It's right here." Sergeant Mallory walked around to her keyboard and studied the screen. "Here." He pointed to an open share file. "The results came in around November of his second year in college."

Coleman snapped upright. "That's right before he quit the team and moved to Spain."

"Yep," Nillson said. "And right after the FBI put him in a special registry."

Exhaling sharply, Mallory stepped back and folded his arms. His eyes stayed on the computer screen. "Think he's a terrorist?"

"Let's find out." Nillson jumped up, going to a filing cabinet. "Mike, you take over on my computer and start checking the federal files. Jack . . ." She opened a drawer and yanked a laptop out, handing it to Coleman. "Take over from where we left off. I'm going to reach out to a contact at Homeland Security and access his credit cards so we can track his location." She picked up her desk phone. "There are a lot of flags on this guy."

"Hold on," Mallory said, clicking on a file. "No need to call Homeland. They have his address in the system, but according to the passport records, your killer boarded a flight to London last night."

* * * * *

DeShear leaned against the window of officer Kensington's car, forcing his eyes to stay open. Green and red splotches appeared before his eyes, making him queasy. Each breath was work, and his insides throbbed with pain. During his last coughing fit at the Dockmaster's building, he was puking up blood in the restroom.

DeShear rubbed his eyes, putting it all out of his mind. "Let me borrow your phone again, would you?"

Kensington pulled to a stop light and dug in her purse. "Here, but she's probably quite busy with your Vice President."

He dialed Maya's number. It rang about six times and went to voicemail. DeShear slid the phone into a cupholder by the gear shift, wincing and holding his abdomen.

"Why not try texting her?" Kensington said. "She doesn't know my number, after all. And traffic will get thicker as we get closer to Royal London Hospital. Caprey's visit has the streets closed."

* * * * *

Vice President Caprey waved to people in the hallway as she stepped into a holding room—a small classroom where they could wait until the Secret Service decided her detail was cleared to leave the building. Maya's phone pinged as she followed the Vice President's staff into the room.

"How did it go, Doctor?" Caprey asked.

"Good." Maya smoothed her skirt. "I think."

"She did great," the Secret Service agent approached. "Madam Vice President, may I speak to you for a moment?"

As they walked away, Maya took her phone out of her bag and glanced at the screen.

This is DeShear. Call me at this number.

A jolt of fear went through her. His treatment was nearly due, but the disease didn't run on a schedule. He could be having issues. She glanced at the phone's time display, then mashed the button to call him back.

* * * * *

"Maya," DeShear said, trying not to cough again. He pressed the speakerphone button.

"Hank, are you okay?" Maya asked.

"I think I'll live—at least for a little while longer." He gripped his stomach. "We're near Royal London Hospital. Are you still there?"

"Yes. I'm in a holding room downstairs. How fast can you get here?"

DeShear glanced at Kensington.

The officer stared out at the traffic. "About ten minutes."

"Okay," Maya said. "Call me when you arrive."

* * * * *

Maya ended the call and went to the Secret Service agent. "I need to stay behind when the Vice President leaves."

"No." He lowered his voice, glancing around. "That's all been arranged, *Doctor*. We have to get on to the next stop."

"I have to administer a treatment to the private investigator I'm traveling with. Vice President Caprey knows all about it."

"Well, she didn't say anything to me, and we have a schedule to stick to. I—" His hand flew to the side of his face, pressing his earpiece. "What's that, sector two? Are we all clear for Eagle One to depart?"

Maya stepped away, pulling out her phone. There were a lot of procedures involved when traveling with the Vice President, but very few to exit a public hospital. She opened a web browser and found a site map of the hospital campus, then typed a message for DeShear.

The Vice President will be leaving from Milward Street, so

She stopped typing. Maybe it wasn't a good idea to broadcast Caprey's exit strategy.

Deleting the first message, she started again.

My ride leaves from Milward Street, so I will travel on foot to

Flipping to the browser, she zoomed in and found a street a block away.

. . . Cavell Street, and head north. Meet me there.

She sent the message and waited for the reply. When DeShear's okay came back, she slipped the phone into her pocket and headed for the classroom door.

* * * * *

"There she is." DeShear pointed to Maya as she walked along Cavell Street. Officer Kensington honked the horn and pulled to the curb. Propping himself up, DeShear waved.

Maya opened the back door and climbed in, her jaw dropping when she saw DeShear. "Oh, Hank. You look awful. What happened?"

"What didn't?" DeShear said.

Putting her hand to his neck, Maya checked his pulse. "You're freezing. We have to get moving." She faced Kensington. "Officer, I have a temporary medical facility set up in an apartment a few miles from here, on the northeast end of town. Would it be possible for you to take us there?"

"Yes, ma'am. MI-6's orders." She pulled away from the curb. "We have to watch for the Vice President's motorcade route, though. They'll have the streets blocked for it."

Maya nodded. "She's headed to the airport, I think. But we came in at a military base, so maybe—"

The car lurched to the right as a large white van swerved in front of them. Kensington stomped the brakes, spinning the wheel to avoid a collision. DeShear banged into the window. Maya fell sideways, grabbing the headrest of the front seat. The car rammed the curb, slamming them sideways.

The van stopped short, then it's engine revved. Its tail lights lit up red, then white, as its tires screeched. Smoke filled the wheel wells as the big van rocketed backwards at them.

"Hold on!" Kensington shouted, grabbing for the gear shift.

The rear of the van smashed into Kensington's car, the crushing *boom* of the impact filling the air. The passengers launched forward, heads and arms flopping.

DeShear unbuckled his seat belt as the van doors flew open. Two armed men with big barrel rifles jumped out.

"Everyone, get down!" DeShear shouted, sliding to the floor. "Maya! Get on the floor!"

Kensington reached for her sidearm. The windshield shattered. Rapid fire gunshots filled the air, sending bits of glass all over the inside of the car. Kensington bounced back and forth in her seat, her blood splattering the windows. Her hands fell to her sides as she slumped to the door.

"Kensington!" Shattered glass rained down on him. Bullets ricocheted off metal. Keeping his head low, DeShear reached toward the far side of the vehicle, across Kensington's body and to her weapon. Shot after shot blasted through the car, sending bits of fabric and upholstery into the air.

DeShear squeezed his eyes shut and lunged forward, ramming his hand onto the officer's gun.

The shooting stopped. A few bits of glass fell from a shattered side window. Cold air blew through the car.

They're reloading.

"Maya, are you hit?" He pressed himself forward, his fingers slipping off the wet gun. When he pulled his hand back, it was covered in blood. Kensington's hand hung at the side of her seat, her head on her chest. He grabbed her wrist and felt for a pulse. His heart sank. There was none.

DeShear glanced into the back seat. Maya lay on the floor. Blood seeped from the side of her head.

Outside, a man shouted orders in a foreign language.

DeShear unholstered Kensington's gun and threw himself into the back seat. Glass bounced off the upholstery as he landed. He shook Maya. She raised her head, her eyes wide.

"Stay down," he said. "I'll cover you. I'll— I'll get the car going and get us out of here. Just stay on the floor."

He peeked over the seats.

If I can fire off a few shots, I might be able to send them into a defensive position, get myself into the front seat and get us out of here.

Outside, a single shot fired. DeShear crouched down. There was shouting, and then another shot.

Then it was quiet.

DeShear's heart was pumping. Keeping low, clutched the gun tightly.

Jump over the seat. Push the body out of the way. Start the car.

There wasn't enough time.

Footsteps came to him through the broken windows. His heart pounded as they got closer—hard shoes on concrete, growing louder.

The attackers had probably reloaded. He couldn't make a run for it—couldn't leave Maya to die—but he might be able to stay low and get the car started before he took too many shots.

He swallowed hard. The killers would open fire the second his head popped up.

He shook his head, looking at Maya. Their chances were bad.

A bad chance is better than no chance.

Holding his breath, he inched upwards. Maya groaned next to him.

Smoke from Kensington's wrecked sedan streamed skyward. The van doors were open, but the men weren't visible. On the street around the wreck, people ran and screamed, jumping for cover.

One person moved slowly and smoothly through the chaos. A woman, in a leather jacket, with dark brown hair. She walked toward DeShear, holding a gun at her side.

The lady from the pier. The one who bombed the truckload of gas cylinders.

DeShear threw himself into the front seat and reached around Kensington's blood-soaked torso to turn the ignition key. The engine made a clicking noise.

He tried it again. Nothing.

He gripped the gun and looked at the gear shift. The car was still in drive. He slid across the seat, pressing Kensington's body to the door and shaking the wheel. He stretched a foot out to the brake and rammed the transmission into neutral.

The woman walked forward, raising the gun and pointing it at him. "I told you to stay out of my scene."

DeShear leveled Kensington's sidearm at the stranger.

She shook her head. "There are more guns than mine pointed at you."

The passenger side door opened on the sedan, and two large men grabbed DeShear. One slammed a fist into his gut while the other yanked the gun from his hand. The men hauled him out of Kensington's vehicle, holding him tight as they dragged him to a small white car.

Down the street, an ambulance sped toward them.

As they shoved him into the back of the car, the woman went to her motorcycle. She swung her leg over the seat and the engine roared to life, whining as she raced down the street. As the little white car pulled away, DeShear peered out at the wreckage. Two armed men lay on the ground by the van, blood pooling around their bodies. Kensington's bloody corpse rested against the door of her car. Maya was nowhere in sight.

CHAPTER 15

The dark-haired stranger read her phone screen as she got off the motorcycle and walked toward the old warehouse, a rag tied over her upper triceps. The two thugs dragged DeShear from the car, holding his arms in a vise-like grip. He struggled for air, his gut still aching from getting punched.

Bending over, the woman grabbed the handle of a roll-up door. "Your friend is alive." She flung the door open and walked inside. "Severe concussion and possible brain swelling. Looks like a bullet grazed her. They're talking about a medically-induced coma." She stuck the phone into the back pocket of her jeans.

A thin man in overalls approached her. "So? How's the coat?"

Trinn pulled off her leather jacket and tossed it to him. "Needs more Kevlar—and a warmer lining." She disappeared into the shadows.

The warehouse contained rows of broken-down assembly lines and rusty manufacturing machines. A small office stood off to one side, probably for the manager of whatever the place used to produce. Spider webs filled the building's hazy, broken windows, and dirt lined its ancient concrete floor.

One of the DeShear's captors spoke to the shadows. "Trinn, what do we do with this guy?"

"Take him downstairs." A different woman's voice echoed off the walls of the empty space. It was softer than Trinn's, with a trace of a Spanish accent that made it slightly familiar.

The man walked toward a staircase. "Follow me."

The other man raised Kensington's gun.

"No, I don't think so." DeShear winced, holding his abdomen. His heart racing, he squared his shoulders. "If you're going to kill me, skip the dramatic flair and just do it here."

"Kill you?" The woman from the motorcycle reappeared on his left, frowning. "I saved your life—twice. Get downstairs."

She turned and headed down the staircase. The man with the gun unloaded it and set it on an old wooden work table, then went back outside.

The other man stared at DeShear. "You heard what Trinn said. Downstairs."

"You ambushed us," DeShear called after her. "You got Kensington killed—the port authority officer—and you nearly killed—"

Trinn wheeled around on the stairs. "We interrupted that ambush. Those weren't our guys in that van. I saved you when I took out those two assassins firing the automatic weapons that were turning your car into swiss cheese. And you'd be a smoldering briquette if I hadn't knocked you into the river last night when that truck blew up."

DeShear narrowed his eyes.

"Yeah. Now do you want to get some first aid on that injury, or do you want to bleed all over the place?"

"If that chaos back there is any example of your ability," he huffed, walking toward her, "I might be better off with the people who ambushed us."

"Fine by me," Trinn said. "It wasn't my idea to—"

"Mr. DeShear." The other woman's voice was calm and even.

"You know, you're pretty ungrateful." Trinn glared at DeShear, climbing back up the staircase. "You should thank me."

His jaw dropped. "A woman is dead because she helped me. I'm a little short on gratitude at the moment."

"Mr. DeShear." The second woman stepped out of the shadows, her petite figure cloaked in a white physician's jacket.

DeShear's jaw dropped. "Dr. Carerra."

She nodded. "I'm very sorry about all this drama, but I felt it was . . . necessary." She stepped forward, taking his hand in hers and studying his face. "And we are all very sorry about the loss of the port officer. Her death is, of course, a tragedy. But it could not be helped. We weren't able to act any faster than we did."

Dominique Carerra was beautiful, with dark curly hair and even darker eyes, but she looked older than she did a week ago in Indonesia. More lined, and much more tired.

"Maya is my friend, too," Carerra said. "She was extracted from the scene as you were, and will receive the best care possible—for both our sakes." She looked into his eyes. "I don't want you to worry."

DeShear fought the urge to ask questions and demand answers for the moment. It wasn't the time.

"And according to the text she sent me this morning," Carerra glanced at her phone. "You are due for a second round of treatment. Is that correct?"

"I . . . yes." He swallowed. "I'm sorry—"

"It has been a bit much." Carerra shook her head. She glanced at Trinn. "For all of us. Please, come downstairs. We will start your treatment, and I have something I would like to show you."

The basement of the old warehouse was small, a bunker of sorts, with no doors or windows to the outside. Two examining tables had been set up, with lights and some medical equipment nearby.

"All this for me?" DeShear said.

"Unfortunately, no." Dr. Carerra opened a drawer on a cabinet and pulled out a bottle and some large bandages. She handed them to Trinn. "Because of the nature of our relationship with Dr. Hauser, we had to use this facility for some treatments in the past."

DeShear stood upright. "Hauser?"

Trinn went to the first examining table and hopped onto it, pushing her sleeve up to expose the blood-spotted rag tied around her triceps. She undid the makeshift bandage and let it fall to the surface of the table, reaching for a jar of cotton balls.

"The drugs required for your treatment are unique," Dr. Carerra said. "And very specific to your condition. Of course, we have developed a few of our own—Maya, in particular, was instrumental in that. But if . . . the *right eyes* were to see certain purchases, they would know what they were for, and they would have a way to find us."

Carerra guided DeShear to the second examining table.

He sat. "But if Hauser is dead, who would . . ."

"Are you comfortable?" Carerra pulled an IV drip rack to him. "I have something I would like to show you." She gestured to Trinn.

Pulling her phone from the back pocket of her jeans, Trinn pressed a button and held the screen in front of DeShear. "This is only part of the message," she said. Cell service is spotty over here, so I assume there's more, but I don't know."

Dr. Carerra viewed the blurry image, a sad expression on her face. "We do know that this was taken covertly by a person at the event—no phones were allowed in the room—but we don't know precisely when it was recorded, or by who."

The video appeared to be shot across the top of a table, toward a speaker in front of a projection screen. The dim lighting didn't allow the camera lens to focus, so the speaker wasn't clearly visible.

"We already regenerate skin for burn victims."

DeShear bolted upright. Dr. Hauser's gravelly voice was clearly audible on the phone.

"We can replace nearly any organ in the body," the old man said, "including the heart, via transplant. Any organ, except the brain." The blurry silhouette waved a hand toward the projector screen. "What amazing things mankind has accomplished! Things that, a hundred years ago, were impossible. The stuff of fiction. Fantasy. I ask you, fellow scientists—fellow pioneers—what else is science capable of? What is the next step?"

The silhouette paced back and forth in front of the projector, limping. "Look at the screen behind me. Innovations like 'talk to text' are a miracle. As I speak, my words can be instantly interpreted by the computer and written, translated into any language in the world."

The words "any language in the world" appear on the screen in English. Below it, appeared

En Español: Cualquier idioma del mundo.

En Français: N'importe quelle langue du monde.

Auf Deutsch: Jede Sprache der Welt.

The delighted, blurry man chuckled. "And if I were to ask another computer to read it out loud, it would." He leaned over the projector to a laptop. A different male voice repeated his words. "And if I were to ask another computer to read it out loud, it would."

The audience laughed. From the acoustics, there were maybe fifty to a hundred people in the room. DeShear leaned forward, peering into the phone's shaky display.

At least it's a ballroom and not a stadium.

"Synthesizers," the speaker said, "are able to grab the specific sound patterns for a violin—or a church organ or a barking dog—replicating them so perfectly that someone with almost no musical talent at all can entertain us with a violin concerto just by doing little more than learning to play the piano. In a similar way, a specific human voice print can be grabbed—and now the computer can read my words and sound exactly like me."

He pushed another button and his voice came over the PA, reciting what he had just said, in his exact voice.

"Now, my friends, what if we were to take this one step further?"

The limping silhouette shuffled toward the screen, the sound of a cane hitting a hard surface coming through the phone's tiny speaker.

"What if we were to bridge the gap between my thoughts being spoken, and move one step closer, inserting a microscopic array of sensors inside the lobes of the brain responsible for speech? Then, I wouldn't have to actually *say* the thoughts, I could simply *think* them, and in the same way that my brain delivers the electrosensory commands to make my larynx, mouth and lips move so the words come out—we send a signal to the computer and it does it instead."

He stood, mouth closed, as the PA announced, in his voice, "Would that not be amazing?"

An audible gasp went up from attendees in the room.

"In a similar way, if we were to harness the visual receptors in the brain and the auditory receptors, the sensors for taste, pleasure and pain—we could, with enough computer power, re-create the entire human experience and pass it from one person to another. We could transfer all the comprehensive information of a library straight into your brain at age five, making schools as we know them all but unnecessary."

The blurry man raised a hand, shaking it at his audience like Moses at the Red Sea, his voice booming. "We could do what man has yearned to do since the beginning of time. We would essentially become immortal, because what is a person other than the sum total of all their memories and experiences, stored in the computer that we call their brain?" The group began to applaud. "If we were to harness that information," he shouted, "we could download the greatest minds that ever lived, and allow them to continue to live."

Cheers erupted from the crowd.

"Einstein would be able to take his research further! Aristotle! Curie! Edison! Mozart!"

The crowd roared like it was a sports event.

When the noise died down, he lowered his voice. "In such a way, one need never die. As I say, replacement components are available everywhere. Titanium hips and knees. New cartilage for arthritic elbows. We can give you an entirely new skeleton that will never break down, and a fresh set of skin and muscles to cover it! All that exists today. But inside . . . Why not also a fresh brain—one that is programmed with what you need? The sum total of your experiences. Like taking the wisdom of a seventy-five-year-old man and resetting the physical odometer to age twenty-five. Fresh skin. New hair. A bladder that doesn't get you up ten times a night."

More laughter.

"Any aspect you wish to amplify would be available, but most important would be *you*. The aspect of the individual would be maintained. Permanently. Indefinitely."

The blurry man stood in the center of the room as the crowd jumped to their feet in a standing ovation, and the phone screen went black.

CHAPTER 16

Officer Davis rubbed his eyes and leaned back on his chair. "Oof. I need a break. What about you?"

The security video of Royal London Hospital rolled by on monitors in front of Officer Grant. "You go ahead, old timer." He smiled at his partner. "When you get back, I'll take a walk to stretch my legs."

"Fair enough." The gray-haired man stood, putting his hands on his hips and twisting. "Might stop by the cafeteria, too." He patted his belly, dropping a paper coffee cup into the trash. "I'm too old to be sitting in uncomfortable chairs. We should see about something with cushions, but then I'd probably—hold it." He leaned forward, tapping the edge of monitor two. "Back this one up."

Grant clicked a button on the keyboard. The screen displayed images of people in the hospital lobby walking backwards.

"There. Stop." Davis stared at the screen. "Can you zoom in on this corner? This lady right here." He extended a finger and drew a circle around a slender brunette as she walked into the lobby.

The image grew larger as Grant clicked the mouse.

"Yeah, there," Davis said. "Does she look familiar?"

Grant nodded. "It's agent Pomeroy, from CIA. So what?"

"Watch. Let the video roll."

The two officers viewed the screen. Pomeroy went into the restroom. People in the lobby milled about. A red-haired woman hassled a nurse at the admitting desk.

"Speed it up. Twice speed."

Grant clicked the mouse. "What are we watching for? Pomeroy's good-looking, but it's kind of creepy to be—"

"Shh." Davis folded his arms. "Just wait."

"For what?"

"That." A blonde woman exited the ladies' restroom, wearing large round glasses and dressed in a white nurse's uniform.

Grant narrowed his eyes. "I didn't see anything."

"Pomeroy never comes out of the bathroom. Mark that spot and play the video forward at ten times speed."

Grant clicked the mouse a few times.

"Okay, stop." Davis pointed to the corner of the screen. "See the time stamp? By this time, we were already upstairs—all three of us, you, me, and

Agent Pomeroy. Look at the other videos. There we are, walking down the hallway on the eighth floor, and Pomeroy joins us. But she never came out of the bathroom downstairs."

Grant backed the video up.

"See?" Davis pointed to the screen. "Brown-haired Pomeroy goes into the restroom, and a blonde nurse comes out. None of the videos show either of them onscreen at the same time."

"She—Pomeroy—is wearing a disguise." Grant nodded. "Why?"

"That blonde nurse beat up a big security guard," Davis said. "Now, why is a nurse dodging security at her place of work, beating up a security guard, and carrying a taser? The Chief of Hospital Security interviewed the staff. None of them recognized that blonde nurse. Pomeroy reappears on the eighth floor, stays with us for the interview—and even leaves the hospital with us—and the blonde nurse is never seen again. After taking down the security guard, she just fell off the face of the earth."

Grant shook his head. "Pomeroy got into a cab and got right back out of it after we left—after that bizarre interview. What's the CIA up to?"

"I don't know," Davis said. "Go get the security sergeant. The nurse they were looking for is Agent Pomeroy."

* * * * *

The British accountant paced back and forth across her kitchen, hugging herself and biting her fingernails. Each time a car passed by on the street, she jumped from the center of the room and peeked around the edge of the window until its headlights faded from view.

She stepped onto her back stoop and lit up a cigarette, dialing her phone again. After a few rings, the pre-programmed, generic response played again. She took a deep breath and let it out slowly while she waited for the tone. "It's Lily Anders in accounting at Royal London Hospital. We have a problem. I need to talk to you right away."

She stared at the phone, her hand trembling, and lifted the shaking cigarette to her lips.

A car drove down the street. Lily held her breath, watching as it came closer. A line of white trailed upwards from her cigarette.

She breathed a sigh of relief as the car went past, taking another drag on her cigarette. "Bloody nonsense. Scaring myself to death."

The car's tail lights lit up, and the vehicle reversed, pulling to the curb. It was half a block away, near the corner, but it wasn't a car she knew. Most of her neighbors took the tube to work and back—and everyone was home by now.

She gazed at the car. No one got out. A white cloud of exhaust flowed from the tail pipe.

Lily dropped the cigarette and crushed it under her foot, going back inside her kitchen.

Her phone rang in her hand. She jumped, gasping, then closed her eyes and shook her head. The screen displayed "JT." Heart pounding, she pressed the button and put the phone to her ear.

* * * * *

Lily's voice wavered as she spoke. "Jaden! Oh, thank you for calling me back."

"You shouldn't be calling me." Trinn lowered her voice and stepped away from Dr. Carerra and DeShear. "What's happened?"

"I was worried. A doctor from the American CDC came to my work. They said the shipment we stole was contaminated and anyone handling it might get cancer. I called Randy, but he—"

"Randy?" A jolt of fear shot through Trinn. She squeezed her eyes shut. "Get out of your house. Now."

"What?"

"Do you have a car?" Heart racing, Trinn slapped her pockets for her motorcycle key. "Or a friend's place close by that you can go to?"

"No. Why?"

"You're in danger." She held the phone away from her face and checked the time. "Turn out your lights and lock the doors. Get in the bathtub. I'm on my way."

"But, I don't understand."

Trinn threw on her leather jacket and raced up the stairs, heaving open the warehouse door. A cold wind swept over her. "You have to trust me. Now, go. Get off the phone and—"

The sound of breaking glass came over the line. Lily screamed.

Fear gripping her, Trinn threw her leg over the motorcycle seat. A British man yelled at Lily from the background. "Right, girl. You've done botched it now."

"Lily!" Trinn started her motorcycle. The engine noise drowned out the call. "Lily, who is it? Tell me who's there!"

Lily screamed as the phone jostled. "No! No, get away from me!"

"Come on, Lily," the man said. "Let's have that."

There was a loud crash in the background. "Jaden! Help me!"

"I'm coming." Heart pounding, Trinn dropped the bike into gear, squeezing the phone to her head to hear over the engine. "How many are there? Who do you recognize?"

"It's Randy and Hollings. They've smashed the window and they're coming inside. What do I do?"

"Fight. Use whatever you have and fight for your life." Trinn revved the engine and held the phone with two fingers, grabbing the handlebars and sending a spray of gravel up behind her. She raced down the dirt road of the warehouse, her hair whipping in the wind.

An icy blast of air bit her face and hands. When she reached seventy miles per hour on the straight away, she pressed the phone back to her ear. She couldn't hear anything.

Trinn glanced at the screen. The line was dead.

* * * * *

"Here," Officer Davis said to the Chief of Security at Royal London Hospital. "We've isolated Pomeroy's movements. She doesn't stay in the cab after we split up. She gets out and goes around the side of the building."

The large man folded his arms and stared at the computer screen. "Why didn't facial recognition pick her up?"

"Not sure, but once we put her in your system, we got this." Davis glanced at the Chief. "A port authority request went to the MI-6 lab last night. Pomeroy is a ninety percent match for their Jane Doe 135, a suspect in an explosion on one of the piers. We checked cell phone traffic on the pier towers. That time of night, it's pretty quiet. There were about two dozen pings from phones near the time of the explosion, and all but three were port employees. Of the three that weren't, two phones belonged to men. The other phone was only at the tower around the time of the explosion. Local police talked to every person who was authorized to be on the docks over the last twenty-four hours, and captured those interviews on video. Nobody saw a brown-haired woman in a dark jacket. Not working, not smoking, nada—until she appears on the security cameras immediately after the explosion."

The Chief nodded. "So, either twenty-plus dock workers and security guards are lying sods, or Jane Doe 135's cell phone is this one. Did we trace it?"

"You bet we did," Grant said. "To Amelia Dansing, who rents an apartment on the edge of town. According to the driver's license registered with her rental agreement, Ms. Dansing is a ninety percent match for Jane Doe 135 and for Agent Pomeroy."

"That's pretty air tight." The Chief patted Grant on the shoulder. "Nice work, mate."

Davis stuck his head into the security Chief's office. "Excuse me, sirs."

"Yeah?" Grant said.

"You asked me to track the phone we isolated from the pier tower and see where it goes." Davis swallowed. "It's currently moving at over 160 kilometers an hour on the A-11."

* * * * *

"Lily, dear." Hollings twirled the bread knife between his fingers like a baton as he paced back and forth across the living room. The Christmas tree lay on its side, the lights still on, broken ornaments scattered across the floor. "We can't have our people running off making stray phone calls. Randy here tells me you've absolutely been burning up the phone lines. Called him, and made about six calls to that American lady, Trinn."

Lily sat in the love seat, her hands under her thighs, trembling. Her legs were bound at the ankles by the cord from her TV. Duct tape had been wrapped around her waist, trapping her elbows to her sides.

Her gaze went to Randy.

"Sorry, love." Randy walked from the kitchen, stuffing a piece of ham into his mouth. He flopped onto the couch. "Family phone plan. I can see all your calls, in and out, on my computer."

Hollings stroked the side of Lily's face. "Let's see how sharp a knife you keep, lass." He pushed her blonde locks back, holding them tight in his fingers as he exposed her ear. A tiny gold earring shined in the lamp light.

The edge of the knife gleamed. Hollings held it up to her face, easing it past her nose and across her cheek. His breath was hot in her face, smelling of ale and fried fish.

He jerked the knife upwards. Lily gasped, shutting her eyes.

"There, girl. Nothing to fear." He dropped a clump of blonde hair into her lap, turning to Randy. "Nice and sharp, that is." He leered at Lily, leaning in close. "Might have to keep that bit of cutlery after we're done carving things up with it tonight."

Lily turned her face away, a faint whimper escaping her lips. A tear rolled down her cheek.

"I think she's due for a haircut." Hollings licked his lips. "What do you think, mate?"

Randy leaned over to peer around Hollings. "Might have a go. Looking a bit shaggy now you've done the one side. Best even it out, yeah?"

"Aye. She is a shaggy one." Hollings dragged the edge of the knife lightly along Lily's cheek. "She's a right filthy gossip, she is, running that tongue of hers all day to that Yank woman."

Lily breathed hard, her eyes on Hollings and the knife.

He traced her lips with a dirty fingertip. "I wonder how we could fix her so she don't go blabbing no more?"

"A big mouth, you're saying?" Randy said.

Hollings scowled. "Big mouth. Big blabbing tongue." He clenched his teeth. "Big bloody headache, this one."

"Please, Mr. Hollings." Lily quivered, her heart in her throat. "I'll do whatever you want from now on."

"What I want is to get back them calls you made to Trinn. How you going to give me that? Eh?"

"I . . . I didn't . . ."

"You did, Lily. You called her and called her. The Yank that done tried to kill me, and wanted to kill your boyfriend here."

"Threatened to sizzle me brains with a taser."

"That's saying he had any." Hollings turned around and plunged the knife deep into Randy's belly, twisting it and dragging it upwards to his chest. The boy lurched forward, holding his guts with both hands as he howled.

Lilly screamed, her eyes wide.

"That's it." Hollings smiled at her. "There we go."

Randy rolled off the couch, gasping, holding his guts. Blood gushed over his hands as his head hit the floor. Hollings grabbed the boy by the arm and held him upright, stabbing the blade into the young man's throat and sawing it open.

Randy's eyes opened wide as his jaw dropped, blood running from the massive slash under his chin. His hand flew to his neck as he fell to the floor.

Lily screamed again and again and again, her cries filling the air.

"That's it, yes." Hollings stood in front of her, the knife dripping with blood. He stepped toward Lily. "Now, let's finish that haircut."

CHAPTER 17

DeShear lay on the examining table, an IV drip in his arm. Chest stickers held thin, colored wires that ran to an EKG.

The basement room was warm and quiet. Dr. Carerra put a finger on the side of his face, inspecting the cut.

"You could use a few stitches—as long as I'm here. Unless you want a manly little scar." She picked up the first syringe.

"One thing at a time. If it's not bleeding, I'll stick with it as is."

* * * * *

Trinn darted around the sparse traffic, leaning forward on the bike to cut the wind. The jacket was doing its job, but with no gloves or helmet, the frigid air still sliced right through her.

Another icy gust rocked the motorbike. Up ahead, a flatbed truck sped along the highway. Trinn opened up the motorcycle's throttle and closed in behind the big vehicle. The bulk of the truck cab blocked some of the wind and steadied her bike.

She glanced at her speedometer, shaking her head. 160 kilometers per hour, but it wasn't fast enough. Her gaze went to the phone. It was useless now. Even with the truck blocking some of the wind rush, the engine noise from the motorcycle was too loud to make a call. She'd never hear Lily's voice over the phone, and at this speed, Trinn couldn't risk trying.

She had to go faster. That was the only thing that mattered now.

Trinn tossed the phone into the bed of the truck and opened the throttle again, soaring out from behind the truck and into a wall of icy wind.

* * * * *

DeShear folded his hands over his abs, staring at the ceiling as he prepared for the long treatment. The hum of the EKG machine was the only sound in the room.

"What do you make of Hauser's recording?" he said. "Do you think there's a chance he could still be alive?"

Carerra finished dabbing the side of his face with an iodine sponge and applied some gauze, holding the bandage in place with a piece of tape. "I am worried about Tristan. He will search for Dr. Hauser if he thinks that evil old man is still alive."

DeShear nodded. "It's tricky. Hauser is literally talking about a machine that could mimic him perfectly. Any audio from now on will be suspect."

The doctor turned away, checking little brown bottles in cabinet drawers and filling the syringes that would be plunged into his veins over the next few hours.

The EKG machine buzzed next to him, starting another printout, but his gaze remained on Carerra. This small, unassuming woman was the main reason he—and a lot of other people—would stay alive. He had questions for her, lots of them, about his treatments, and what awaited him on the other side of the gamma sequence. Would he still be his old self, running on the beaches of Tampa Bay at dawn every day, as if nothing had happened? Or would there be changes? With so many of his internal organs under siege, and so many drugs being used to combat that, for so many months . . . what complications would he be dealing with later?

Will I die in the next few months, and what will my new life be like if I don't?

He stared at the IV needle in his arm. His questions were keeping him awake at night. Maybe no one had the answers.

Across the room, Dr. Carerra picked up the same bottle for the third time, and set it down again.

He took a long, deep breath. He had questions, but now was not the time for them.

Now was the time to see a human being worried about losing someone she loved. DeShear knew a little about that.

* * * * *

Officer Grant put his hands on the dashboard as the squad car's siren wailed. Two Specialist Firearms Units followed in heavily armed vehicles.

Gripping the steering wheel, the Chief glanced at Grant. "The A-11 is a direct route into London. That bombing at the port makes your girl Pomeroy a suspected terrorist, so we'll be stopping her—and the big guns will be drawn."

Grant pulled his weapon out and checked the clip. "Fine by me."

An officer's voice came over the radio. "Chief, the suspect has slowed down and turned into a residential neighborhood. Any changes in the plan?"

The Chief grabbed the receiver and held it to his mouth. "No. Steady on. Lots of show once we get inside, but we want her alive." He frowned, lowering his hand. "What's she up to?"

*   *   *   *   *

"You and I, we've both suffered a lot because of Hauser," DeShear said. "A lot of people have. Maybe I can help Tristan. The Vice President has given me contacts in police agencies here and throughout Europe. Maybe if he talks to her—"

"He won't." Carerra stopped fidgeting with the bottles, her shoulders slumping. "He can't. He won't risk coming forward. Certainly not for a politician. He's wanted for a dozen murders in the United States, a few in Spain, some here in Britain . . . the instant anyone learns who he really is, he risks being put behind bars for the rest of his life." She turned toward DeShear, but her eyes were elsewhere. "He said he'd be going away, but he could not tell me where, or for how long—and during that time, I know he could be imprisoned, or hurt or killed. But that is information that will never reach me. I may never see him again, and I will never know what happened."

* * * * *

Trinn raced down the street, peering over the handlebars toward the near-dark residence that Lily called home. The row of town houses filled the block on both sides, but the neighborhood was quiet. No one was walking the dog; no joggers pounded their way down the sidewalks. A few parked cars dotted the side of the street, but no moving vehicles were in sight.

The neighborhood looked calm and safe.

She stopped about half a block away, cutting the engine and parking the motorcycle next to a car, under a tree. Hopping off, she slinked along the front of the row houses until she got to Lily's unit.

* * * * *

"Losing a loved one." DeShear gazed at the back of the doctor's white jacket. "The heart never really heals, not completely. We learn to go on, but we're always wounded."

Carerra's shoulders went up and down with a sigh.

He slid his legs over the edge of the examining table and sat up, being careful not to disturb the wires and tubes attached to him. "I don't think The Greyhound will die for a long time. It's not his style. And staying away from a fight isn't, either."

"Or yours." She gazed at him. "Why are you here, doing this? You helped stop the infanticide in Indonesia, and the human trafficking. When is your job finished?" She shook her head. "Like his. Never."

"My job was done when we shut down Angelus Genetics in Indonesia, but then they killed Lanaya."

Carerra's hand flew to her face. "Lanaya is dead?"

DeShear nodded. "Murdered, the second she got off the plane from Indonesia."

She buried her face in her hands, letting out a quiet moan. "It will never end." She lifted her eyes. "I'm sorry about Lanaya. I—I didn't know."

DeShear took a deep breath and let it out slowly, staring at the ground. "I told Lanaya she'd be safe, and two days later she was killed. I went to visit her family. She . . ." He swallowed hard. "She wanted her kids to visit me during my treatment— when I'd be fighting for my life—to see what a hero looked like."

He looked away. The EKG machine hummed next to him, its paper report slowly sliding off its cart and onto the floor.

"I made myself go to Lanaya's family, and I looked her daughter in the eye. I told my friend's little girl that I'd find the people who killed her mom." He glanced at Carerra. "And that's what I'm going to do."

Her voice fell to a whisper. "You think that's Tristan."

"I did, but not anymore." He sighed, staring at the many bottles and syringes lined up for him on the table. "Things don't add up that way now. If what you just said about The Greyhound—about Tristan—is true . . . you risked a lot by telling me. You love him, but you believe in justice and fairness, too. Him killing Lanaya wouldn't have been that, and then you wouldn't be here helping me."

Carerra slipped her hands into the pockets of her white jacket, her eyes on his.

"I think Tristan has a plan," DeShear said. "But he wants you to be prepared for the worst-case scenario."

She nodded slowly, her tired eyes far away. "How do you know?"

DeShear shrugged. "That's what I'd do."

* * * * *

Lily's front door was cracked open an inch, each gust of cold wind pushing it back and forth over the tiny gap.

Trinn held her breath. No noises came from inside.

Lily's attackers could be expecting Trinn to barge in, but she sensed otherwise. The noise of the attack had been on purpose. The attackers wanted to scare Lily—and they did. The sounds Trinn heard over the phone were those of a woman who was terrified out of her mind.

So far, this quiet room didn't fit with that.

Trinn crept to Lily's front window, keeping low and out of the light. Her breath went out in little white puffs in front of her. Inching her head up, she peered inside.

The edge of the curtain hung from its broken curtain rod, shielding part of the living room, but not all of it. The Christmas tree lay on its side, a broken window behind it. The pictures on the wall were knocked sideways and a desk lamp lay on the floor.

* * * * *

The Chief's radio squawked in the squad car. "Our ETA is about two minutes, sir. Cut lights and sirens?"

"Aye, you'll be silent on approach," the Chief said. "Let's not scare everyone too badly until we're all in place." He glanced at his speedometer as trees and parked cars whizzed by outside his window. "My car will take the front. I want full tactical, fanned out around the residence, front and back, before I knock on the door. And blast her to bits if she blinks, boys. No telling what this woman's capable of after that bombing."

* * * * *

Trinn lifted her head higher. A couch. A loveseat. No obvious attackers in the home. At least, not downstairs. The table and bookcase had been upended.

She craned her neck a little further. Her gaze fell onto the face of a man, his eyes open but unmoving, and his neck covered in blood.

Trinn's heart jumped. It was the truck driver from the hijacking. Hollings' partner.

Lily didn't do that.

And if Hollings had killed his partner, then .

. .

Trinn jumped up and stared into the window to view the rest of the room, her jaw dropping.

* * * * *

Carerra administered another IV drip and prepped the next syringe. "What do you think he wants?"

"Hauser?" Deshear exhaled, staring at the ceiling as he lay on his back. "Hierarchy of needs.

Food, shelter, like that. Then, once you're as far up the power and money ladder as he is, I think you expand your horizons. You look at your legacy, what you accomplished and what you'll be remembered for. But I think what he said on the recording is right. I think he wants to live forever. He has everything anyone could ever want, and he means to keep enjoying it. Based on what he said, he may even have the technological resources to pull it off."

"I think it is much simpler." The doctor cleaned DeShear's arm, pushing the syringe and sending the medicine through his vein and into his system. "I think he wants love." She sat on the stool next to the examining table. "Something went terribly wrong in his life. Especially a doctor, who is sworn to do no harm. He's filling a hole inside of him. Gaining knowledge and becoming a physician didn't do it. The prestige of building a world renown organization didn't. He had money, power, fame— but it wasn't what he really craved, deep in his heart. He wants love."

"You can't discount the fact that he might just be crazy," DeShear said.

"Love makes everyone crazy." Carerra lined up the next syringe. "The lack of love can open the darkest shades of the soul."

* * * * *

Trinn ran inside the townhouse, but she knew what she would find. She shut the door behind her, staring at the scene.

Lily lay face down on the floor, a knife sticking out of her back. Trinn dropped to her knees, feeling Lily's cold neck and wrist for a pulse. She found none, her hands coming away coated in blood. The dead woman's eyes were frozen wide with horror, etched into her face from her last moments alive.

The gaping slash on her throat told how she had died, and the massive amounts of blood staining the rug answered any questions about what message her killer wanted to send. Trinn stood, her knees wet and red, staring at the wall.

Drops of blood trailed from Lily's chair and across the room, where a bread knife pinned a human tongue to the wall.

* * * * *

The Chief's car slowed down as he eyed the residence.

"Pomeroy's position has remained stationary, Chief," the officer said over the radio. "Our tactical officers are in place, front and back. We are ready on your go."

"Right." The Chief took a deep breath, letting the car idle forward. "It's nearly time, officer Grant. You'll stay in the car, out of sight, until we've swarmed. And if any shooting starts, try not to hit me."

* * * * *

A police car pulled up in front of Lily's townhouse, with its lights flashing. After a moment, the lights went off, and an officer stepped from the vehicle. He walked slowly toward Lily's front door.

Trinn slipped away from the living room and stepped into the kitchen. She pressed herself to the wall, glancing around. A red smear marked the paint where her elbow had been. She glanced at her arms and legs. Her knees and hands were covered in blood, and red footprints tracked from Lily's body to the kitchen.

* * * * *

The Chief stood at the front door of the townhouse, adjusting the Kevlar vest under his coat. The earpiece broadcast the movements of his officers as the last few tactical officers rushed to get into place.

"Good to go, sir."

He reached out and pressed the doorbell.

* * * * *

Trinn scanned the kitchen. It held no weapons. The knife block stood empty on the counter, and opening cabinets to search for something useful would make too much noise and waste too much time. The utensil drawer had been dumped. Tea towels and an apron littered the floor.

The doorbell rang a second time. Trinn grabbed a towel from the floor, wiping her hands off and staring at the back door.

* * * * *

The officer's voice boomed through the small home. "Police. We've had a complaint about the noise, and I see you've got a broken window. Now, if you don't open up, I'll be coming in anyway."

* * * * *

Trinn's hands were clean enough, if the officer didn't look too closely. The apron might hang low enough to cover her bloodstained knees. She held her breath and leaned over to pick it up. If she opened the front door an inch, and wedged herself into the gap so the officer couldn't see past her to the rest of the room, she might be able to keep him from coming inside and discovering the bodies—and taking her away on suspicion of murder.

Or…

She eyed the back door again.

* * * * *

The Chief put a finger to his earpiece.

"Suspect is approaching the door, Chief."

He nodded, swallowing hard. A chill wind blew across his face as the lock made a metallic thump and the knob turned.

His pulse thumped in his ears.

As the door inched open, the Chief threw his shoulder forward, knocking the occupant backward. He jumped inside, windows crashing on all sides as the tactical unit leaped into the house. The back door burst open and several uniformed officers raced inside.

"Get on the floor! Get on the floor!"

The middle-aged woman's hands flew to her face. She screamed, backing away from the entrance. A fat, gray haired man jumped up from the couch, a newspaper in his hand. "What's all this!"

A dozen officers poured into the room, weapons aimed at the couple.

The Chief stared at the woman, his jaw hanging open.

Officer Grant raced in. "Where is she? Where's Pomeroy?"

The chief frowned, grabbing his shoulder radio. "Deakins! Where's Pomeroy?"

A young officer entered the home, a computer tablet in his hand. "I don't understand it, sir. The phone is pinging right there in the driveway."

The chief stormed from the house, staring across the walk at a large, flatbed truck. One of his officers stood in the bed of the vehicle, holding Trinn's phone in his hand like it was a dead rat.

* * * * *

"Miss!" The officer rang Lily's doorbell again. "I'm coming in!"

He flung open the door and ran into the room, nearly tripping over the fallen Christmas tree. Stopping, his jaw dropped as he viewed the gruesome murder scene.

Trinn wrenched the knob on the back door. It opened an inch, then slipped from her hand and slammed shut again.

"You, there!" The officer ran toward her. "Stop!"

She pulled the back door open as far as it would go and pressed her face to the gap. The knob had been tied to the iron railing on the stoop.

A heavy hand came down on her shoulder.

Trinn whipped around, dropping low and driving her shoulder upwards into the officer's gut. She pushed him backwards, crashing both of them into the wall. As he sagged to the floor, she leaped onto the counter and crawled to the window over the sink.

The officer groaned, reaching for his shoulder radio.

The latch on the window frame didn't budge. Layers of paint held it in place.

Turning her head, Trinn closed her eyes and smashed the glass with her elbow. She put her hands on the sides of the frame and leaned back, staring into the darkness outside. A cold gust of wind blew into the kitchen.

The officer got to his feet, coming toward her.

Trinn ducked her head and took a deep breath, throwing herself out.

She landed sideways, rolling over the cold, hard ground. As she glanced back, the officer's face appeared in the window. Trinn jumped to her feet, sprinting around the corner of the unit, to the rear of the building. A wooden fence lined the back of the long, skinny lot, not twenty feet from Lily's back door, and spanning the length of the building. Trees on the other side created shadows for hiding. She gritted her teeth and pumped her legs.

A hundred yards to the motorcycle, and—

The fence flashed white as a gun fired. Pain burst forward from Trinn's back like she'd been hit with a baseball bat. She crashed forward, her face hitting the grass as two more blasts jolted her.

Trinn rolled over in the frigid grass, surging in pain and fighting to breathe.

A shadow raced toward her.

"Now, Miss." Hollings held up his shotgun, leveling it at Trinn's face. "Let's see what's really going on in that pretty head of yours."

The officer crashed into Hollings. The gun fired sideways, flashing white and filling Trinn's ears with a deafening blast that made them ring, but she was otherwise unhurt.

Trinn gasped for air, her back on fire with pain, as the officer leaped onto Holling's chest and cracked his baton over the old man's head. Panting, he turned around, blood tricking from his nose. He reached for the taser at his side. "Now," he gasped, "you stop, Miss."

She shook her head, forcing herself to her feet. "Thanks for the help." She winced, holding her side as she limped away. "But I gotta go."

CHAPTER 18

The lights in the warehouse basement flickered as Dr. Carerra unhooked the empty IV bag and set it on the tray table. Putting his hand over his mouth, DeShear yawned.

"Don't try to fight sleeping." The doctor's voice was soft and calm. "Sleep is what you need. It is when the body heals itself best." She lifted a new IV bag to the rack and adjusted its drip. "The next injection will put you out anyway, but you will awaken with renewed energy. Maya said Tristan slept for days when she gave it to him."

"How is Maya?" DeShear asked. "Do we know? Trinn said she was in a medically-induced coma."

Dr. Carerra shook her head, pulling the little stool over to the examining table and sitting. "She's not. We used that as an excuse to move her out of the emergency treatment center and into specialized care, where she is under the direct watch of people I know and trust. From there, we can transfer her to specialists at a hospital with facilities specifically for that type of brain injury—in this case, the Ludvika Lasarett, in Sweden. A place that is safe, and far away from any prying eyes."

"So, Maya is okay?"

"Not yet." Carerra took a fresh syringe from the tray table and jabbed it through the rubber stopper in the top of a little brown bottle. "She was struck in the head with a bullet. She has sustained a major concussion and possibly brain swelling."

"That's . . . what Trinn said when we came in." He frowned. "How did she know? It had only happened a couple of minutes before."

"Jaden was reading the instructions I sent to the ER physicians and ambulance paramedics."

"You arranged for the ambulance," DeShear said. "It was waiting."

She nodded, filling a second syringe from a green bottle. "We knew the attack was coming, we just didn't know when. But you got in the middle when you went to the port—and you put Maya in the middle, too."

"So." He rubbed his chin. "You blew up the truck at the port. Why?"

"Jaden did, yes." The doctor set the medicine on the table and rested her hands on her knees. "Tristan explained the tactics this way. If you're a bad guy and the police come after you, you hide—but if you're a bad guy and another *bad guy* comes after you, you fight back. Capone in Chicago, Medellín in Miami. You make a statement, written in blood, out on the streets."

"Tristan wants the streets of London flowing in blood?"

"He wanted to stop the bad guys before there was any blood. For that, we needed to start a fight that looked like a rival moving in. Jaden did that by imbedding herself with the hijackers. They led her to an accountant at the hospital. Then Maya just backtracked the paper trail."

"Hold on." DeShear sat up. "How do you get the drugs for this warehouse, to do your treatments?"

"Lay down." She put her hands on his shoulders. "We use resources from around the world. Private resources."

"But you're acquiring and using pharmaceutical medicines that are specific to treating the gamma sequence, and you buy a lot of them. So this place can be tracked down, too."

She leaned back, her jaw dropping. "We've been here for nearly a year now . . ."

DeShear shook his head, sitting up and sliding his legs off the examining table. "You were too small an operation to notice. That's changed." He stood, pulling the EKG wires from his chest. "The people you picked a fight with can locate us the same way we located them, by following the purchases. Now it's a race to see who finds the other first." He reached for his shirt. "You said Trinn knows their operation best. Where is she?"

"I . . ." She shook her head. "I don't know. She always has to leave on sudden notice to keep up appearances with the hijackers."

"Okay." DeShear fastened his buttons and glanced around. "Can the last part of this treatment wait? We have to get out of here."

"It's three vials. I can administer it from almost anywhere, but you will—"

"Their attack this morning shows they know about your group—which means if they don't know about this place, they will soon. If they had the firepower to attack a car on the streets of London in broad daylight, they won't hesitate to come here, and you have no defenses that I've seen. We need to move. Would that skinny guy upstairs have heard from Trinn?"

"Maybe." She turned to the stairs, raising her voice. "Mr. Redlins, have you heard from Jaden?"

"No, mum. She left in a rush, a while ago. Hasn't called in."

"Can we call her?" DeShear asked.

"We aren't supposed to," she said. "In case someone has been apprehended or their cover has been blown."

He nodded. "What about a backup system?"

"We use the Savoy in downtown, on the river."

DeShear grabbed the railing and limped up the stairs. "Mr. Redlins, we need to get out of here. How fast does this place pack up?"

"I don't know, sir," Redlins said. "We've never tried. But what do we pack it into? We'd a need a truck."

DeShear winced. "Do you have a car?

Redlins pointed to the warehouse door. "It's just outside."

181

Leaning over the stairwell railing, DeShear called downstairs. "Doctor, have those two gorillas that mugged me box up whatever is essential. Mr. Redlins and I will be back in an hour."

* * * * *

Redlins' rusty white Mini Cooper bounced along the road like the car had been built before shock absorbers or springs. DeShear clung to the little handle over the passenger window with one hand and put the other one on the dashboard, his head hitting the roof. "We need to find an area with lots of vehicles, Mr. Redlins." The car hit a bump, making DeShear wince. "Any ideas?"

Redlins hugged the wheel, pulling his wool derby cap down over his forehead. "There will be lots of people out at Claybury Park today, but not yet."

The tiny vehicle rolled past a residential street lined with two-story row houses.

"Whoa," DeShear said. "What's that?"

Redlins hit the brakes. "Here? It's, ah . . ." He glanced at the street sign. "Clayhall Avenue, sir."

DeShear shook his head. "No, that." He pointed down the street to a massive, red double-decker bus.

"That?" Redlins faced DeShear. "It'll stick out like a red thumb!"

"Out here, yeah. But not in town. Turn."

Cranking the steering wheel, Mr. Redlins forced the little car around and pointed it down the residential avenue. "How we goin' to get a rig as big as that?"

DeShear ran his hand over his chin, eyeing the giant bus. "I'm going to ask the driver really nicely."

* * * * *

Trinn walked fast and steady, past the Waterloo Bridge and down the wide, concrete walk that ran along the Thames. She held her jacket tight against her, shuddering in the harsh, frigid wind that blew across the river.

Stopping at a magazine stand, her gaze wandered over the merchandise. She picked up a red canvas bag with a white image of a boat on it and the wording "Wood's Silver Fleet," a pen, a small sketch pad, and a roll of mints, setting them near the cash register. Behind the old man at the counter, a plastic oven showcased an array of sausage rolls under its warming lights.

"Just this, then, Miss?"

Despite the awful look of the meat-pastry, Trinn's stomach growled.

"And a sausage roll, please." She hunched her shoulders against the wind and dug into her pocket for some cash.

The clerk rang up her sketch pad and placed it in a bag. "Nice day for drawing."

"Mmm. Yes." Each word left her lips in a stream of white, carried away from the icy river.

Raising a set of tongs, the man reached into the plastic oven. "You an American?"

She nodded. "Yes."

"Welcome across the pond. Sorry it's so cold for your visit." He handed her a bag and counted out her change. "A happy New Year, to you, Miss."

"Thank you. Happy New Year to you, too."

Trinn walked another hundred yards or so before cutting across the street and going through a short, iron fence that separated long rows of manicured hedges. She passed a stone-lined pond and a round patio, strolling through the Savoy's rear entrance and into the warm air that awaited inside.

The front lobby bustled with business. Tourists followed crisp-suited bellman past the massive Christmas tree and across the immaculate, black-and-white checkerboard lobby. Tasteful vases on pedestals adorned wood-lined walls. The grand, arched ceiling of the main hallway stretched out in a welcoming seafoam green.

She stopped before getting to the front desk, sitting at one of the polished, dark wood tables that dotted the near corner. Opening the tiny shopping bag, she took out her sketch pad and pen.

With winds of white and starry nights
I lay beside my firelight.
A chance to meet the one who'll keep
A promise to my heart's delight.

She wrote fast, filling the first page with rhyming lines and the second with text like a diary entry, mentioning typical tourist areas and her alleged observations of them.

Seeing London bridge by water taxi was better than walking, but the abbey across from Big Ben would have been fun for Dad. We saw Buckingham palace and the changing of the guards . . .

On page three, the coded message began.

When we visited New York last year to see grandma, we took a trip to little Italy. They had the best pizza! I got one with artichokes and onions, which I would never usually do, but it was a-may-zing. Here, the pizza has sucked, but the pubs are awesome. I plan on going to as many as possible . . .

By page four, she was out of ideas—and getting a cramp in her hand. She picked up someone's leftover newspaper from the chair next to her and copied the middle of an editorial about the upcoming election and which politician was the most inept.

She finished, tucked the pad into the canvas bag, and headed to the claim check.

* * * * *

"Stealing a bus," Redlins said. "You're mental."

"I'm not stealing it." DeShear unclipped his seat belt. "I'm borrowing it. Just pull in front and hit the brakes. I'll take it from there. As soon as the passengers get off, head back to the warehouse and help Dr. Carerra pack. I'll meet you there."

"Right." Redlins tugged his cap and stomped the gas pedal. The little white car zipped along the side of the long red bus. "Have you ever driven a bus, sir?"

"No, but it can't be too different from a car, can it?

"I suppose we'll find out, eh?" Redlins gripped the wheel. "Good luck. Ready . . . steady . . ."

He swerved the Cooper in front of the bus and pressed both feet to the brake. The little car's tires screeched as they came to a stop, the roar of the giant bus's air brakes hissing loudly behind them.

DeShear glanced over his shoulder, flinching as the rear window filled up with the red and black diagonal stripe of the bus's front bumper. He snatched Redlins' cap and opened the door, waving and smiling as he ran toward the bus.

* * * * *

Trinn thanked the bellman and tipped him £5, exiting the Savoy through the front entrance. The surrounding buildings kept the wind gusts at bay while she went to the last planter box on the right and tucked the claim check tag in the front corner.

Tugging her jacket tight around her, she turned and disappeared down the street.

* * * * *

"Thank you for stopping!" DeShear grabbed the stainless steel railing and pulled himself into the bus, keeping his face low. He dropped Redlins' derby cap over the security camera. "And now I'm afraid I have to tell you, there's a bomb on board." He reached past the driver and turned off the service radio, grabbing the receiver wire and yanking it out.

The bus driver turned white.

"You've been trained for a bomb threat," DeShear said. "What's the procedure?"

The man shook his head, trembling. "I—I—I . . ."

"You have to evacuate the vehicle and all passengers, is that right?" DeShear nodded at the man.

"Y-yes."

"Okay, then. Out." He turned to the passenger seats. About half a dozen people sat reading their phones. "Passengers! I am wearing a suicide vest filled with explosives. I'm hijacking this bus. This is your only chance to escape unharmed."

The passengers looked at him for a moment, then scrambled for the exits.

DeShear stared at the driver. The man jumped up and ran out the door.

Pushing the yellow button, the doors closed. DeShear dropped himself behind the big steering wheel. Ahead of him, the little white Cooper drove away.

DeShear rubbed his hands together, gazing at the dashboard of the bus. He set his foot on a wide, flat pedal, and pushed. The engine roared.

Grabbing the giant gear shift, he stepped on the clutch and jerked the massive vehicle into motion.

* * * * *

"Cheeky bugger." One of the men who abducted DeShear stood next to a stack of boxes and medical equipment in front of the warehouse. "You stole a bloody bus."

"Barely. Load it up." DeShear tossed him a key. "We don't have a lot of time before the police arrive."

The man scowled. "Maybe if you'd have taken something a little less conspicuous, eh?"

"Unless you're bullet proof, I'll take my chances against the police rather than the rival drug gang. They already shot up one car I was in today. Where's Dr. Carerra?"

"Here." She stepped from the warehouse, a large leather bag over her shoulder.

"Okay, ma'am. You and I are going to leave now."

Redlins threw his car keys to DeShear.

"The rest of you." DeShear opened the door for Dr. Carerra. "I bought us a day, if that. Find a place to stash this equipment, then drive the bus to the edge of town and dump it. The doctor will update you with a more permanent location."

The big man scratched his head, staring at the equipment he'd dragged outside. "Where are we supposed to hide all this gear?"

Shaking his head, DeShear raced around to the other side of the car. "Anywhere but here."

* * * * *

DeShear studied the highway while Dr. Carerra drove, his eyes darting to every car that appeared, in front or in back of them. After a few minutes, he relaxed.

"We can go to a hotel," Dr. Carerra said. "After we go by the Savoy to see if Jaden left a message. I have money and a fake identification. We'll be safe. We can give you the rest of your treatment then."

"She wasn't alone," DeShear said. "Trinn, on the pier."

"Our people were assisting. You met some of them. They take her to a location, or get her a nurse's uniform. She was able to imbed herself in with the hijackers, and—"

"This wasn't a helper." DeShear shifted on the seat. "And it certainly wasn't one of those two big thugs or Redlins. This guy rode in when the bomb went off, running up to the flames to find her and get her out. I wouldn't call that a helper. I'd call that . . ." He pursed his lips, watching the doctor's face. "I think it was Tristan. I thought so at the time."

"It can't be." Her eyes flashed. "He—"

"Why not? If I were your husband, I'd stay close." He lowered his voice. "Even if I couldn't talk to you, or if it was best that you didn't know I was there, for your safety. You say we're alike, he and I. When I was a rookie at the police department, I worked shifts, so sometimes I'd drop my daughter at preschool in the morning." He took a deep breath and let it out slowly. "I liked to swing by during recess and park across the street, just watching her play with the other kids on the playground. I wanted to be as near as I could be." He shrugged. "I think Tristan is close by, too."

They approached the sign for the bypass to London. Carerra took the turn and headed into town, almost automatically. Her mind was elsewhere.

"Tell me about the plan for the hijackers," DeShear said.

She sighed. "Find one city with a facility. Stop the supply lines, to draw them out. No supplies, no activity."

"Simple and effective." DeShear nodded. "And it sure worked. You drew them out. I had Maya tracking their purchases. I suppose she told you that. What happens next?"

"Track the purchases to find any other locations," she said. "Then repeat the process. No medical facility can survive without a constant stream of pharmaceutical supplies—disinfectants, medicines, gasses for surgery, equipment. You saw what we stockpiled in that warehouse, and we're a semi-mobile unit."

"Oh, that's it!" DeShear bolted upright. "The equipment." He faced Carerra. "Doctor, there can't be more than a few places that make the specialized equipment necessary for surgeries. If Hauser set up another facility somewhere, they'd be buying equipment like they were building a hospital. We need to find out who has been supplying things for new hospitals, specifically ones with major surgery centers. In the States, those would all be registered with the CDC. Where would they be registered in other countries?"

"It's the National Institute of Health here in the UK. In Spain, it's *Ministerio de Sanidad, Consumo y Bienestar Social,* the MSCBS . . ."

"I may be able to ask the Vice President's office to open any doors we need. Do you have friends there?"

"In Spain, yes." She glanced at him, biting her lip. "But before you make any further plans, there is something I must tell you. Something you deserve to know."

CHAPTER 19

Rising eight stories over the Thames and surrounded by trees that were as old and established as the building itself, the Royal Horseguards looked more like a castle than a hotel.

Trinn shivered as she walked through the pristine, white limestone entrance.

The gray-haired doorman tipped his top hat, bending slightly as she passed. His long coattails fluttered in the wind. "Good afternoon, Miss."

"Good afternoon."

The lobby was slightly smaller than the Savoy's, but every bit as regal.

"I need a room for a few days, please." Trinn slid her passport and credit card across the counter to the desk clerk.

"Yes, ma'am, Mrs. Barclay." The young man leaned forward and typed on his computer.

"Something up high, with a view of the river—if you have it."

"I think we just might be able to arrange that. We've had a few late cancellations for the new year's celebrations because of the weather . . ." He smiled and looked up from the keyboard. "Sixth floor. Will that do?"

"That will be perfect."

* * * * *

Dr. Carerra swallowed hard and stared out at the road. "When Tristan first found out about the horrible things Angelus Genetics was doing, he worked hard to get them to stop—through proper, legal channels. When that didn't work, he took matters into his own hands."

DeShear knew that, but he also knew that all confessions needed a starting point, and sometimes they needed to gain momentum to get to where they were going. He watched her eyes and waited for her to continue.

"I knew what he was doing. I disagreed with the methods, but I convinced myself it was somehow better to try to control the damage he wanted to cause, by guiding him, than to walk away and let him wreak havoc on the targets he located."

The doctor's pained face displayed her remorse. It always had.

"As we found other people with the condition," she said, "we formed a kind of network. Some could get information or do research, as Maya did, or lend assistance by forging hospital records, or stealing medications. Tristan led them, with the understanding that together they would do the difficult things necessary to stop Angelus, but that he alone would kill the ones responsible for the deaths of so many. Nothing else had worked, but he wanted no blood on anyone else's hands." She sighed, adjusting her hands on the wheel. "Of course, we soon learned that it takes more than one person to carry out such things and remain under the radar of the authorities. And since it was primarily Tristan risking his life every time, it became necessary to implement additional groups who could carry on if Tristan were killed or imprisoned."

She swallowed hard again. "I love my husband. Like a soldier in a war, he believed the lives he took were morally right and necessary for justice to prevail. When he saw things had changed—that his methods were no longer necessary to take down Angelus—he stopped." She glanced at DeShear. "You did that. You and your people changed his heart, and gave my husband back to me. I will always be in your debt for that." She blinked a few times, sniffling. "But there were others who disagreed, who felt we should finish what we started—and finish the list."

DeShear spoke softly, looking at her. "That list had people on it who weren't involved in the infanticide and illegal organ harvesting, or the human trafficking—people who were working to get all that stopped."

"To some, that mattered." She shook her head, glancing out the window. Open fields had turned to houses, and then buildings. "Others' hearts were too hardened by then. Those are our rogue elements. And that is who Tristan is also trying to stop."

"That's who killed Lanaya?" DeShear said.

Carerra nodded, pulling to a stop near the Savoy Hotel. "It seems I am not done causing you pain."

* * * * *

Trinn strolled through the lavish suite. High ceilings, plush carpet. The big, soft bed called to her, as did the oversized bath tub, but she still had work to do.

A few blocks away she was able to acquire a new phone and some clean clothes. A computer came next—and another sausage roll from a street vendor—before heading back to the hotel.

* * * * *

DeShear walked with Dr. Carerra to the planter box closest to the street, the façade of the Savoy rising tall behind them. Wind gusts battered the little green bushes as she reached past them and plucked a claim check tag from the mulch.

"That is a good sign." She brushed off the little white tag and held it up. "I will be right back."

His eyes stayed on her as she went down the long walk and disappeared into the regal building, returning a few minutes later carrying a red canvas bag.

"What happens now?" he asked.

She kept walking, taking his arm. "Now we go to a warm café and see what Jaden wants us to know about her situation."

"Can't she just call? They sell disposable phones around here somewhere, I'm sure."

"She would if she could. So, for some reason, she feels she can't, or shouldn't."

They walked around the corner, crossing the street a block away and entering a coffee shop. A small table near the front windows was empty.

Carerra sat down and opened the bag, taking out the sketch pad. "The first page is usually inconsequential—a way to encourage others to think it is a college student's journal or a diary that's been left behind. We will look for a reference to Jaden's code word." Carerra scanned the pages, dragging her finger along until she saw what she was looking for. "Here, it mentions New York. That's her."

DeShear glanced at her. "Trinn is New York?"

"Yes. If she mentions it in a conversation, she is indirectly trying to tell you something about herself, or to see if you are in the network. If you are not, it won't mean anything to you."

Nodding, DeShear watched the doctor's finger continue over the writing. "This pizza reference," she said. "First, it indicates the pizza is good—'the best'—and then it says it is bad. She is saying that she had a safe house, but she has torched it now."

"Torched?" DeShear said. "She didn't burn it down."

"She means she left it, but first removed anything that could tie it or her to us. Saying 'the pubs are awesome' and 'I will visit as many as possible' means she is in an expensive hotel and will be there for several days."

"Simple and effective. I like it." DeShear sat back. "Seems like a lot of work to convey a message, but I get it. If they found her place, they may have found yours—and a text from a new phone might set them back on her trail."

"Exactly." Carrera stood, checking the time on her phone. "Jaden will likely be at the Goring or the Horseguards, and since this is plan B, she will be registered under the name Barclay."

DeShear got up and pushed his chair in. "Why one of those two?

"Because her flat was dismal. If you saw it, you wouldn't think to look for her next at one of the most expensive hotels in London." The doctor walked to the exit, dropping the sketchpad in a trash can by the door. "The Horseguards is about a block away from the Savoy."

"Okay." DeShear flipped his collar up as he followed her out the door. "After we locate Trinn, I'll go dump Mr. Redlins' car."

"Jaden can do that. If we don't finish your treatment, you won't be walking around under your own power."

* * * * *

As Dr. Carerra crossed the lobby of the Horseguards hotel, a dark-haired woman in sunglasses walked up to the desk clerk. Her knit cap covered the top of her head, and large, round glasses covered most of her face. Leather gloves and an elegant full-length wool coat covered the rest of her, down to a pair of black high heeled boots.

"Mrs. Barclay," the woman said. "Room six twelve. Any messages?"

The clerk peered at his computer. "No, ma'am."

"Thank you." She turned and left the building.

DeShear and Carerra followed.

Half a block away, she stopped and faced them. "Thank you for coming, Dominique. You, too, Mr. DeShear."

"Are you okay?" Carerra asked.

"Fine." Trinn nodded. "I wasn't followed, and the hotel room is clean." She handed Carerra a plastic key. I was able to get a computer, but I haven't logged into the safe site yet. You?"

Carerra shook her head. "We had to evacuate the ware—"

A gray van screeched to a stop on the road next to them. The side door opened, revealing a man with a shotgun.

DeShear leaped in front of Carerra. Trinn turned, running into the barrel of a pistol held by Hollings. He held it close to his jacket, smiling. "Go on, try it. I'll put enough holes in you to make Lily seem spotless by comparison."

Behind DeShear, another man said, "I've two barrels aimed at you and the Misses, Yank. Get into the van."

DeShear grabbed Carerra by the collar of her coat. "Do what they say, Doctor." He stepped backwards toward the gun. When it hit the small of his back, he pushed the doctor toward the building and spun around, shoving the shotgun in the direction of the street. The man fired, his blast going into the open van.

DeShear grabbed the smoking end of the gun and shoved it backwards into the man's gut. As the attacker doubled over, DeShear drove the wood stock upwards into the assailant's chin. The stranger sagged to the ground.

DeShear whirled around and stepped toward Hollings.

"Stop!" Hollings kept his gun in Trinn's chest. "I'll put one through her heart if you take another—"

Trinn grabbed the pistol with both hands and dropped to her knees. Swinging the shotgun like a baseball bat, DeShear landed the stock on the side of Holling's face. The fat man's head whipped backwards. Trinn thrust his gun upwards as he fired.

The shot ripped DeShear's jacket, sending white-hot pain through his shoulder. Hollings landed on his back, with Trinn jumping on top of him.

DeShear glanced into the van. The man inside had dropped his gun and was staring at the red spots oozing blood all over his chest and arms. DeShear reached out and slammed the door shut, glaring at the driver. Turning white, the van driver floored the gas, and the van peeled away from the sidewalk.

DeShear glanced at Carerra, his shoulder throbbing. She sat on the sidewalk, her jaw hanging open.

She's fine, just a little surprised.

Stepping past the doctor, he checked the man sprawled out behind her on the curb. No movement, and only a slow gurgle coming from between his bloody, broken teeth. He was no longer an immediate threat.

DeShear turned back to Trinn. She sat on Hollings' chest, pinning his head to the concrete with the pistol.

Gritting her teeth, she leaned over and drove the tip of the gun into Hollings' forehead. "I should have killed you the first time I had the chance."

"You haven't the guts." He smiled, blood trickling from his ear. "Then or now."

"No? I disagree." She lowered the gun, put the barrel to his left wrist and pulled the trigger.

Hollings howled in pain.

Trinn grabbed his other arm and put a shot through his right wrist. She got to her feet as he rolled around on the pavement, screaming.

"But unlike you," she said, tucking the gun in her belt. "I'm not a murderer."

Carerra sat on the sidewalk, her jaw hanging open and her face white. DeShear put his hand out to her. "We need to get out of here, ma'am. Now."

On the street, people ran in all directions. The doormen were shuttering the hotel.

Breathing hard, Trinn stepped to DeShear and Carerra, her head down. "These streets have surveillance, so the police will be here soon. We need to get out of sight and split up."

"No," Carerra said, trembling. She got to her feet and knocked the dirt off her hands. "No. We stay together."

DeShear glanced around. "Well, whatever we're doing, we need to do it quickly." He put his hand on Carerra's shoulder and pointed to a nearby alley. "Step in here."

Trinn followed them down the narrow, brick-walled space, as DeShear slipped behind a dumpster. She joined him, yanking off her long coat to reveal her leather motorcycle jacket underneath.

"I can steal a car off the street." DeShear faced Trinn. "Did you leave anything incriminating in your hotel room?"

"No. I have my wallet and phone."

"What about clothes, computers, papers?"

"Nothing traceable to me. The computer is hard locked with a twelve-digit alphanumeric password. No one's getting into that. We're good."

"Okay." DeShear glanced toward the street. "Redlins' car is off limits. It's been seen in a crime earlier, and the surveillance cameras will eventually connect it with this attack, so we can't use it."

Carerra pulled the keys from her pocket and dropped them into the dumpster. "Mr. DeShear, you were a police officer. If you were looking at this situation, where would you expect the people involved to go?"

"Anywhere but here."

"Then what if we stay put? The Goring is a few blocks away. If I go there and get a room under a new name, we are right back in business. Jaden can get a new computer, and I can administer the rest of your treatment."

"I don't know," Trinn said. "What if they don't have a room? The clerk at the Savoy said—"

The doctor shook her head, patting her wallet. "If I wave enough cash under the right nose, they will have a room, don't worry." Her eyes went to Trinn's hat. "Now, no one has seen me do anything except get attacked on the street—if they even saw that. I can use your hat and glasses to mask me enough to check in. You two can come in a few minutes after me and hide in the lobby. When I get the room, follow me up."

"But—"

"You said we don't have time." Carerra took Trinn's jacket. "You're right. We don't. I'm going."

She turned to walk back to the street.

"Hold on," Trinn said. She held up her long coat and turned it inside out, handing it to the doctor. The hat and glasses followed.

DeShear was impressed with the transformation. Reversed, the wool coat looked much less fancy. The silvery lining was a far cry from the sleek beige exterior, but with the hat and glasses, Carerra looked different enough to walk right past the scene of the attack and not get noticed.

As the doctor went back toward the street, Trinn and DeShear went the other way down the alley.

* * * * *

Fast-walking along the windy sidewalk that hugged the Thames, DeShear checked out Trinn's leather jacket. "Do you always wear two coats in winter?"

"If one's Kevlar." She hunched her shoulders against the cold.

"What?"

"This one has a Kevlar lining," Trinn said.

His gaze wandered over the coat. The dark leather didn't show the lumpy thickness usually associated with bullet proof gear. It hugged Trinn's curves like a regular jacket.

She jammed her hands into the pockets, shuddering. "It's not as warm as wool, but it's a lot safer."

CHAPTER 20

Dr. Carerra approached the rich, carved-wood front desk at the Goring hotel. She swallowed hard to suppress the butterflies in her stomach, and did her best to stand tall. "Hello. I realize it's short notice, but I'd like to see if I could get a room for the night."

The young man behind the desk stood up straight. "Oh, I'm terribly sorry, madam. We've been booked for months—New Year's celebrations and all."

"I understand." Carerra set her wallet on the counter and dug through it. She'd seen her husband do this a few times, but she didn't like it, even though she desperately hoped it would work. "It is a bit of an emergency. Any room would do. Maybe you have a guest that hasn't checked in, who might decide not to come?" She pulled out a wad of hundred-dollar bills and held them close to her chest, fanning them out like a deck of cards. She cleared her throat and silently counted out five bills, laying them down.

The man bristled, lifted his chin. "I'm very sorry . . ."

"Oh, I completely understand." She continued counting out bills, trying not to let her fingers tremble, until twenty were laying on the desk. She peered up into the clerk's eyes. "Please help me. I was under the impression that my friends, the Franklins, are here. I would love to stay here with them."

He stared at the money, his mouth hanging open. "We're completely booked . . ."

She counted out ten more bills. "The Franklins are such a large family. I know they'd appreciate it if you looked at your computer again."

Three thousand dollars lay on the counter.

The man licked his lips, lowering his voice. "Madam, I—I simply cannot . . . The hotel has strict rules—very strict . . . rules . . ."

"Or have my friends gone to one of your lovely competitors?" She picked up the bills and folded them, cupping her hand over the cash. "I realize I'm asking you to go through a lot of trouble for me, by checking again. But I'd be appreciative—very appreciative—if you did."

The front desk manager walked over, her dark hair pulled back in a tight bun and her dark blue suit tailored perfectly. She smiled at Dr. Carerra. "Hello. Is there a problem, Mr. Jennings?"

"No, ma'am. I was just apologizing to this nice lady that we have no available rooms."

The young lady beamed again. "Oh, he's quite right, madam. We've been booked for months. Very sorry."

"Yes," Dr. Carerra said. "Mr. Jennings was very apologetic about that. That he would love to accommodate me, but that you were full."

"Yes, I'm afraid that's right."

"But I suggested that maybe you could check the computer again." Carerra uncupped her hand and held the folded wad with one finger. "Computers are such pesky things, you might see something you'd missed. I'd be very appreciative if you looked again."

The woman stared at the wad of cash. "Looked . . . again?"

"One tiny room." Carerra looked at the manager. "Anywhere in the hotel."

The young woman blushed. "Well, I . . . I suppose it can't hurt . . . to just look." She glanced at Jennings. "Do you think, Mr. Jennings?"

His face was just as red as his boss's. "I suppose, Miss, if we were to both look . . ."

The manager swallowed hard, facing Carerra. "Yes. What if we both looked?"

The doctor smiled, whispering. "Then I would be equally appreciative to both of you." She slid the money to the manager and reached back into her wallet. "That was understood."

"Yes. I can see that you would be." The young lady tucked the money into her vest pocket. "As it happens, there has been a cancellation. A small room, as you said."

Carerra didn't look up, counting out more cash. "On an upper floor."

The manager's cheeks glowed a darker red. "That, that, that . . . I—that—could . . ."

"Yes, there it is." Jennings typed quickly on the computer. He stood up, smiling. "We've just had a cancellation. Fourth floor, with an excellent view of the skyline."

"It sounds lovely." Carerra slid the money across the desk to him. "This really is my lucky day. May I check in immediately?"

He smiled. "Of course, madam. I'll just check you in . . ."

"Thank you for choosing the Goring," the manager said, pulling out a business card from her pocket. She handed it to Dr. Carerra. "If you should need anything else during your stay, here's my card."

"And mine." Jennings slid his card across the desk.

* * * * *

DeShear pulled his sleeve up to expose his wound.

"Take your shirt off," Dr. Carerra said. "I'm not risking an infection over modesty."

She sat in the chair next to DeShear, carefully pressing a needle and thread through the side of his upper arm. Hollings' bullet had left a deep cut, but nothing more. DeShear alternated between wincing and exhaling hard as she went about stitching him up. He gritted his teeth, trying not to make any audible noises.

Trinn sat in a third chair across the suite, arms folded and legs crossed, staring out the window at the gray skyline. An intermittent firework popped off over the darkening city.

Carerra dabbed the wound with a washcloth. "We will complete your treatment in a moment. It may knock you out for a while."

"I can sleep over there." DeShear glanced at the couch.

"Nonsense." Carerra shook her head. "You may be asleep for more than a day. You'll sleep on the bed. I will finish giving you the medications there. Jaden won't mind sleeping on the couch."

He peered at Trinn, then turned back to the doctor. "What about you?"

"A chair will be fine," Carerra said. "I'll be very limited on access to medical equipment while I tend to you. I don't expect to get much sleep."

Trinn uncrossed her legs and stood up, walking over to them. "It's a big bed. You can both use it. There's room."

Snapping the thread, Carerra got up and went to the dresser, picking up each of the brown bottles there and reading the labels. She drew a syringe from her bag.

Trinn turned the chair around backwards and straddled it, folding her arms across the back and leaning on them. "Besides, you earned a bed."

DeShear cocked his head. "How do you figure?"

She sighed, looking away. "Back there, on the street. I hesitated when Hollings and his crew jumped us." She gazed at DeShear. "You didn't. That made the difference."

He inspected his stitches. "You did fine." He gently touched the skin around the wound.

Trinn's eyes wandered from DeShear's cut, moving over his biceps and lingering on his firm torso.

"I got you shot because I froze up," she said. "It won't happen again."

He got up, shaking his head. "You know, this bunch is schizophrenic. They use automatic weapons on the street in front of the hospital, but they use rusty shotguns this afternoon?" He stepped to the window and stared down at the street.

"The attack at the hospital was gangland style," Trinn said. "This time, it was like the first time Hollings pulled a gun on me. That time, he wanted to make sure I didn't take his job. What did he want this time? We know he's a killer. He carved up Randy and Lily."

"He didn't want you dead. Not yet, at least." DeShear leaned on the windowsill, rubbing his chin. "Although he may have changed his mind after you shot him—twice." He turned to Trinn. "Why *didn't* you kill him the first time?"

"It wasn't the plan," she said. "Tristan wanted us to draw out the hijackers. We do that by taking their drugs, so we're on their radar screen as a threat, by appearing weak at the right moments—like the first time I had a gun to Hollings' head. I fired into the ground and told him to find a new line of work, so he'd come after me later."

DeShear leaned back against the window and folded his arms. "And pull his whole operation into the light with him." He nodded. "And now Hollings goes back to his bosses with this story, and a whole new level of rage. Tristan made up a good plan—and made a good decision to put you in charge of it." He stroked his chin. "Where did he find you?"

"Tristan and Jaden found each other." Dr. Carerra filled the first syringe. "At a hospital."

"You . . . lost someone." DeShear pursed his lips, nodding. "I'm sorry."

Trinn walked to the window, shoving her hands into the pockets of her jeans. She narrowed her eyes as she gazed outside, and leaned on the window frame. "My older brother was my lifeline, growing up. My dad died when I was very little, in Operation Desert Storm. My mother used me as a punching bag after that, whenever she got drunk—which was every day. I was in high school before I realized I was constantly living in fear, and that other kids lived differently. I'd hide behind a big wall in the alley at school, because bullies seemed drawn to me. Even in college, I was always on edge—but David was the one person who always watched out for me."

She put a finger on the glass, staring past it to the fading light of the sunset. "One day, he asked me to help him out with a new business. A mixed martial arts place he was starting." She smiled, glancing at DeShear. "I thought it was crazy, but he was all excited about it. He'd taken some classes and had gotten very dedicated. Anyway, he wanted me to do the books. I ended up becoming friends with one of the instructors, who started teaching me things. Come to find out, my brother had been diagnosed with the gamma sequence earlier that year." She swallowed hard, her voice wavering. "He bought the business and asked the instructor to help me." Her voice fell to a whisper. "So I would be okay after he was gone."

DeShear took a deep breath and let it out slowly, staring at the floor. "I think you're more than okay." He glanced at her. "If anything were to happen, I'd want you by my side for it."

She smiled, her eyes brimming with tears. "Remember that whenever your arm is throbbing in pain."

"It is time." Carerra held up a syringe. "To give you your last treatment. Get in bed."

DeShear watched Trinn a moment longer, then pushed himself away from the window and strolled toward the bed. "This one takes me out for a while, huh?"

"You're done for the day," the doctor said. "And maybe longer—but maybe not. You aren't as worn down as Tristan was."

"Wait," Trinn said, walking over. She raised her nose, sniffing. "You stink. Get a shower first. I don't want to be smelling that all night." She grabbed his uninjured arm and pulled him toward the bathroom.

DeShear looked at Dr. Carerra. She lowered the syringe. "When was last time you had a shower and some food?"

"I, uh . . ." He shrugged. "I don't know."

"Okay, take your shower." Carerra set the needle on the dresser and picked up her purse. "I will see about getting us something to eat from the café in the lobby."

As Trinn turned the water on in the shower, DeShear slipped off his shoes. He winced as he pulled off a sock, glancing at the hand he'd injured at the pier.

She stared at him. Wounded shoulder, wounded hand.

"Here." Trinn squatted and pulled off his other sock. Standing, she reached for the button of his pants.

He caught her hand and turned his back to her. "I can manage from here."

"I'm sure you can."

The door closed. DeShear took a deep breath of the warm steam, slipping off his pants and briefs. When he turned to enter the shower, Trinn was standing in front of him, naked.

He took a half step backwards, his jaw dropping. "Jaden, I don't think . . ."

"Good. Don't think." She took his hand and pulled him into the shower. "Just get in."

* * * * *

In the lobby hallway, Dr. Carerra pressed the button on her phone and held it to her ear. After a few rings, the call was answered, but no one on the other end spoke.

"I did what you said." She closed her eyes, pressing the phone closer. "Damsel in distress. The first sign of me worrying that you wouldn't come back, and DeShear couldn't help himself. He was tripping over his feet to assist."

"I thought so," The Greyhound said. "That would've gotten me to help."

She sighed, staring out at the lobby. "Now I've lied to him."

"You did what was necessary. He'll understand later."

The lobby of the Goring bustled with people preparing for their evening. Nice cars pulled up out front; well-dressed couples went out to them. Outside, the flag of the offices across the street flapped in the wind.

"Darling, I know this is difficult," Tristan said. "There are no easy choices for any of us, but . . . You can afford to trust DeShear. I can't."

CHAPTER 21

Trinn lay sideways on the bed nibbling a bagel. Her dark, wet hair fell gracefully over the white hotel robe.

At the desk, Dr. Carerra wrote in a notebook. "I can send your blood to the lab from here if I call for a courier. It won't be traceable. I could leave the samples at the desk and access the results online."

"Go for it." DeShear clapped the crumbs of a chocolate croissant from his hands, rising from the bed and shoving his fists into his pockets. "You know, I keep running it over in my mind. The two attacks—the one on the street just now, and the ambush near the hospital . . . It's like the cops in Minneapolis told me—the different styles mean it was different attackers. There was me, Maya, and officer Kensington in the car, attacked without warning and without a chance for the attackers to take hostages. So they wanted us dead. Assuming the port officer was an unfortunate accident, who would want to kill me or Maya?"

Trinn sat up. "I've been embedded with the hijackers for weeks. I never saw any of those guys at the hospital attack before."

"Doctor," DeShear said. "You said Lanaya was killed by the Greyhound's disciples. Are you sure?"

"We are almost certain." Carerra set down her pen. "But we don't know which one."

Trinn looked at DeShear. "Then the attack at the hospital was to get rid of you. The disciples have figured out you're here. They still want Hauser's people dead, and you got in the way of that when you got Tristan to stop killing them."

"Okay." DeShear rubbed his chin. "The hijackers seem to want you alive, Trinn. They probably think you got the cylinders unloaded and blew up an empty truck. That would explain why they keep putting a gun in your face, but don't pull the trigger—they want to know where their merchandise is. Meanwhile, they still need to supply Hauser's operation, so there's another order being put together somewhere. If we can locate it, we can ask MI-6 to let it slip through the lines—and follow it to Hauser."

Trinn swept her hair over her shoulder. "Like your original plan."

"Yeah," DeShear said. "Well, Tristan's a fighter, not a detective." He picked up Trinn's phone. "Maya was working with the NIH to track purchases. Time to ask my new friends in the Vice President's office to give them a call."

He dialed the number he'd been given to memorize, and waited.

Some rustling came over the line, followed by a small groan. "This is Jameel Pranav."

"Sir, it's Hank DeShear. My handler gave me this number. I'm sorry. It must be pretty late over there."

"It's okay." The Vice President's Chief of Staff cleared his throat. "They gave you this number to call for a reason. How can I help you, Hank?"

"Well . . ." DeShear pursed his lips. "I guess I need you to wake up the Vice President."

* * * * *

"Hank, I'm not gonne lie to you," Vice President Caprey said. "I've been hearing about a lot of gunplay on the streets of London ever since you got there. I'm not happy about it."

DeShear rubbed his eyes. "Madam Vice President, that's all tied to Hauser. We need to see if we can have NIH watch for combinations of gas cylinders being put together as a replacement order for the shipment that was destroyed. Hauser's people will be collecting it soon, if they haven't already."

"In politics, you can't wait until you're up to your neck in hot water. If my toes get wet, I'm going to pull the plug on this thing. Understand?" Caprey said. "But . . . I'll have Jameel make the call. You'll hear from someone in the Prime Minister's office as soon as they know something."

"Thank you, ma'am. But, uh . . ." he glanced at Carerra. "It might be better not to have too many politicians directly involved in this."

"Yeah." Caprey chuckled. "Trusting a politician is about as smart as trying to build a house on shifting sand. Fair enough. I'm sure the head of Royal London Hospital can get it done. I'll have Jameel set it up."

"Can MI-6 let it get over the border, ma'am? We need it to travel freely to its destination, if we can."

"If it's through allied countries, that won't be too difficult. Anything else?"

"No." DeShear took a deep breath. "Thank you, Madam Vice President."

"You're welcome. Try not to shoot up so much stuff. How's the illness?"

He nodded. "I've been able to receive mobile treatments so far."

"Okay. Stay safe. Goodnight."

"Thank you, ma'am. Goodnight." DeShear lowered the phone and ended the call.

"Speaking of treatments." Dr. Carerra approached him, holding a syringe. "It's time to say goodnight here, too."

As she wiped his arm with an alcohol swab, DeShear glanced at Trinn. "Think you can keep us from being attacked until I wake up?"

"Nobody knows we're here." Trinn smiled. "Go to sleep. I'll keep you safe."

* * * * *

DeShear woke up to a ring tone, sunlight streaming in through the window. Trinn was pacing back and forth, holding the phone to her ear.

"Got it. Thanks." She put her hand on her hip and looked at him. "How are you feeling?"

DeShear propped himself up on his elbows, the bedsheets falling around his chest. "Pretty good."

"Yeah, Dominique said you might." She went to the bed, sitting near him. "She's getting us some sausage rolls for lunch. We got a call from MI-6 a few hours ago. A shipment was arranged that was nearly identical to what was stolen in Macclesfield the other day. It's on a barge to Amsterdam, labeled as U. S. Military cooking supplies."

"Hours ago?" He threw back the sheets and sat up. "How long have I been out?"

"Easy, tiger." Trinn put her hands on his shoulders. "It's a twenty-four-hour boat ride. We have plenty of time to get there by plane before it docks."

* * * * *

The Vice President's Chief of Staff cursed and slammed the phone down, jumping up and going to the window. He stared over the lush green lawn, biting his fingernails.

The cell phone on his desk rang. He lunged for it and read the screen, then pressed the button and jammed the phone to his ear. "It's about time! I've been calling you all night."

"Hey, the nation has demands other than yours for its Director of National Intelligence."

Jameel paced back and forth, swearing. "That stupid private investigator has asked to track a certain shipment. He thinks he can follow it to our special friend."

"So? I can put CIA assets wherever we need them. If he gets too far, he'll be stopped."

"Stopped?" Jameel wiped sweat from his brow. "He'll need to . . . go away. The drones are ready. We can't allow a—"

"When we stop someone, it's very effective. And very permanent."

"I just . . ." He shuddered, loosening his tie. "She has asked for this directly, so he needs to be allowed to proceed. But if he gets too close, I need it handled. Quickly and effectively. The drones need to be kept secret until Hauser says otherwise."

"Listen, if the time comes, this private detective will get drunk and have a fatal one-car accident—okay? Stop worrying. My people are very good at this sort of thing."

* * * * *

Trinn shivered as she stepped through the big glass doors at Amsterdam airport, glaring at the gray sky. Her phone pinged with a text message. "We don't need to place a tracker on the truck. MI-6 just gave me the access code to their satellite that's going to be tracking it."

DeShear followed her, his breath sending long, puffy clouds of white into the frosty air. "A satellite that watches one truck?"

"Drones and the satellite alternate feeds. We do it in all covert actions."

He glanced at her. "We?"

"We. The United States." She pointed to a row of taxis. "Time to do some shopping. We need a burner phone and a computer—and a hotel with a view of the port. The barge docks in about two hours."

* * * * *

DeShear leaned over Trinn's shoulder and frowned at the computer screen. The satellite offered a fuzzy overhead view of the truck as it sat in the unloaded freight area. Nobody met it. Instead, it sat for three hours in the freight zone until a short, thin man climbed behind the wheel. The truck had since entered the line to exit the property.

"What now?" He picked up a pair of binoculars they'd purchased, and paced across the hotel room. Outside, an airplane landed in the distance. The freight area was barely visible from their window, but DeShear could make out the top of the truck cab.

The sunlight hurt his eyes. He lowered the binoculars and stared at the horizon. It swayed, as green and red splotches appeared in his vision. His stomach churned, a queasy feeling swelling inside him.

He put his hand on the wall to steady himself, glancing at Trinn to see if she'd noticed.

She watched the computer, gathering a strand of her hair together and brushing the ends over her lips. She clicked to a road map of western Europe. "If he gets on the A-30, he's leaving town. We'll just have to keep our eyes open and ask British intelligence to keep the satellite over him."

DeShear took a deep breath. The queasiness subsided. "We won't be able to get there in time if he meets another truck—or several trucks. We'll have to take turns watching, to see where he is at all times." DeShear's phone rang. He took it from his pocket and answered it. "Hello, Doctor. How am I doing?"

"Your T-cell count is very high," Carrea said. "And so is your white blood cell count. Your body is acting like it's trying to fight an infection. How do you feel? Any headaches? Or fever?"

He glanced at Trinn. "No. None of that."

"Good. Maya's protocol is working well so far. The steroids and HGH will help repair and regrow any organs that are under attack, but don't be fooled. The strength you feel is temporary. Your body requires a constant supply of the meds, or the dam may burst, so get as much rest as possible. We will be reaching a very critical phase soon. I want you to call me twice a day, morning and evening, unless you feel pain or start showing symptoms—vertigo, migraines, vomiting—anything like that, yes?"

He squeezed his eyes shut and nodded. "Will do. Thank you, ma'am."

"There is one other thing. I would try to accompany you on this journey, but . . ." She sighed. "My past has found me. Today, my office received a subpoena. I am to appear before a U. S. Congressional inquiry to discuss the many illegal business dealings of Angelus Genetics. The whole board has been summoned. I expect I will be publicly flogged and humiliated, then stripped of my license. I fear I may soon be calling you from a prison cell."

DeShear put his forearm on the wall and leaned his head into it, trying to ignore the pain welling in his abdomen. "Fight it, Doctor. I can talk to the Vice President. Nobody knows how big a role you played with The Greyhound, and—"

"But I know the role I played. I am ready to pay for my crimes," Carerra said. "I will do what I can for you. Then someone else will take over."

She ended the call. DeShear stared at the phone. Carerra wasn't innocent, but she was the last person on the Angelus Genetics board who should be in prison.

Trinn didn't look up from the computer. "How's the prognosis?"

"Peachy." He dropped the phone onto the mattress and sat down next to it, unsure of what details to disclose. "I guess I should try sleep while you watch the truck. Doctor's orders."

"Sleep fast," Trinn said, frowning. "He's on the A-30. If he turns onto the A-1, we're leaving."

DeShear flopped back on the bed and closed his eyes. "And going where?"

"To a rental car agency. He can take the A-1 all the way across Europe." She leaned closer to the screen, clicking a road map overlay.

The brown truck turned from the A-30 to the A-1.

"Yep. Nap time's over." Trinn jumped up, grabbing her coat. "Call your friends at MI-6. We're going to need a computer with a satellite uplink."

CHAPTER 22

DeShear exited the taxi, staring at the rental car building. It was a shiny glass structure with very little concrete or steel showing—like a lot of other buildings in Amsterdam. Everything looked like it was built either four hundred years ago or in the 1970s.

Trinn pulled her jacket tight and glared at the car—a Volkswagen Jetta with a stick shift and a big sunroof.

"Sunroof," she said. "Because it's so warm and sunny."

"Hey, it's all they had. At least it's got the steering wheel where I'm used to seeing it." DeShear opened the passenger door and set the equipment bag inside. "I'll get the computer up and running."

The streets outside of town were wide and smooth, but as they got further along, the side streets got narrower. In less than an hour, they were crossing the border into Germany. Occasionally the satellite image got fuzzy or blurry, but it stayed on the brown truck.

Snow flurries flittered across the road. Gray clouds moved over a grayer sky as the sun tried to peek through.

Trinn gripped the steering wheel and glanced at the computer. She followed from a mile away so they wouldn't appear in the truck's rearview mirror.

The sunlight overwhelmed his eyes again. DeShear winced, turning to look out the side window. Red and green splotches cascaded over his eyes. He faked a yawn, closing his eyes until the colors went away and the urge to puke faded.

A few more deep breaths and the feeling passed. He sat upright, shading his eyes from the glare of the gray sky. "You know, I have to wonder how far this guy's going."

"Doesn't matter," Trinn said. "We have a full tank of gas. Where he goes, we go." She pressed a button on the dashboard, sending more warm air through the car. "This stupid sunroof is irritating me." A slight hiss came from the gap in the sunroof's weather stripping, allowing an occasional snowflake to float down onto Trinn's lap. She scowled, making a fist and pressing it to her mouth. Exhaling hard, Trinn sent hot breath over her fingers.

"That's a long-haul truck, with two reserve tanks." DeShear felt normal again, like the wave of sickness had decided not to stay after all—like it had never started in on him in the first place. He balanced the computer on his lap, folding his arms. "He can drive to China. How long do you think MI-6 will keep us linked up?"

"Hopefully, for however long it takes." She glanced at him. "What's got you worried? We can—"

The rear window exploded. Cold air rushed through the car.

"Gunshot!" Trinn ducked her head, swerving the car hard to the right. DeShear crouched, his heart thumping. He slid to the floor and slammed the computer shut. Accelerating, Trinn glanced in the rearview mirror. "Stay low."

He peeked over the back of his seat. "Where's our gun?"

"Here." Trinn opened the center console armrest and handed him the weapon. "We only have four rounds."

Another shot hit the trunk of the car with a loud *thump*.

"Then floor it," DeShear said.

Trinn gritted her teeth and stomped the gas pedal, rocketing the Jetta forward. Her hair flying in the wind, she swerved left and right, weaving around the other cars.

"It's a black sedan, about fifty yards back," Trinn shouted over the wind noise. "No front license plate."

DeShear looked out the front windshield and pointed at a van. "Get in front of that guy, so the shooter doesn't have a clear shot."

Trinn raced the engine until she was in front of the van, then cut over.

The van driver slowed down, shaking a fist at the Jetta. The attackers' vehicle kept their distance, firing another shot. It hit DeShear's headrest and went through the windshield.

He glanced at the hole. "That's a large caliber rifle. This isn't gonna work. They can follow us anywhere on this road, and if we go any faster we'll get spotted by the truck. Make a turn."

"Okay. Get ready." Trinn swerved again. "I'm going to punch it, and as soon as they start to close in, I'll hit the brakes and force them alongside of us. When I do, empty the gun into their car."

"Got it." DeShear looked out Trinn's window. Snowflakes swirled around the inside of the car. "I'm getting in back for a clear shot. Punch it."

As he dived over the seat, Trinn pressed the gas pedal to the floor. The Jetta raced ahead, its back seat covered in broken glass. DeShear crouched low, clicking the button on the door to lower the window.

The sedan closed in, firing another round. The bullet seemed to miss the Jetta.

"Ready?" Trinn shouted.

DeShear gripped the pistol, the icy wind pounding the inside of the car. "Ready!"

"Now!" Trinn slammed on the brakes. The momentum thrust DeShear forward and brought the sedan close.

DeShear bolted upright and leveled the gun at them. The shooter was a young man with a goatee. He raised his rifle and swung the barrel to point at DeShear.

Holding the pistol with both hands, DeShear rested his arm on the bottom of the open window and took aim. The frigid air sliced into his exposed skin. He took a half breath and held it.

The gunman fired. The shot whizzed over DeShear's head and shattered the window on the other side of the car.

DeShear squeezed off three shots in rapid fire. A red splotch appeared on the shooter's forehead, and the rifle barrel lowered. The man swayed, slumping forward onto the dashboard, his gun dropping into the car.

"One down," DeShear shouted.

The driver's jaw hung open as she looked at the shooter, then to DeShear. She was a young woman, maybe twenty-five years old, with short, dark hair.

DeShear lined her up in his sights. She was no more than twenty feet away.

You can stop this right now, lady—but if you move, I shoot.

The woman swerved the sedan to the right, smashing into the Volkswagen. The cars boomed with the impact, sending DeShear backwards. He pulled the trigger as he fell, firing upwards and to the right, missing his target.

"Hang on!" Trinn shouted. She slammed on the brakes again and spun the Jetta hard to the right. It skidded sideways, and the sedan roared past them. Slapping the wheel, Trinn punched the gas and dropped the car into a lower gear, launching them down the exit ramp.

DeShear grabbed the backrest and pushed himself over into the front seat. "Are you hit?"

Trinn hugged the steering wheel, shaking her head. "I'm good. You?"

"Fine. Get us out of here. They may not be alone, and we're out of ammo."

She nodded. "I got this." She turned onto a smaller road. The street was narrower, cutting through a hilly area with rock walls on either side. Greenery slapped the car as it went by.

"How's the car?" DeShear asked. "Hit anywhere important?"

"We took one near the trunk." Trinn said. "I smell gas. We may have a leak."

DeShear sniffed. The wind was rushing in too hard for him to notice any gasoline odor. "Keep an eye on the gauge." He glanced at the road signs. "Let's ditch this car up ahead somewhere. Anywhere with a crowded parking lot. I'll steal us another one."

"There's a touristy area nearby. That ought to have—uh oh." Trinn glanced in the mirror. "Looks like our friend in the black sedan is back."

DeShear whipped around. The driver was steering with one hand and holding the rifle with the other, resting the barrel on the dashboard. She fired, shattering the front windshield of the sedan, then fired again. The rounds sailed past the Escape.

"There!" DeShear pointed to a smaller street. Walls from the medieval-age lined the sides; tourists meandered over a stone-paved road. "Turn there."

"It's too narrow!" Trinn shouted.

Another shot bounced off the roof of the Escape.

"We can make it." DeShear reached over and shoved the wheel.

Trinn turned, sending the vehicle careening down the ancient, skinny street. The Jetta bounced over the stone road, slamming DeShear and Trinn into the roof. Pedestrians leaped out of the way as the sedan followed.

Trinn laid on the horn. The stone walls came closer on each side.

The driver of the sedan fired again, taking out the side mirror next to DeShear.

Ahead, an arched walkway loomed over the road, connecting two fat towers. A massive wooden gate hung beneath the arch. The road's stone walls curved inward, narrowing as they got closer to the gate.

"We can't make it." Trinn leaned back, grimacing as the Escape raced ahead. "It's too thin."

DeShear leaned forward, putting his hands on the dashboard. "We can make it."

The stone walls got closer and closer.

The sedan driver fired again, hitting the wall outside DeShear's window and blasting bits of shattered rock into his cheek.

Trinn gritted her teeth and punched the gas.

The gate loomed in the crack-filled windshield. The stone walls were a speeding blur, inches away from the windows on each side of the car.

The Escape jolted to a stop, the crunching sound of metal filling the air. Trinn and DeShear were thrown forward as the engine cut out.

DeShear looked over his shoulder. The sedan was speeding forward. He grabbed the door latch and heaved his shoulder into the car door, but it didn't move. The doors were stuck shut, the car wedged between the stone walls.

Behind them, the sedan crashed into the narrow walls and stopped. The rifle slipped from her hand and skidded across the hood, followed by a giant dust cloud that enveloped the car.

The Escape bounced as the top layer of the rock wall came loose, landing on the back half of the car and blocking the rear windows. DeShear shoved the laptop into the equipment bag and jammed the button on the armrest. The window didn't go down.

"No power," he said to Trinn.

The sedan driver pounded on her door, unable to get it open.

"Sunroof!" Trinn swung her legs around and leaned back, turning her head and thrusting her feet upwards. Her heels hit the glass panel, knocking it open. "Let's go."

She hoisted herself up and out the top of the car. DeShear followed. They jumped from the roof to the hood of the Escape, racing down the stone street and around the corner.

The little shops of the village were filled with patrons. Trinn grabbed DeShear's hand, slowing to a walk to blend into the crowd. She pulled them into the first shop. "Get some clothes to disguise yourself," she whispered, plucking a colorful shawl from the rack.

DeShear grabbed a gray trilby hat with "Oktoberfest" printed on the band, placing it on his head. The next rack had sweatshirts and caps. He found a black windbreaker as Trinn wrapped a dark blue scarf around her neck.

DeShear swiped a trembling finger along the rim of the old-style hat. "Think 1950 Frank Sinatra is going to mind that I borrowed this?"

With the shawl covering her shoulders, Trinn walked to the counter. The cashier was a gray-haired man with a bristle mustache and a dark brown wool sweater.

"Wir werden diese kaufen," Trinn said, peeling off several bills and handing them to him. "Kaltes Wetter heute."

"Ya," the old man said. "Kalt für das neue Jahr."

She waved her hand up and down her legs. "Hast du lange Mäntel?"

He nodded as he rang her up, pointing across the narrow street. "Sie können dort einen kaufen."

Trinn smiled. "Danke schoen, mein Herr."

"Bitte, fraulein." The old man handed her the change. "Gutten Abend."

Trinn took DeShear's hand again, leading him away from the counter. "Auf diese Weise, meine Liebling."

He pulled on the windbreaker and adjusted his hat, then wrapped the scarf around his neck. "Ya."

The streets were still full, but the two wrecks around the corner were gaining attention. People pointed and walked that way.

"How we doing?" Trinn said. "You okay?"

"Yeah," he lied. The knot in his stomach had grown to the size of a basketball. "What about you?"

"I'll be okay. We'll be harder to spot if we aren't dressed the same as when we got out of the car." Trinn led him to the shop across the street. "This store has long coats. Find one and let's go."

DeShear glanced over his shoulder. "I didn't know you spoke German."

"Now you know." She entered the shop. "Get a coat—a long one. We need to appear as a married couple, to blend."

After buying a coat for each of them, they reentered the streets looking more like the locals. The center of the village had a wide-open town square, paved with bricks. At the center was a large, round fountain, with a tower rising high over it, and a small statue on top.

Even in the cold weather, pigeons clustered around the tourists, looking for food crumbs.

"So." Trinn slipped her arm around DeShear's, scanning the crowd as they walked farther away from the wrecks. "You can get a car for us?"

He nodded. "Yep."

"Then give me the computer and I'll meet you at the corner. Hopefully, our truck hasn't met anyone in the last few minutes."

CHAPTER 23

DeShear pulled up to the corner in a red Ford Escape. Trinn glanced up from the small bench at the corner, where she had been studying the computer. She closed the laptop and walked toward the car.

"How's it look?" DeShear asked as she got in.

"I can't say for sure. From my best estimates, the truck hasn't stopped moving." She clicked to the road map overlay and pointed to the screen. "He traveled this far while we were following him, and . . ." She slid her finger across the green line that represented the highway. "He's gone about this far since. That's pretty consistent."

DeShear chewed his lip. "If I had to guess, we were out of commission fifteen to twenty minutes. There are a lot of heavy cylinders on that truck. If he stopped and unloaded, it'd be the fastest delivery ever. Plus, I don't know if a guy hauling stolen medical supplies would keep going in the same direction after he dropped off the merchandise."

"Not for very long, anyway. Okay, let's keep following him." She reached for her back pocket. "Think I should phone it in? Are we the only ones watching this guy? Is MI-6 on this, or anyone else?"

DeShear drummed his fingers on his knees. "If anyone else were watching that truck, we'd be getting all sorts of calls right now if he unloaded. I think it's just us."

"And I think he didn't have time to unload."

"So do I."

She put her hands back on the laptop and sat upright. "No point in making ourselves look bad, then."

* * * * *

The truck drove through the night, passing through the south of Poland and into Ukraine. DeShear handed off driving duties to Trinn when they stopped for gas, ostensibly because he needed sleep—but the red and green splotches had started again, and he couldn't fight them and drive. This time, the energy drained out of him the moment he got into the passenger seat.

He woke up as the sun peeked over the tips of distant mountains, casting a yellow-orange glow over the sky. The hum of the engine had stopped.

DeShear sat upright. His wave of nausea had passed again. The Escape was parked on a hillside, surrounded by trees. "What happened? Did we run out of gas?"

Trinn stared at the horizon. "Look."

A flat, beige parcel of land spread out in front of them for miles. A stark white mountaintop rose from the horizon, towering majestically over a walled city built centuries ago.

DeShear narrowed his eyes as the fields grew brighter. "Is that a castle?"

"I think it's an old monastery." Trinn sat with her arms folded over the wheel, her chin resting on her hand. "The internet and phone got spotty after we crossed into Ukraine, so I sent a text of our current location. We lost our connections completely about an hour ago, but since it was dark, I figured I'd keep visual contact and follow from as far back as I could." She picked up the binoculars and handed them to DeShear. "He drove up that little road a few minutes ago and parked in the courtyard, then he went inside. From what I could see, about a dozen guys unloaded the truck. That's it, so far."

"We need to get a closer look."

"If we go any further by car, we'll be able to be seen."

DeShear cleared the sleep from his throat. "What did you have in mind?"

Trinn shrugged, slipping the strap of the equipment bag over her shoulder. "We have warm coats. Want to go for a walk?"

* * * * *

Trekking through the massive, flat field was colder than he expected, but the rows of plants allowed relatively quick passage. The wind swept down from the mountain, blasting everything in its path.

"What is this stuff?" DeShear cut between the rows of husks, sinking in clods of dirt. Some of the plants were as tall as he was. "It's too skinny to be corn."

"Sunflowers, I think." Trinn lowered the binoculars and slid them into the equipment bag next to the pistol and laptop. "They must leave the stalks up after they harvest whatever it is."

"If they leave the stalks up, that means they harvest by hand." He gazed down the long row. "I can't imagine picking all these plants one at a time."

"You could if you didn't own a modern tractor. I don't think Ukraine has seen much modernization since the end of World War II."

"Leave it to Hauser," DeShear panted, "to pick the poorest places on earth to do his dirty work."

She pushed a broken stalk aside as she moved forward. "He's a businessman. He's keeping costs down, and probably oversight at a minimum. The government here had a reputation for being pretty corrupt."

DeShear nodded, blowing on his hands as he followed her.

An hour later, they were near the edge of the monastery. Two other pickup trucks had come and gone in that time.

DeShear stared up at the wall surrounding ancient campus. Built on a small plateau, the monastery was about twenty feet higher than the surrounding fields. Its walls stretched two stories into the air, but the tops of the buildings inside were visible. White structures with blue dome roofs, and towers with green tops, peeked over the ancient walls.

The sound of another engine came to them from the distance. DeShear crouched, eyeing a small pickup truck as it drove up the dirt road and stopped at the gate of the walled city. A man in a long, dark coat came out from a hut nearby and went to the vehicle. After a moment, the truck passed through.

DeShear peered through the binoculars, checking out the big wall.

"What do you think?" Trinn asked.

"I don't see any cameras." He frowned. "But that doesn't mean they don't have them."

Trinn tried her phone. "There's still no cell signal, so the laptop won't be getting anything from the satellite feed."

"Let's find another way to get into this place," DeShear said. "It's time to see what Dr. Hauser has on the other side of those walls."

A diesel engine roared to life. DeShear crouched, peering through the rows, as Trinn came up next to him.

On the other side of the monastery, a shiny new tractor drove down the little hill, to a large pasture where the sunflower stalks ended. It lowered a row of tilling discs into the short grass there, and drove forward, turning the soil. After driving a few hundred yards along the tall stalks, it made a wide arc and headed back. When the second row was done, it started a third.

One of the pickup trucks pulled to the edge of the freshly churned dirt. Another shiny tractor drove past, pulling a wide, metal bin that was mounted over rows of rotating pipes. The pickup truck driver climbed into the bed of his truck and lifted a big bag, cutting it open and pouring its contents into the tractor bin. When several bags had been emptied out, he waved, and the tractor rolled down the row, its pipe wheels rolling over the ground.

The truck driver held his jacket closed against the wind and jumped down from the truck bed. Opening the cab door, he pulled out a large thermos. He carried it to the roof of the cab, where he sat down and took a cigarette from his pocket. He lit up, then opened the thermos and poured himself a steaming cup of its contents, staring at the machines as they slowly went about their task.

"That's our way in." DeShear said. "If we can overpower the pickup truck driver, I can swap clothes with him and you can hide in the back with the empty bags. We should be able to drive right in from wherever he came out."

"How do we take him? He'll see us coming, and so might anyone else watching."

"My guess is, at this hour, he's drinking coffee. Sometime soon he's going to walk ten feet to water the sunflower stalks instead of driving all the way back inside."

* * * * *

They crept closer to the edge of the sunflower field, eyeing the truck driver between the rows. Beyond him, an arched gate served as the rear exit of the monastery. A few well-dressed people appeared at the open gate, one of them pointing at the tractors. The others nodded, then they walked back inside the wall.

"What do you think that was about?" Trinn asked, shivering.

"No idea." DeShear blew warm air over his fingers. "Somebody's getting a tour, maybe?"

Eventually, the truck driver got up and slid off the cab roof and onto the truck bed. He walked to the tail gate and jumped to the ground.

As they lay in wait, the man walked toward Trinn and DeShear, shoving aside the tall stalks and entering the sunflower field. The roar of the tractor engines obscured any sounds.

When the truck driver stopped walking and pulled off his gloves, DeShear jumped up and pointed the gun at him.

The man's eyes moved slowly upward, as if in a daze. He stared at DeShear, not moving.

Trinn attacked from the side. She swung her forearm across the driver's throat, leaning back and squeezing his neck with a choke hold, until his arms went slack and his head sagged.

Panting, she lowered the man to the ground. "Okay," she said to DeShear. "Get changed."

* * * * *

While Trinn kept watch, DeShear ripped his shirt into strips, gagging the driver and tying his hands and legs.

Standing, DeShear adjusted the sleeves and waist of his new attire. He handed his long coat to Trinn and glanced at the distant tractors. "How's everything look out there?"

"Quiet." Trinn lowered the binoculars. "Get into the truck and back up this way before you turn to drive back to the wall. I'll grab our gear and jump into the bed. Then I can cover myself with the empty bags."

"Done."

He reached behind his back and tucked the gun into the waist of his pants, pulling the jacket down to hide it, then walked to the truck and slipped inside. On the seat was a radio and a lunch box. DeShear started the truck and backed up, glancing in the rearview mirror. When he stopped, Trinn dashed from the plant stalks and dived into the truck bed, pulling seed bags over herself. When she had covered up, DeShear pressed the clutch and dropped the truck into gear, driving toward the arched gate on the side of the wall.

The inside of the monastery was clean and well kept, as if it served part time as a museum. The area between the ornate structures was dirt, but the buildings themselves were clean and bright.

DeShear parked the pickup next to another truck, and stepped from the vehicle. Aside from the dim hum of the diesel tractors, the place was silent.

On the far side of the compound, a wooden roof covered a staircase that disappeared into the earth. Beside it stood a steel dumpster.

He reached inside the truck bed and tapped Trinn's leg, a knot forming in his stomach. "Come on out."

She slid a bag from her face. "Where we going?"

"Hauser's Indonesian facility was huge. He hid it in the middle of the jungle, on a dozen acres, because it housed so many people. This all looks too small to be a second site for that."

"Well." Trinn sat up and moved to the back of the truck, handing him the long coat she bought him at the market. "Put this back on, and let's have a peek in the windows."

DeShear took off the driver's jacket. "You don't like my trucking attire?"

"I love it. Sure looks warmer than this." Trinn held up her sleeves. "But I bet he's not allowed in as many areas as the nicely dressed folks on that tour. This is closer to what they were wearing."

DeShear put on his long coat and hid the driver's jacket between the seed bags. Trinn ran across the east side of the compound, her long wool coat flapping as she checked each building. Scouting the buildings on the other side, DeShear glanced at the gate in case anyone entered. He found a chapel with old pews, a bunk house with wooden beds, rooms with hand-carved tables and chairs—nothing to indicate the monastery was anything other than what it appeared to be, except the constant flow of trucks in and out.

Trinn waited for him at a wooden cart at the far corner, crouching low to stay out of sight. The wind blasted over the walls. Shivering, she reached inside the wool coat and tugged her leather jacket lapels closed. "Well?"

"Basically nothing." DeShear leaned on the cart, catching his breath. His hands were turning white from the cold. "You?"

"Prayer rooms, writing rooms, an unused dining hall." She shook her head, glancing across the top of the wall. "Those medical cylinders didn't come here for no reason. There are plenty of better places than this place to distribute them from, if that was the goal."

"Yeah. Let's check the basement." He hooked a thumb over his shoulder, taking her hand. "This way."

They crossed the compound. DeShear grabbed the wooden railing of the staircase, looking down. No sounds came from below.

A car horn honked. The front gates inched open, rumbling as its old hinges struggled to support its heavy wooden doors. Trinn stepped behind the dumpster, DeShear following. Another pickup truck drove in. Its driver got out and walked toward them.

DeShear held his breath, squatting.

The driver approached the staircase, a glassy look in his eyes. He grabbed the railing and turned, going down the stairs, where another man met him. They said nothing, staring at each other, then they both walked off and the monastery was quiet again.

DeShear rubbed his neck, gazing at the staircase. "Seems like whatever Hauser has here, it's down there." He turned to Trinn. "Did you see their faces? It's like they're drunk."

"That's not drunk," she said. "That's *vacant*. There's something wrong with these guys."

CHAPTER 24

Jameel gripped his phone, biting his nails as he paced back and forth across his office. He took a deep breath and closed his eyes. "I don't seem to understand, Mr. Director. I—"

"It's pretty straightforward, Jameel," Bob Richards said. "Caprey's private operator—that detective from Tampa you asked me to allow to run around Europe as a favor to her—has located the Ukraine site and is now on property. So, we've got a situation to deal with."

"I . . ." Jameel swallowed hard. "What do you recommend, sir?"

"Me? This was your idea. We remove him, as planned. Protect the drones, remember?"

"I—I don't recall making any such request."

Richards huffed. "This ain't my first rodeo, son. Removing the PI was your idea, so you're going to give the order. Don't try to weasel out of your responsibilities now that the dirty work needs to be done. You're the one who wanted to play with the big kids. I'm advising you of what to do. I have an asset in close proximity that can resolve the problem as originally agreed." He cleared his throat. "Now, are you unclear about anything we've discussed? Because we can certainly get your boss on the line and see what she thinks about your extracurricular activities."

"No." Jameel's shoulders slumped, the wind going out of him. "That won't be necessary."

"Then do your job and order the hit. Remember, this was a courtesy call. I'll forget your rudeness in the matter, but you'd better remember something. When you ask this department to do something, it gets done. But you have to ask."

Jameel rubbed the back of his neck. "What about continued funding for the upcoming campaign? Any issues there?"

"Hauser's money will continue flowing through his online shell contributors, same as it always has." Richards chuckled. "There are over ten million of them now, so we can funnel all the cash we'll need to get your boss into the Oval Office next year."

"With you as her VP."

"That's right. And you'll be very rich—as long as we all do our jobs. Like making problems go away if they might mess with Dr. Hauser's cash flow, right? So stay focused—and order the hit."

"I, uh . . ." Sweat gathered on his brow.

"Order the hit, Jameel!"

"Okay! Do it. Take the PI out." He took a deep breath and let it out slowly, leaning on his desk. The phone shook in his hand. "Kill Hank DeShear."

"There. Was that so hard?"

Jameel squeezed his eyes shut, biting his nails as a lump swelled in his stomach.

"Now, everything can get back on track," Richards said. "Uh, I think the words you're looking for are 'thank you for all your great advice.'"

"Yes." Jameel swallowed hard. "Thank you. For all your . . . help, Mr. Director."

"You're welcome, *Fuego*."

* * * * *

The Vice President walked into her Chief of Staff's office, staring at the stack of papers in her hands. "I can tell when you're worried, Jameel." She peered at him. "What's bothering you that you don't want your Vice President to know?"

He winced, shaking his head. "Just . . . some push back on a budget item, ma'am. But it will be okay."

"You sure?" She set the papers on his desk and looked into his eyes.

"Yes." He forced a smile. "It's a minor issue. I've been assured it will be handled."

* * * * *

DeShear crept down the steps, his eyes darting across the large underground room as warm air drifted up the staircase. The massive area below was at least fifty feet wide, all concrete, with recessed lighting and corridors going off in all directions. Monitors had been mounted on a far wall, displaying views of hallways that ended at steel-framed doors with large, glass windows.

Trinn studied the monitors. "Where do you suppose this video feed goes?"

Footsteps echoed from one of the hallways. DeShear searched for a place to hide. The concrete was bare, with the exception of the entrances to its many corridors. Trinn pointed to the closest one. He nodded and followed her into it.

Holding his breath, DeShear pressed himself to the wall as the footsteps came closer.

A man in tan coveralls took a few steps into the center of the main room, then turned and headed toward the corridor where DeShear and Trinn hid. His glassy eyes seemed to look at nothing as he neared them.

He slowed at the entrance, his arms at his sides, then walked quickly into the corridor—and went right past them. At the end of the hallway, he stopped, his reflection glowing dimly in the overhead light.

"Think he's deaf and blind?" Trinn whispered.

"I don't know what his deal is." DeShear swallowed hard. "But if he doesn't care that we're here, that's fine by me."

The steel door slid open, and the man entered the dimly lit room on the other side.

Trinn stepped away from the wall. "Want to try our luck on the same door, or another one?"

"I think it's Russian roulette no matter what door we go through." DeShear rubbed his chin. "But

I'm going through one. I've got to know what's going on here."

The steel door slid open again, and a woman in tan coveralls stepped out. She walked toward Trinn and DeShear as an old man's gravelly voice echoed out from the room behind her.

"In these ways, we can conduct the necessary surgeries that allow our wonderful program to sustain itself."

DeShear snapped upright, a jolt of adrenaline going through him. He'd heard the voice before.

"And together we will create what has only been dreamed of before."

His heart in his throat, DeShear crept forward, down the long hallway, with Trinn on his heels, toward the entrance of the dim room and the firm, decisive sound of Dr. Hauser's voice.

He peered around the entrance. Rows and rows of people sat in a dimly lit auditorium, the seats descending toward center stage where a large screen displayed an inert blue rectangle. White text crossed the screen, matching the words of Dr. Hauser as his voice filled the room.

"We have what you need."

The screen turned dark, then a tiny white light beamed forth from the center. It illuminated a human form, the silhouette of a man, as the screen got brighter and brighter.

"Genetics is the science of what is possible."

The silhouette rotated, turning brown, then beige, until it displayed the full detail of an adult male.

"Concentric genetic engineering, or CGE, is the actualization of the possible, in real time. Real people, designed specifically for you, in any way you want, and any age you want. Tall, short, strong, soft, male, female. Whatever race, whatever body type."

As he spoke, the image on the screen turned from a slim, naked man to a wide-shouldered bodybuilder, then to a woman with blonde, shoulder-length hair. Her hair became darker and longer, turning straight and black. The skin changed from Caucasian to African American, then to native American, and finally Asian. She got shorter, then taller, then her belly swelled and another silhouette appeared next to her.

Then another, and another.

"But you need not take my word for it."

The screen went dark, disappearing upwards into the ceiling as the stage lights came on.

"See for yourselves."

The curtains parted and a slender man stepped out, dressed in tan coveralls. He was followed by a wide-shouldered body builder dressed the same way, then a blonde woman—all identical to the images displayed on the screen moments ago.

The crowd gasped.

Another woman walked out, with long dark, hair, followed by a twin whose hair was straight and black. A nearly identical woman stepped forward through the curtain, but with Caucasian skin, followed by her African American twin, and their native American triplet.

When the Asian version took her place on stage next to the others, the crowd was on its feet.

The shorter one came out, then the taller one, and finally the pregnant mother holding the hand of a child.

All of them were real. Living, breathing humans, with Hauser's voice booming over them.

"We have what you want, for whatever you want."

The applause went on for nearly a full minute—a standing ovation—as the well-dressed members of the crowd waved white cards with black numbers on them.

Dr. Hauser's gravelly voice came over the speakers, but he was nowhere to be seen. "Before you place your order, allow us to take a few questions."

The house lights went up. Hundreds of people stood, their voices drowning out the presentation. Trinn nudged DeShear, pointing to a row of empty seats at the back of the auditorium. With their newly-acquired coats, they didn't stick out too much in the auditorium. He crouched low and followed her between the seats. Near the front of the stage, a microphone was passed to an Asian-looking man.

"How real are these prototypes?" He gestured with his white placard, number 121. "Do these drones feel pain, or bleed?"

"We prefer the term prototype, as opposed to drone—but indeed they do feel pain," Hauser said. "Please watch the stage."

A young woman in a grey business suit walked onstage carrying a long, wide briefcase. Another woman followed her with a small table, placing it on the right side of the stage. Laying the briefcase flat, the first woman opened it and stepped back, sweeping her hands over its contents. The video screen lowered as a camera zoomed in on an array of weapons. Knives, brass knuckles, a leather whip, a handgun, and an Uzi submachine gun gleamed against the red velvet inside the case.

The crowd grew silent.

"You may see for yourself, Mr. Kagemushi. Please—perform a test of your choice."

The Asian man walked around to the right side of the stage and went up the steps. Onscreen, his eyes wandered over the weapons inside the case.

He picked up a knife and walked toward the slender man at the far side of the stage.

Kagemushi lifted the drone's arm and pushed up the shirt sleeve. The camera zoomed in close, showing the exposed flesh on the big screen.

Stepping back and forth, Kagemushi tugged at his collar. The slender man stared straight ahead.

"It's quite alright," Hauser said. "Please go ahead."

The screen showed Kagemushi licking his lips, his breath coming in short pants.

With a jerk, Kagemushi dragged the knife across the drone's exposed forearm. On screen, the skin opened wide, and a stream of blood ran down the arm. It cascaded across his palm and over his thumb, dripping onto the stage.

Kagemushi gasped and stepped back; the slender man stared straight ahead.

"They do indeed bleed. Thank you, Mr. Kagemushi."

The crowd applauded as Kagemushi exited the stage.

DeShear eyed Trinn as she shivered, reaching inside her wool coat to tug her leather jacket lapels tight. An uneasy feeling grew in his gut. Trinn's reaction was probably as much from being cold as it was from witnessing the sickening display happening onstage.

"There was also a question about pain," Hauser said. "We can have any unit display as much or as little pain—or pleasure—as you require."

The stage curtain pulled back further to reveal a man at a computer. Several monitors were above him, each displaying the face of one of the people on stage, with a second monitor underneath showing lines of code.

He typed rapidly on the keyboard underneath the image of the dark-haired woman. She turned to the blonde and stroked her cheek. The blonde smiled. Then the dark-haired woman frowned, grabbing the blonde's hair and yanking it hard. The blonde shut her eyes, yelping as the brunette violently jerked the hair back and forth. The blonde shrieked and cried, but did nothing to resist.

The technician typed again. Raising a fist, the brunette landed a blow to the blonde's face, knocking her to the ground. She lay on the stage, glassy eyed and crying, blood dripping from her nose.

"Or, we can remove the pain completely."

As the blonde drone lay on the ground, two other women stepped forward and kicked her. She bounced and jerked with each impact, but no longer cried out. She made no sound, her face as blank as if she were a bored employee in the middle of a long business meeting.

A woman in the crowd waved her placard and stepped forward. "Shcho z emotsiyamy?"

"They can, madam Zelnikenski. Later models will offer quite a wide range of emotions—but let's not get ahead of ourselves. Most of you need workers in—shall we say, various trades. The current model will work quite well for that goal, allowing for the exact desires of your clients to be met from the moment of initial contact."

The woman put a finger to her earpiece, nodding. She pulled out a paper and made notes.

"And of course, every unit is fully guaranteed to carry out your most explicit orders, whether that is a mining operation that requires long hours at the bottom of a dangerous coal shaft, a government that needs firefighters to enter a burning building, or a business that wants to ensure its world-wide client base receives the kind of horizontal recreation your upscale establishments are known for."

As the technician typed, the bodybuilder walked to the briefcase and pulled out a gun, pointing it at the slender man. He fired a single shot, and his target jerked backwards, a hole opening in his head. He slumped to the ground, blood pouring from his temple.

The body builder turned and replaced the weapon in the case, then stepped back in line, his expression never deviating from a blank stare. Two assistants came from behind the curtain and dragged the dead man to the side of the stage, a red smear marking their path on the floor.

The crowd swarmed toward three women dressed in white shirts, waving their placards and shouting their orders.

"What am I watching?" Trinn hissed.

"Dr. Hauser at his finest." DeShear gritted his teeth. "This is what we came to stop."

"Any range of pain will be available," Hauser said. "And you simply pre-program the response to have the unit laugh or cry accordingly. A client with a torture fetish could spend hours horsewhipping a single unit, and all he would hear was squeals of ecstasy from her—even as her flesh came off in chunks and fell to the floor. It's all in the programming."

The screen showed two men boxing, then cut to a shot of bodybuilders lifting weights.

"Of course, there are many other applications of this technology."

An army platoon ran across a field, grenades exploding all around them. Gymnasts and marathon runners, steel workers, sky divers—image after image appeared on screen to demonstrate what Hauser's latest products could do.

The last scene was of an operating room, where a graphic showed a cartoon kidney moving from its glassy-eyed donor to the smiling elderly recipient on the next operating table. The heart followed, and the lungs, with titanium knees and hips flying in from off screen. Finally, a skin graft moved the younger unit's face to the highlighted bone structure of the older patient, and he stood, smiling, a strong, healthy, younger version of himself. He walked toward the camera, slipping out of his hospital gown to show leisure clothes, as he took the hand of another patient—a beautiful, curvaceous woman with flowing hair who had just undergone her own reconstruction. They walked away, hand in hand, along a wave-filled beach, toward a glowing sunrise.

The two assistants came forward with trays of phones.

"For your convenience, we have provided private system cell phones, so you can call anyone in your respective organizations to assist with your order."

The mob pressed forward, grabbing the phones from the trays, shouting and waving their cards as they barked numbers and cities, delivery dates—all as Dr. Hauser's gravelly words echoed through the room.

"We have what you need."

CHAPTER 25

As the frantic mob made their phone calls, DeShear tugged Trinn's arm and headed toward the corridor.

She walked through the doorway and put a hand on the wall, her head sagging. "I think I'm going to be sick."

"Keep your lunch down a while longer if you can." DeShear walked ahead of her. "I have a feeling we haven't seen the whole show. Those other hallways lead somewhere. I want to know where."

At the main room, he peered around the corner. No one was in sight. DeShear dashed to the next closest hallway and headed for the large steel door at the end. It didn't open when he approached. He moved to the side and glanced through the glass.

The room was fairly dark, with large metal racks like a warehouse.

DeShear put his hands on the door frame and tried to slide it. The door didn't move.

Trinn cupped her hands around her eyes and pressed her face to the glass. "What do you think?"

"Some kind of storage." DeShear glared at the shelves, pursing his lips.

Trinn jumped back from the glass, flattening herself against the wall. "Somebody's coming out."

The door slid open and another glassy-eyed man walked out. He went down the corridor and into the main room.

Trinn stood up. "Guess no one cares we're here."

"They're holding a kind of open house." DeShear stepped into the room. "Maybe that's part of it. They expect their buyers to inspect the grounds."

"They're holding a slave auction."

The room was longer than it appeared from the entry. Rows of shelves went from floor to ceiling, as far as he could see, with barely eighteen inches between them.

The nearest one was covered in a sheet. DeShear lifted the corner and rubbed the material between his thumb and forefinger. "Cotton. It's bedding." He pulled the sheet back to reveal a plywood surface. The next bunk was about twelve inches above the first—just enough room for a person to slide into.

Stepping back, he stared down the long row. "It's a warehouse, all right. They cram them in here when it's time to sleep." He made a rough count of the shelves. "Twenty-four by thirty. That's about seven hundred and twenty people that this room can hold." He turned to Trinn. "How many corridors did we see?"

"Maybe fifteen or twenty. So that's almost fifteen thousand."

"If they're all beds. He's got to feed them. Let's keep looking."

The next two rooms appeared the same, as Trinn and DeShear peered through the glass. Rows and rows of shelves covered in thin sheets.

DeShear rubbed his eyes, huffing. "I've seen enough. Where do you think the cylinders went?"

"I'm not sure it matters." Trinn shook her head. "We watched an execution. That's enough to shut this place down."

"Vybachte, bud' laska." A woman in a white shirt and gray skirt called to them from the end of the hallway. She gestured for them to come into the main room.

DeShear cocked his head. She smiled, waving her hand again. "Auf Deutsch? Nihongo?"

"American," he said.

She blinked, then smiled again. "This way, please. The reception will be starting soon."

"How about that." DeShear headed toward her. "Just like the old geezer said. They can download whatever they need."

Folding tables were being set up in the main room. Hauser's voice echoed from a different corridor. DeShear glanced around.

"The probe is largely self-guiding . . ."

A set of double doors slid closed behind a man in a surgical gown.

"Hey." He nudged Trinn. "Are you seeing this?"

"Yeah." She turned and walked quickly toward the hallway. "I don't think the folks from the catering department care where we go, do you?"

Trinn rushed down the hallway and through the double doors. Behind a second set of doors, bright lights flooded a huge room. Dozens and dozens of operating tables were surrounded by teams of surgical staffs. Each patient sat upright on the table, a metal band holding their heads in place. TV monitors displayed the surgery over their heads; a laptop computer rested near the foot of each operating table.

Dr. Hauser's voice came from speakers in the ceiling. "Using the robotic arm, guide the final probe to the cerebral cortex. When it is in place, you may test the system."

Almost in unison, the surgeons stepped back from the patients. The tip of a mechanical arm lifted from the patient's head and disappeared behind the operating table.

In the nearest group, a man in a surgical gown reached for the computer, tapping on the keyboard. The monitor above him glowed with a green perimeter.

Across the huge room, a few of the other monitors glowed green.

One by one, the other screens—over a hundred in all—glowed red.

"If the insertion procedure has been successful," Dr. Hauser said, "your screen will display a green indicator. You may begin the closing process and prepare to send the unit to the recovery room."

The surgical staffs with green monitors pulled off their latex gloves and lowered their masks, moving away from their operating tables.

"If the process falls outside of the required range, your screen will display a red indicator. Please take your staff to the retraining center. Your unit will be collected to the retention area."

The instructions were repeated in Japanese, then a few other languages.

The remaining groups walked toward the rear of the huge room as swarms of men with gurneys came in. At the green tables, the patients were lifted onto the gurney and wheeled off. They went through a set of doors on the far side of the room.

The other patients remained at their operating tables.

Another group of men came in, dressed in the tan coveralls and pushing carts. Their faces expressionless, they went from table to table, pulling the patients into the carts, stacking them like sacks of mulch at a gardening center.

DeShear stared at the carts, unable to take his eyes off them as they collected the units from the tables, one by one, until every cart was full.

He stood, frozen, as the men struggled to push the heavy carts to the rear doors at the room and down the dark hallway beyond.

"Vybachte, bud' laska." The woman in the gray skirt called to them again. When they faced her, she smiled. "This way, please. The reception will be starting soon."

DeShear nodded, walking toward her. "Can't say I'm much in the mood for a party just now."

"Maybe that's because you weren't invited, mate." A man stepped into the entry, holding a gun in his hand.

"Hollings!" Trinn said, jumping back, her jaw dropping.

Fear and adrenaline gripped DeShear's gut. Behind Hollings, two large men brandished rifles. Hollings' arms were bandaged from the wrist to the elbow, and the side of his face sported a large, purple bruise.

"And you, Miss." He scowled. "Remember that accounting clerk from the hospital—Lily? Carved her up nice, I did, and hung her blabbing tongue on the wall." He held up his bandaged arms and glared at Trinn. "Oh, the fun I'm going to have paying you back for this."

CHAPTER 26

"Keep your hands in the air," Hollings bellowed, marching Trinn and DeShear into the noisy auditorium.

The knot in DeShear's stomach tightened.

Hollings is going to pretend we're drones and shoot us while everyone watches.

Most of the buyers were still huddled near the front of the stage with their phones, placing orders with Hauser's assistants.

Their captors hadn't patted them down, so DeShear's gun was still tucked into the back of his belt, but it was out of bullets.

"That way." Hollings waved his gun toward the front row. "So's everyone can see what happens to you lot."

Trinn swallowed hard, her voice wavering. "Hollings, if . . . if you were gonna kill me, you'd have done it already." She licked her lips, panting. "You—you don't have the authorization."

"No?" He leaned forward and whispered in her ear. "When this is over, I'm going to slice your pretty little neck open and hang your head in my garden to scare away the crows."

A bead of sweat formed on her brow. "You're worse than one of these mindless drones."

The crowd quieted as the gunmen approached.

"Nothing to fear, folks," Hollings shouted. "Just a few pesky vermin to be removed. The activities will resume straight away."

The screen over the stage faded to blue as the voice of Dr. Hauser boomed over the room. "Ah, our special guests have arrived. Ladies and gentlemen, allow me to introduce Hamilton DeShear, a private investigator from Tampa, and Jaden Trinn, a covert operator for the United States Intelligence Community."

Pulse pounding, DeShear glanced around the room. They were outgunned and outnumbered.

The attendees of the presentation looked at him, a low murmur emanating from the group.

"I have a message for you," Hauser said. "Stand by."

The screen turned gray with static, then the face of the Director of National Intelligence, Bob Richards, appeared. He narrowed his eyes, scowling as he read from a blue piece of paper. "Hamilton DeShear created an illegal drug operation to transport Chinese opioids through Indonesia and into the United States with his partner, Lanaya Kim of Minnesota—who DeShear recently murdered to assume sole control of their drug operation. Our liaisons in MI-6 turned over a video recording showing DeShear exploding a bomb at the port of London, to interrupt the flow of drugs from a rival drug cartel. At that time, our CIA engaged an asset in Europe to observe Mr. DeShear's activities. DeShear subsequently met with and extorted money from board members of Angeles Genetics, such as Dr. Dominique Carerra, to finance the expansion of his illegal drug enterprise across Europe. DeShear was also a principal in an attempt to assassinate the Vice President of the United States outside of a London hospital during her goodwill mission. The attempt was only thwarted when our asset intervened, stopping DeShear and his associates just a few blocks from Royal London Hospital, where the Vice President had been giving a speech." Richards lowered the paper, glaring into the camera. "These actions make Mr. DeShear a clear and present danger to the interests of the United States. He is to be terminated on sight."

Hollings chuckled, checking the magazine of his weapon. "You trusted the wrong bird, mate."

DeShear glanced around the room, his heart racing. His gaze fell on the weapons case onstage.

I'll never make it in time.

"Agent Trinn," Richards said. "It's time to finish your mission."

Hollings held his gun out to Trinn.

The knot in DeShear's stomach surged, fear pulsing through him as Trinn turned and looked at him.

The henchmen thrust the barrels of their rifles into Trinn's back. Hollings smiled. "And don't get no ideas, hey?" A gunman handed him another pistol.

Trinn stared at Hollings, her mouth hanging open.

"Agent Trinn," Richards growled. "Finish your mission."

She reached out, her hand inching towards the gun. DeShear swallowed hard, taking a step to the side. The crowd behind him moved away.

Hollings cocked his head, looking at DeShear. "You're wondering if she ain't one of them drones the doctor cooked up in his lab—aren't you, mate?"

"Agent Trinn!" Richards shouted.

Trinn grabbed the gun and pointed it at DeShear. She bit her lip.

DeShear leaped backwards, pushing himself between the buyers. Shrieks erupted from the group. He pulled his pistol out of his belt and stood upright, holding Kagemushi by the neck.

DeShear jammed the tip of the gun into his hostage's neck. "Hollings! You can't afford to shoot into this crowd—you'll kill your boss' patrons." He backed toward the stage, dragging Kagemushi with him. "That's bad for business."

The crowd scattered, running in all directions. Hollings darted behind a row of seats.

"Help me!" Kagemushi screamed, his hands at his sides.

"Hold it!" Hollings shouted to his henchmen. "Hold your fire!"

The glassy-eyed men lowered their rifles.

Trinn aimed her gun and pulled the trigger.

Kagemushi's body jerked backwards. He slumped sideways as DeShear released him and leaped onto the stage. As Kagemushi dropped to the floor, DeShear raced for the weapons case on the table—and the Uzi submachine gun he'd seen there earlier.

Trinn fired again. The shot sailed past DeShear as he ran. It hit the wall next to his head, sending up a cloud of debris.

DeShear reached the case and grabbed the Uzi. Trinn fired a third time as he knocked the case over, scattering the contents across the stage floor. DeShear dived behind the wall.

Rolling onto his back, DeShear took a deep breath and ratcheted the slide lever of the Uzi. The computer technician slumped to the floor on stage, a red spot oozing from his back. Sparks burst from his computer.

DeShear thrust himself upright, leaning around the corner and pulling the trigger on the Uzi. A spray of bullets rattled across the ceiling of the auditorium. The customers screamed, running for cover or ducking their heads and dropping to the floor.

Hollings' gunmen stood firm and unmoving in the melee. "Shoot him, you idiots!" Hollings smacked the leg of his gunman, frowning.

In front of them, Trinn raised her weapon at DeShear.

He held the Uzi with both hands and pointed the barrel at Trinn's chest. A customer ran into Trinn as she fired, sending her shot past DeShear's ear. He gritted his teeth and held the gun firm, squeezing off two rounds. Two holes exploded in the chest of Trinn's long wool coat, sending bits of material into the air as she fell backwards. She crashed to the floor, eyes wide, clutching her chest and gasping. She rolled over and put a hand out, her head sagging as she raised herself a few inches.

Then she collapsed.

Trinn remained unmoving on the floor as the buyers fled. DeShear swallowed hard, his breath leaving him. Customer after customer raced past Trinn as she lay face down on the floor.

He frowned, his gaze moving to the gunmen. They remained motionless. Behind him, sparks continued popping from the computer.

Hollings quivered between the seats, glancing around with his mouth hanging open. Bolting up with a grunt, the fat man launched himself down the aisle and into the mob. He brandished his gun and shouted, pushing through the crowd and scurrying out of the auditorium.

DeShear leaped off the stage and sent another spray of bullets into the ceiling, scattering the crowd. He ran down the aisle and burst through the doorway, racing down the corridor and into the main room.

Hollings shouted. A mass of soldiers and rifles rushed toward DeShear from inside the far corridor. He opened fire again, hurling lead into the hallway and sending the soldiers diving to the ground. DeShear turned and bolted up the stairs. Legs pumping, he hurled himself past the pickup trucks and toward the rear gate. In the corner of the compound, flames roared into the night sky from DeShear's stolen Escape.

Shouts echoed from behind him. He dashed through the rear gate, the massive field of tall, dead stalks looming just a few dozen yards ahead in the fading light. Gunshots pierced through the biting wind, sending up splatters of dirt in front of him. He pointed the Uzi over his shoulder without looking back, firing until the chamber clicked empty.

DeShear hurled himself through the field, the dead stalks slapping and slicing him as he ran. The icy wind burning his lungs, he cut across the rows and sprinted deep into the tall recesses. Behind him, soldiers barked orders, their footsteps thundering through the air. Shots ripped through the husks to his left. He dived to the right, crashing through the brown plants and scrambling to his feet again.

His legs churned over the cold, loose clumps of ground. Far ahead, the stalks parted and the gray sky met the brown earth. His insides ached as he raced on through the cold, splashes of green and red dotting his vision.

"Oh, no," DeShear put a hand on his abdomen, staggering forward. "Not now."

He narrowed his eyes, forcing himself forward as the horizon swayed back and forth, focusing only on the grey patch of light at the end of the row. Queasiness churned in his stomach.

He fell to the ground, gagging and gasping, holding his face away from the frozen ground until the red splotches overtook him. Pain erupted in his abdomen, doubling him over as he spit up blood.

The thunder of dozens of boots grew louder.

* * * * *

Jameel Pranav bit his fingernails, viewing the laptop on his desk. Over his shoulder, the Director of National Intelligence stood, frowning at the satellite images of the Ukrainian monastery.

Jameel leaned forward, his voice wavering. "Okay, this looks good. The Ukrainian militia groups are moving in under the direction of our CIA advisors . . ."

"No, it's not good, Jameel."

"But they're swarming all over the place. You said—"

Roberts buried his face in his hands. "I said the Ukrainian militias would attack, led by our CIA advisors, yes."

"So . . ." Jameel eyed the screen. Tiny soldiers with rifles raced across it toward a big field. Others were in every corner of the compound.

"Our groups are still twenty minutes away by chopper," Roberts said. "They aren't on site yet!"

* * * * *

As the buyers were ushered into a secured area of the monastery, the men with carts rolled out from the corridor, heading across the main room toward the surgical center. One glassey-eyed drone peeled off, pushing his cart into the auditorium to collect the man shot dead onstage during the earlier demonstration.

Hollings flinched as faint gunfire echoed through the main room from above. Cursing, he ran toward the stairs.

The drone said nothing, guiding his cart down the aisle of the auditorium. Halfway to the stage, he stopped. He pulled his cart to a woman in a long, wool coat. She lay face down, unmoving, her dark hair falling over her face and shoulders.

He put his hands around her middle and lifted, heaving her into the empty cart, then turned it around and headed to the stage. Grabbing the feet of the dead man, he dragged the corpse across the stage and slid it into his cart.

The drone moved to the auditorium exit, pushing his cart as he passed through the main room. Gunshots echoed overhead. He went down another corridor, until the doors opened and the icy mountain wind swept over him. Pushing the cart to the end of the loading area, he pulled the contents onto a pickup truck, then turned his empty cart around and pushed it back inside.

The silent driver started the engine and pulled the truck toward the sunflower field.

A soldier ran in front of the truck, holding his hands up. The truck stopped.

"Zachekayte tut khvylynku," the soldier said. He glanced toward the edge of the field, where three men stood loading their machine guns.

* * * * *

Jameel's jaw dropped as he peered at the screen. "Whose army am I looking at in the monastery?"

"Doesn't matter. There's only one thing to do." The Director slammed the laptop shut. "Your stupid test of our security has gone too far. We need to get out of here—and get to somewhere public, where we can be seen and create some culpable deniability. A bar or restaurant, anywhere we can be noticed. Meanwhile, I'll get on the horn and arrange to get this mess cleaned up."

Jameel was white, his fingers trembling. "It was supposed to test our operational security. I . . . I wanted to be sure—to see if anyone could find anything—"

"It worked. Someone found everything we wanted to keep hidden. Now we need to fix that situation." The Director tucked the laptop under his arm. "Exit the building as fast as you can without drawing attention. Where do you want to meet?"

Jameel swallowed hard. "The Palm restaurant? In the bar?"

"Perfect. It'll be crowded." Richards headed for the door. "Take your car and meet me there. I'll be along in half an hour."

* * * * *

DeShear pushed himself to his knees, listening in the twilight for the footsteps of the soldiers.

Nothing.

Why did they stop?

The wind rushed over him. In the distance, a man shouted.

"Hotovyy!"

DeShear forced himself to his feet, blinking hard to clear his head.

"Meta!"

A jolt of fear went through him. He didn't know the language, but he knew the cadence—like a firing squad getting ready to pull the trigger.

"Vidkrytyy vohon'!"

Machine gun fire filled the air, splattering the withered stalks all around him. DeShear lowered his head, running for the gray patch, sprinting blindly forward out of the row.

The ground disappeared out from under his feet. He fell, covering his head and closing his eyes, landing with an awkward, heavy thud. Not onto the hard, cold ground that he expected, but onto shifting stacks of beige cloth bags. They were soft and warm—heavy, like bags of mud, but with firmness and hard spots. Dirt covered too much of them for him to know what they were.

The machine guns fired again, lighting the sky. DeShear ducked his head, pressing himself into the bags. They gave off a strange odor, like mildew and sweat, with the underlying stench of urine.

The shooting stopped; shouting followed. DeShear put his hands down onto the mushy bags, pushing himself up to peek over the edge of the pit. Far away, the soldiers were swarming the field again. They were looking for him. And they would be here soon.

He lowered himself slowly, to prevent sliding under the shifting bags. They seemed to move with his body weight, sinking down around him, heavy and soft, like gel with structure. The stench of mildew seeped upward from the depths of the pit, filling the air and making DeShear gag again.

He shook it off and looked around. One of the tractors was nearby, its motor off and its driver sitting idle at the wheel, staring at the horizon. He was dressed in the beige coveralls of the stage models, with a jacket like the one DeShear had taken off the truck driver earlier.

DeShear glanced at the bags. They were the same beige material.

As he leaned back, his mouth dropped open. The bags sagged forward. Realization loomed over him and gripped his core. They weren't bags. They were men in coveralls. And women, and children.

The pit was filled with dozens and dozens of living human beings, partly covered with dirt. Their glassy eyes staring at him.

They were alive.

DeShear gasped, holding back the urge to retch, looking around the pit filled with thousands of inert drones in the process of being buried alive.

Some were naked, some were covered with dirt, only a foot here or a hand there sticking out. The wind whipped over the top of the pit, but down below it was warm, heated by the bodies of Hauser's drones—the result of failed surgeries and overenthusiastic sales presentations.

Proof of the lunacy of Hauser's depraved operation—until the tractors covered them up and planted something over the evidence.

He flailed his arms and legs, pushing backwards, trying to get off of them and away from them. The more he struggled, the more he sank into the warm pile of stinking flesh.

The sound of footsteps reached his ears, growing louder again.

With his heart in his throat, DeShear grabbed a handful of material on each side and pulled, sliding the bodies over himself. They were heavy, breathing and moving with the remnants of whatever they'd been programmed with. It was like being at the bottom of a football pile after a fumble, but without the lively action from the other participants. Just the sickly smell and involuntary movements of cast-off human experiments.

Voices came from the top of the pit, followed by the metallic ratcheting of a machine gun being cocked.

DeShear squeezed his eyes shut, hunching his shoulders and gritting his teeth, his heart pounding.

The barrage of bullets exploded into the night, the living corpses on top of him jerking wildly. Thick, warm fluid dripped onto his cheek, making him cringe. Another burst of gunfire sounded further along the pit, and another. Pulse throbbing, DeShear forced himself to remain still.

Flashlight beams swept over the pit. More commands, then the thundering sound of dozens of soldiers as they marched away.

The thunder grew fainter, until he heard them no longer, the night air filling with the wheezes and fading gasps of the wounded victims in the pit.

CHAPTER 27

"Poshyrene!"

The commander at the monastery yelled across the darkening field, and the soldiers spread out, scouring the ground until they reached the road beyond. They continued into the next field, calling to each other, their voices growing fainter and fainter.

The soldier in front of the pickup truck stepped aside. "Rukhatysya." He waved at the driver, pointing to the fields. "Rukhatysya."

The truck drove away from the monastery and down toward the sunflower field.

When she thought the pickup was far enough away, Trinn slipped over the side and ran between the rows of cold, tall stalks.

* * * * *

The setting sun slipped over the horizon as Trinn crawled between the rows to the road on the other side. There would be a town down that road somewhere—and help, possibly, if she didn't get picked up by the soldiers. Her heart pounding, she stopped and held her breath to hear if anyone was following her.

As she neared the edge of the field, a car drove by with its headlights on. Her first instinct was to run toward it, flag it down, and ask for help. She fought the urge. There was no way to know if it had been sent from the monastery to capture her. Her eyes darted across the trees and bushes on the other side. There could be soldiers hiding nearby, just waiting for her to run out into the open so they could shoot.

A soft groan came from her right. She froze, the wind blasting past her, ducking down to zero in on where the noise had come from—and whether it was a soldier.

The edge of a wide pit was visible in the dim light. A man's arm grappled with the soil as he struggled to lift himself out.

* * * * *

DeShear steadied himself, trying not to remember he was standing on other people as he worked to climb out of the pit.

A rustle came from the sunflower rows. He froze in fear, his heart pounding.

The soldiers. They won't make the same mistake twice.

A woman spoke softly. "Give me your hand."

English. Trinn.

She parted the stalks and stood over him, extending her hand.

DeShear didn't move.

She puts her hands on her hips. "I saved your life twice. When are you gonna start trusting me?"

Frowning, he thrust his hand upward at her. She grabbed it and helped him from the pit.

"I trust you," he said, panting. "Even though you shot at me."

She headed back into the tall stalks. "If I had wanted to hit you, I would have. Instead, I put on a show and took out the computer system—for a while, anyway. But you sure didn't miss." She pulled the jacket away from her torso, two holes visible in the night. Trinn rubbed her side. "I think you cracked two of my ribs."

DeShear pursed his lips. "I knew you were wearing that special leather jacket that Redlins made for you. Still . . . " He shook his head. "You never know what a bullet is going to do when it hits. I figured I'd draw them away and you'd slip out eventually."

She narrowed her eyes, staring at him as the wind pushed strands of her hair across her face. "Okay. How are you holding up?"

"I've been better." He glanced over his shoulder. "I thought I saw a road around here somewhere. Let's find it."

"It's right over there." She pointed. Distant headlights illuminated a strip of cracked asphalt.

"Do we risk it?" he asked.

"Still got that Uzi?"

"Yeah."

"Then we risk it." Trinn headed for the road. "Who knows when another car will come by."

When the car got closer, DeShear held the Uzi behind his back and ran into the street.

The car screeched to a stop. He pointed his machine gun at the driver. "Out! Get out of the car."

Trinn sprinted to the driver's door and yanked it open. The old man behind the wheel raised his hands, his mouth hanging open. She grabbed the lapels of his jacket and pulled him from the car, getting behind the wheel as DeShear opened the passenger side door.

* * * * *

DeShear sat on the hotel room bed, getting the Vice President up to speed on Dr. Hauser's Ukrainian monastery facility.

"Terrific work, DeShear," Caprey said. "Absolutely excellent. I'll have a dozen divisions of the Ukrainian army there in a few hours to lock the place down—with a bunch of UN forces leading the way. You did a fine job."

"Thank you, Madam Vice President."

"Your country owes you. Agent Trinn, too."

DeShear smiled. "She's here with me. I'll tell her."

"You know," Caprey said. "I checked you out—can't just let anyone wander onto Air Force Two, you know. You're a former teacher, a former cop . . . If you were twenty years younger, you'd be just what the CIA wants in a recruit—smart, creative, and determined. If you'd like to make your assignment with the Bureau of Diplomatic Security permanent, you just say the word."

DeShear furrowed his brow. "Ma'am?"

"You were attached to my goodwill mission as a BDS contractor, Hank. Jaden Trinn's department. If you'd like to make it a formal gig, say the word."

He leaned back onto the head rest. "I don't know what to say."

"Say yes. It's got to pay better than being a PI—no offense."

"No, no, no. None taken." DeShear stared out the window. The first golden rays of the new dawn peeked over the distant hills. "I'll, uh—I'll talk to Agent Trinn about it." He glanced at the bathroom door, where Trinn was taking a hot bath.

"Fair enough. Thank you, Hank. Let's talk again soon."

DeShear hung up and sauntered to the bathroom, leaning on the door. "What if you didn't find me in that field?"

Trinn held a plastic bag filled with ice against her ribs and lifted a long leg out of the steaming water, soap bubbles dripping off her heel. "Then I'd have found you somewhere else." She dropped the leg back into the bubbles. "Maybe one day you'd have gotten a message through your detective agency asking you to check the flower pot in front of a swanky Tampa hotel for a claim check tag." She shrugged. "If I wanted to find you."

"I'd have gone, too." He smiled. "I'd have brought an Uzi, but I'd have gone."

She lowered herself until the bubbles covered her chin. "I'd have worn that jacket Redlins made for me, too."

CHAPTER 28

Trinn got dressed while DeShear tried a complimentary hotel razor on his beard stubble.

There was a knock at the door. DeShear bolted upright, going for his gun. A woman's voice came through the door. "Mr. DeShear, Jaden—it's Dr. Carerra. May I come in?"

He recognized Carerra's accent. "How did she know we were here?"

"I made a few calls last night while you were sleeping," Trinn said, going to the door. "All that dizziness you've been pretending not to have—it can't be good. You haven't been keeping her up to date, so she decided to make a house call. She and her husband have a jet, you know?"

"Dizzines." DeShear sighed. "You saw that, huh?"

Trinn nodded, opening the door. "You are one lousy actor."

Dr. Carerra walked in, a big leather bag slung over her shoulder. Her jaw dropped at the sight of DeShear. "Hamilton, what has happened? You look terrible."

"Thanks," DeShear said. "Rough night."

Carerra rushed to him. "We must get your injections started immediately. There is no time to waste." She pushed up his sleeve. "Jaden, bring me a washcloth. I can administer a partial dosage before we go to the airport. You can get the rest on the plane."

DeShear nodded. "Where are we headed?"

Trinn came out of the bathroom and handed the doctor a wet towel. She scrubbed DeShear's arm.

Next to him on the mattress, DeShear's phone rang. Trinn glanced at it as she walked back to the bathroom.

Carerra prepped the syringe. "Are you going to answer that?"

He eyed the phone, picking it up and answering it. "Hello?"

"DeShear, this is Tristan Phillips."

He sat up. Carerra glanced at him. "You know him better as The Greyhound," she said.

The line crackled with static as Tristan spoke. "No, no, no. The Greyhound is dead. He went over the Nungnung falls in Indonesia after getting shot and breaking a foot—and they have a saying over there. Whatever goes over the falls, is never seen again."

DeShear listened, not sure what to say.

"My wife says you're having a rough time with the illness," Tristan said. "I know what that's like, so whatever you need, it's yours. But I have a feeling you'll pull through just fine. Jaden tells me you've been quite active the last few days. That's a good sign. You're going to make it."

"That's . . ." DeShear shook his head, shrugging. "That's great to hear. Really. It's a relief."

"You're flying to Sweden, arriving in a few hours," Tristan said. "To Ludvika Lasarett, on my jet. That's where Maya has been recovering. You'll be safe there."

The doctor plunged the contents of the syringe into DeShear's arm. "I can't stay to oversee your treatment directly," Carerra said. "Subpoenas. But I will get you started, and I'll check in with Maya and the doctors every day."

DeShear looked at Carerra. "So Maya's okay, then?"

"She's almost back to a hundred percent," Tristan said. "She can't wait to get back to work—which is what I'm really calling to talk to you about. We're on the same side, you and I. We have been the whole time. I just didn't always know it." He sighed. "I can't do things directly anymore. I brought too much heat onto myself. But there's still a lot of work to be done—if you're interested."

"Listen, I . . ." DeShear rubbed the back of his neck, staring at the ceiling. "I wanted to shut down Hauser, and we did. I wanted to get Lanaya's killer, and unless I'm very wrong, that was the guy who shot up our rental car near the German border. He's gone now, too . . ."

"That's right," Tristan said. "Interpol arrested a young lady who'd jammed her car into a stone wall, with a corpse trapped inside, near some tourist town with a castle. Your worries about those 'disciples' are over." He paused. "Trinn said there were more mass graves. What was in them, exactly?"

"Bodies. His drones. Hauser is hiding his failure rates, just like before." DeShear glanced at Trinn. "But to bury people alive, that's . . ." He shook his head.

"I know. They were created by him in the first place, so he feels they're his to do with as he pleases. Why so many drones, do you think?"

"I don't know." DeShear let out a nervous laugh. "I think I'm afraid to guess."

"I think there's still a lot of work left to do," Tristan said. "Questions to be answered—once you're healthy again, of course."

DeShear pursed his lips. "I'll give that some thought."

"Okay. That's good enough for now. Get healthy, detective."

"Tristan," DeShear said. "Do you think Hauser's still alive?"

Trinn came out of the bathroom with a toothbrush in her hand. Carerra pulled a blood pressure cuff from her bag and looked at DeShear.

"I think," Tristan said, "that Hauser died in Indonesia, just like we were told. But he already downloaded that voice technology, so any of his minions could pretend to be him. You never saw him at the monastery, did you?"

DeShear shook his head. "No."

"If he's alive, he hasn't shown his face. If he's dead, he only lives on in digital voice."

Trinn put the toothbrush in her mouth and stepped back into the bathroom.

"Jaden shot up the computer," Tristan said. "And I have people attached to the Ukrainian militia. The voice files are about to be deleted—and Hauser with them."

* * * * *

As she left the hotel room, Dominique took the elevator to the lobby, where a car waited, its engine running.

She climbed behind the wheel and gazed at the tall, athletic man in the passenger seat. "What do you think? Will he willingly work with us?"

"I hope so," Tristan said. "We could use him. I feel like he's one of us. I have for a while now, actually."

"Me, too." Dominique put the car in drive.

The Greyhound stared out the window, squinting into the bright sunlight. "He'll say yes when he's ready, and he'll be ready soon. He will want to honor the debt he's accrued with you for saving his life."

"More than that, I think he wants to right wrongs." She turned onto the road. "That's what will get him."

"See?" Tristan said. "We're both right."

* * * * *

DeShear stared out the window as the silver Mercedes pulled away. "What do you think? Is Hauser alive? Or is he being downloaded all over the place?"

"We're grabbing the computers." Trinn sat on the bed to tie her shoes. "If they sent the voice files somewhere, there'll be a digital footprint to follow. It may take a while, but even if he sent it to a dozen locations and bounced it off a hundred servers, we'll eventually find every last one of them."

DeShear smiled at her. "We?"

"Uh . . . yeah. We."

He crossed the room to the bed, lowering himself to one knee in front of her. "Who are you, Trinn? You don't do the books at a mixed martial arts place, do you?"

She looked up at him, sweeping a strand of dark hair from her cheek. "No, I don't."

"You work for the Vice President, you work for The Greyhound. What's really going on with you? Who are you really?"

She gazed into his eyes. "You've seen who I am. I wasn't always what I said I was, but I was always me."

He cocked his head, looking at her out of the corner of his eye. "You lied about almost everything."

"Not everything." She got up, going across the room to the window. "It's a long story. I'm not sure I want to tell it."

"Trinn . . ."

"I live in a rough world, DeShear. I don't kid myself. But a guy like you—"

"Jaden."

She stopped, looking at him.

DeShear stood, staring at the floor as he folded his arms. "I have a very long overseas flight

283

soon. Sweden, for however long, then Tampa, I guess. If I recover from this disease anytime soon, I planned on taking a fishing trip to the Bahamas. So . . ."

"Yeah." She turned away. "Yeah. You want to have a normal life. Okay."

"I'm just saying." He looked up at her. "That seems like a perfect time to hear a long story about someone I'd like to get to know better."

She narrowed her eyes. "Tampa and the Bahamas, huh?"

"Yeah."

"Sounds . . . warm."

He nodded slowly. "It is."

"Well, I love deep sea fishing." She walked back to the bed, pushing him down onto the mattress. "It's a date."

* * * * *

Vice President Caprey paced back and forth across her office, her phone in her hand. "Where's Jameel, Catherine? He's never late for meetings."

"He hasn't answered his phone for hours, ma'am," her secretary said, looking at the other staffers. "None of us have heard from him."

There was a knock at the door. An aide stuck his head in. "Madam Vice President, the Director of National Intelligence is here for you."

"Bob is here?" Caprey glanced at her watch, then to Catherine. "Do we have a late appointment scheduled with DNI?"

"You don't, ma'am," the aide said. "But he says it's important."

"Of course." Caprey stepped behind her desk, taking a seat. "Show him in, Anthony."

The aide stepped away and Bob Richards walked into the office.

"Mr. Director," Caprey said. "How nice to see you—and so late. What can I do for you?"

Richards stood rigid, his face dour. "I'm afraid I have an urgent matter to discuss, Madam Vice President. May we speak . . . privately, for a moment?"

"Of course." Caprey nodded. "Catherine, would you and the others please wait outside?"

The staffers left. Richards stood in front of the Vice President's desk, his hands clasped behind his back.

He sighed, lowering his head. "I'm afraid I have some bad news, Hunter. And I sure hate to be the one to have to tell you."

"Bob, you're scaring me."

Richards cleared his throat. "Jameel is dead. He wrecked his car on the way to a meeting late this afternoon. Apparently, he had been drinking."

"Oh, no. No." Caprey's hand flew to her mouth. "I knew he was stressed about things, but—"

"I've asked the police to keep it quiet. The report will say it was an accident, and no one else was hurt . . . but with the alcohol and the link to your office . . . word will always get out about that sort of thing."

Caprey sat in her leather chair, her hands hanging limply over the sides. "He's been with me forever, Bob. Since Indiana." She shook her head. "I—I can't . . . This is terrible."

"I'm sorry, Hunter. I know this is a shock."

"A one-car wreck? No one else involved?"

"That's right."

"Ohh, Bob . . ." Caprey closed her eyes and put her face in her hands, taking a long, deep breath. Sitting up, she shook her head. "Well, if you had to do it, you had to do it. He screwed up, and he paid for it. Stupid, testing our security that way—but the others will tighten up the ship from this example." She got up from her chair. "Everything okay with the Ukrainian fundraising operation? Hauser's money bought the Indiana Governorship for me and the VP slot. We can't lose that cash flow now."

Richards nodded. "They started taking everything out through the tunnels as soon as the shooting started. By now they're already at the back up site, and you still maintain culpable deniability about the whole thing. It's clear sailing, *Madam President*."

"We really are that close to achieving it, aren't we? Everything I've dreamed about and worked so hard for." She smiled, crossing the room to a tall, antique cabinet. "But let's not get ahead of ourselves. It's a long way 'til November."

Richards chuckled, following her. "And to think, there are people out there who say you crashed your plane just so you'd have a good story to tell when you ran for public office."

"Hmm." She opened a cabinet and took out her purse. "People can be quite cynical, can't they?"

He went to the door and put his hand on the knob. "You know, a funeral for your Chief of Staff could make for an amazing campaign event."

"It certainly could." She reached for the lights. "I like the way you think, *Mr. Vice President.*"

THE END

DeShear, Trinn, Carerra and The Greyhound will return in
The Gamma Sequence 3:
Terminal Sequence

Note to Readers

If you have the time, I would deeply appreciate a review on Amazon or Goodreads. I learn a great deal from them, and I'm always grateful for any encouragement. Reviews are a very big deal and help authors like me to sell a few more books. Every review matters, even if it's only a few words.

Thanks,
Dan Alatorre

ABOUT THE AUTHOR

International bestselling author Dan Alatorre has published more than 26 titles and has been translated into over a dozen languages. His ability to surprise readers and make them laugh, cry, or hang onto the edge of their seats, has been enjoyed all around the world.

Dan's success is widespread and varied. In addition to being a bestselling author, he achieved President's Circle with two different Fortune 500 companies, and mentors grade school children through his Young Authors Club. Dan resides in the Tampa, Florida, area with his wife and daughter.

Join Dan's exclusive Reader's Club today at DanAlatorre.com and find out about new releases and special offers!

DAN ALATORRE

OTHER THRILLERS BY DAN ALATORRE

The Gamma Sequence
Terminal Sequence, The Gamma Sequence Book 3, *coming soon*
Double Blind, an intense murder mystery
An Angel On Her Shoulder, a paranormal thriller
The Navigators, a time travel thriller

Made in the USA
Monee, IL
16 June 2023